BRILLIANT OBJECTS

Brilliant Objects

—

Mark Lamb

LENDAL PRESS

First published in 2021 by Lendal Press
Woodend, The Crescent, Scarborough, YO11 2PW
an imprint of Valley Press · lendalpress.com

ISBN 978-1-912436-92-7
Catalogue no. LP0005

Copyright © Mark Lamb 2021
All rights reserved.

The right of Mark Lamb to be identified as the
author of this work has been asserted in accordance
with the Copyright, Designs and Patents Act 1988.

A CIP record is available from the British Library.

Cover and text design by Peter Barnfather
Edited by Paige Henderson and Jo Haywood

Printed and bound in Great Britain by
Imprint Digital, Upton Pyne, Exeter

*There is no more
virtuous endeavour
in the universes
than the dignified
braiding together of
Brilliant Objects*

Ariel Tzu-Chi
prophet, Jade Period

Prologue

Ink on Paper
New York, NY – August 7 2083

I was born sixteen years ago; on the day the island of Manhattan took to the skies. It's a coincidence which grants me no special perspective, except for feeling no real sense of loss for a past I never knew. To begin with at least, the island was just a beautiful chariot, a shining reward from the gods, sent to swing me over the horizon and carry me home. It was only later I recognised that every Eden carries within it the potential for self-destruction; a tipping point where self-interest outweighs the common good, where a haven becomes a prison cell, and the bruising realities of our shattered world are thrown into sharp relief.

Sometimes, in my dreams of leaving, I'm drawn to the ragged edges of our home, where the remains of wharves and freeways dangle over the side of the monstrous slab like limp spaghetti. Other times, I imagine witnessing the same horizon upon waking, or riding the train to Montauk to taste the sea air, or maybe jumping in a car and driving north to Albany. Mostly though, I'm happy to spend my days collecting clouds and waiting for fragments of the planet's former crust to float by, like devotional lights thrown into a mystic river. Maybe I'll witness the orbit of a mountain range or focus on a tiny, self-contained lake, or look down on a scrap of farmland where a family has made their home in a rusty pickup. Once, I saw the emaciated body of a child, starved to death, on a section of concrete no bigger than a hearth rug; an image that haunts me every day.

Yesterday, we passed under a hundred-acre railway yard, dripping ore-stained water from its underside and dragging a mess of twisted tracks and wooden ties behind it. These smaller fragments are rare though, occupying pride of place in every child's first log book because, when it comes to defying gravity, it seems nature prefers to work on a much larger scale, like it feels the need to impress us. The bigger slabs, the really immense fragments like Prairie Seventeen or the Hiramic Badlands lumber along at walking pace, their monstrous underbellies scarred by jagged mountain tops or pitted with the remains of cities they have demolished during their travels.

Our favourite childhood story was the one about our own home; the city that tore itself from the earth and wandered up past Newfoundland to take a peek at the Atlantic. Mom would linger over the part where the island began to lift. The shrieking noise of disintegrating subways. The foetid heaving of sewers wrenching themselves apart. The yellow-blue lightning leaping between sheared power cables. Then she'd get all tearful. The rifts forming in the Hudson and the East River; how New Jersey and Brooklyn lifted briefly but dropped back again and got left behind like tardy children. We'd cry over the loss of family from Hoboken and Coney Island who we'd never known, Mom pulling us in close, assuring us we were both very special and lucky to make it into the air. Tales of plague-panic overrunning Cairo and Lyon; how some of the early adopters such as Seoul and Jeddah crashed pitifully soon after take-off. That part would always make us sad, but not for long. Excitement would quickly follow when we got to hear about mysterious places like Alice Springs and Dungeness making it into the skies only to sail over the horizon and never be heard from again. Thoughts of them landing safely in some remote Shangri-La provided us with comfort on those deep winter nights when the taste of starvation was in the air.

And so, we survive, finding beauty in what little we have. The boundless skies. Wind-song running over taut cables. The low howl of air playing hide and seek in the desolate shells of tall buildings. Sometimes though, when my empty stomach screams for mercy or I'm submerged in despair by yet another act of senseless cruelty, I wonder if this is something we deserve. It's then, when I'm at my weakest, when belief in beauty falters and emotions are laid waste by darkening skies, that I'm tempted to stop for a moment and pray for the reversal of whatever blessing it is which holds us aloft.[1]

The Psychohistory of Spectacle
– a 60th Century Perspective

Hagstrom-Xi-Hawking Institute
Programme: Module 101, 5983.117 CE

Professor: Teja Foucault-Spark PhD
Institute for Psychohistorical Studies
Luminous Fan

London. England. It is five minutes past two on the morning of December 16th 1944 in parallel 81.03.17. In many similar existences on many similar Saturdays, it is snowing heavily, but in this particular parallel the roads leading to the gabled house in Crouch End are clear. Nobody hears or sees the thief approaching, and despite a squealing sash window and creaking floorboards, the widow, Holt, sleeps on; a solo violinist dreaming of her younger self, lost in the rhythmic freedom and imagery of 'The Lark Ascending'. Downstairs, the intruder moves with silence and precision, identifying each piece on his list and carefully stowing it in a linen bag. Finally, his mission complete, he escapes on a stolen bicycle in the direction of Finsbury Park and is never apprehended by police.

In parallel 81.03.07, however, the burglary goes horribly wrong when the widow wakes and is beaten to death by the intruder. In 81.03.19 she remains asleep, but the thief is spooked by voices from next door, panics, and uses the eiderdown to smother her. In both cases, the intruder flees empty handed. In parallel 16.16.49 the thief never makes it to the house in Crouch End. He is killed during a V2 rocket strike on New Cross a month earlier.

Each one of these events represents the true history which unfolded in that parallel.

The widow in parallel 81.03.17, wakes later that morning and rises to make a cup of tea. It is then, passing through the living room towards the kitchen, she notices her violin is gone from its armchair resting place and numerous mementos are missing from the mantelpiece. A lock of hair from a stillborn child, her late husband's Distinguished Flying Cross, a hand print made in red paint, a signed playing card, train tickets, photographs, postcards and other ephemera, nothing of monetary value, but all of them gone. The widow is inconsolable. In the coming months, she scours pawn shops, salerooms and musical instrument dealers in search of the stolen violin, while simultaneously trying to rebuild her personal history from fading memories. Without her treasured possessions to help though, the widow has no points of reference, no triggers and no personal touchstones with which to access the past. This cruellest of thieves has stolen her entire life.

Today is 5983.117 CE in Parallel Zero and, like the widow of four thousand years ago, we too have had our memories stolen, not by an opportunistic thief, but by fate. The Phage of 2053 CE was a vile, creeping disease whose symptoms included facial disfigurement and the relentless destruction of the victim's musculature. Reputed to be man-made, it evolved into a worldwide pandemic; the agony of destruction being drawn out by its tortuously slow progression. Millions of refugees were thus able to flee from the advancing front, only to be surrounded months or years later and inevitably consumed.

Nowhere on the surface of the planet was safe. Hundreds of millions were wiped out directly; billions more died from disease and malnutrition as society crumbled. The populations of major cities in Europe were reduced to the low thousands, and when the plague finally crossed the Atlantic, mass panic ensued. The southern states of America were thought to have been infected by a refugee boat from Haiti that landed people in swamplands, whilst the northern infection is thought to have come ashore on Long Island. It surely cannot be coincidence that less than an hour after this news hit New York City, the entire island of Manhattan tore itself from the ground and took to the air. If the Phage came from hell then whatever enabled the island to lift itself out of harm's way must surely have been sent from heaven.

This physical lifting of the Earth's mantle in 2067 CE became known as the Inception. It is one of the few proven events in our own parallel's history, as indicated by the broken slabs of planet which were incorporated into the design of the Orb. Records of other historical events did not fare well, and much that survived the Phage and Inception was subsequently lost in the coronal mass ejection of 2158 CE. An outpouring of plasma and massive magnetic fields emanating from the Sun caused the failure of every major system on Earth and the planet-wide destruction of electronically stored data. Although some data survived in buried time capsules and other underground repositories, most disappeared completely and society was effectively returned to a pre-industrial age. Our impression of history became reliant solely on what could be remembered by survivors and whatever text or imagery was stored by physical means. Books, magazines, engravings, printed papers, paintings, photographs and so on, already ancient and fragile, became our only way to interact with the past.

Recent developments in technology though have made it possible to observe our past in a unique manner. Time travel is a proven impossibility, so we are unable to look back along our own timeline. We are, however, able to witness events in other parallels, some of which are similar to our own whilst others are vastly different. The story of widow Holt is the result of early experimentation in this field. By observing actions in parallels similar to our own, we can build up a picture of what most likely happened in our own history. Indeed, in some of these parallels, the entire course of history pivots on the actions of a single striking individual, and it is these lives we choose to study whenever possible.

The recovery of our past is thus a work in progress; an evolving flux of ideas, sometimes magical or fanciful, sometimes unlikely and apparently unconstrained by logic. Our past is distant, unreliable, intangible and, at best, half-remembered. But it is also essential for the well-being of our society. How are we to know our true place in the universe if we are ignorant of our own origins?

We begin this module with an introduction to two highly significant yet very different lives from the distant past. Interleaved with these, we will see short glimpses of the lives of those who experienced Inception and Fragmentation first hand.

Try to keep in mind the time scales involved. In the thousands of years since these events took place, the world has seen the razing of the pyramids, the evaporation of the oceans, and the emptying and destruction of the cities. We have witnessed the construction of The Orb and the foundation of The Holy Edifice. We have mined the moon, settled the Martian city of Nüwa and dispatched generational missions to distant solar systems, achievements due in no small part to the contributions of our actors and participants.

In this newly reorganised module, we will attempt to extract new data, make sense of competing evidence and re-analyse a variety of existing sources including historic media, written memories, thought streams, third party recollections, official transcripts, soma babbles and subjective views. Your task is to herd these tantalising puzzle fragments into a cohesive narrative. There is no inherent order or context which controls how these pieces of evidence are presented, indeed, many new observations have been made by re-examining the apparent causal relationships between fragments. Recent research, for instance, indicates that some previously reliable 'histories' were based on ancient stories intended to entertain, whilst a re-examination of the Immutable Cities transcripts has yielded new and exciting information regarding their nature and those who are believed to have built them.

Primary sources in this module originate with the Baem Historic Archive:

- Hannah Keter – The Manhattan Clips
  (Parallel 00.11.82, 2083 CE)
- Diaries –
  eye witness holo-clip accounts from multiple parallels
- Otto Katz – from ink on paper letters
  (Parallel 00.07.29, 1934 CE)
- Otto Katz – translations of *The Immutable Cities*
  (Parallel 00.07.29, 1934 CE)

Bear in mind that the majority of your course material is sourced from two distinct parallels, each with its own timeline and, in the case of Otto Katz, its own calendar. Parallel universes do not evolve at the same rate, so a year in our native parallel may go by whilst only six months passes in another. We will cover this phenomenon in more detail towards the end of the course, but we need to understand the principle in order to explain how the diary entries and personal statements presented here are dated differently whilst often referring to a similar event. The process of Inception caused physical fragmentation in many parallels, but also led to the widespread fracture of spacetime.

It's also important to appreciate that contemporary cultural idioms are rendered literally and physical locations and measures refer to the systems extant at the time of data gathering.

Many events studied in this course run contrary to sacred teachings, but students are indemnified from prosecution by special license. In recent years the planet's surface has become bearable, if not habitable, so students will be given the opportunity to take part in supervised excavations where possible. Above all, enjoy this opportunity for study and enlightenment. These historic and often harrowing events are held safely at arm's length by the inevitable passage of time, so cannot hurt you.

TFS
5983.117 CE

Immutable Cities 1

AEROPI – *The Ancient Theatre of Dreams*
A loose association of floating islands which form the basis of a carnival. As is common with other itinerant cities, mapmakers supply a kit of intricate micro-mosaic fretworks which allow the enthusiastic geographer to model the component parts of the city and mark its current whereabouts on conventional maps as it tours the globe. All the expected circus fare is here, but the main draw is undoubtedly the freak show, an attraction which pairs doubtful nobility and unimaginable cruelty to yield an unmissable spectacle. Here you will see Siamese triplets travelling in a huge glass jar. Witness the uncanny movements of Jana-Dee the Kineticatrix from the Ice Islands; see Pyrax, the man consumed by continual flame; Lady Endora the cartomancer; Eldine the tattooed woman; the famed wish caster known to the kingdom as Honorabilis. See the transparent Perspective family and the ninety-year-old doll woman with a porcelain visage. Come face to face with Lady Vyper, the enchantress whose ten arms are snakes from the elbows down and

which end in venomous heads. Her toxic glance can halt moving projectiles in mid-air. Fully sated in the sideshow of wonders, take a ride on the four-dimensional carousel, where horses with wings of transparent leather and bodies of knitted bone canter away into the evening sky.

D'NI-CORAX, D'NI-HYMEK – *Cities in Mourning*
The cities lie on opposing banks of a mighty river and are linked by a vast filigree bridge plaited from cast iron. Although they evolved in each other's pockets, the cities have their own languages, opposing musical cultures, differing currency, schooling methods, philosophical outlooks and ideas of art. In fact, they disagree on almost everything of consequence – and everything of inconsequence. Only three things unite them: the usefulness of conch shells as ear trumpets, a complete hatred of everything 'on the other side of the bridge' and an abject horror of ducks. Eight hundred years ago there was a terrible battle at the mouth of the river separating the cities. The opposing navies clashed for an entire lunar cycle until, eventually, one force was wiped out due to the slightly superior firepower of their enemy. Such was the rancour between the combatants that all sense was thrown to the winds; rather than taking the conquered city and its chattels for their own, the victors killed every man, woman and child and slaughtered every item of innocent livestock. Still unsatisfied, they turned to the wanton destruction of architecture, until not a single stone stood upon another. Today the cities of the victorious and defeated flourish in equal measure, the former polished to jewel-like brilliance and the latter rebuilt and re-populated by saturnine folk from the north. Happiness is thus assured or so you might

expect. Instead, the people, and thus their fortunes, are haunted by the souls of the war dead, and this is why every thirteenth clam pulled from that infamous estuary bears the image of a victim's face upon its shell.

ANSHUL TG – *Citadel of the Incurious Mind*
In many of our finest cities there are shamans, priests, celebrants and various other religious leaders who have taken it upon themselves to do our thinking. In the absence of our own ability to reason, they set boundaries and fix eyes upon us to monitor our compliance. Confident that we cannot look after ourselves, they provide guidelines which must be followed on pain of death. Knowing that we cannot divine our own routes, they force us to walk only those paths which have been trodden in the past. And being themselves well acquainted with the sciences, they insist our minds are feeble, unfit to correlate and understand the various mysteries of the universe; that we exist on an island of ignorance in the midst of an infinite black sea. And yet cities like Anshul Tg exist to give lie to the idea we should not stray too far from our beginnings. Instead, this city shows the extent of our creativity and our capacity to explore, an inspiration for all who explore the reasons for and the limits of our existence. The Tg is a towering assembly of exquisite buildings perched atop an ancient needle of rock; it is accessible only by a narrow suspension bridge. Here, the wind approaches with tales of a parched desert and immediately falls into an argument with the breeze from a white-tipped sea. There are many fabulous art galleries in the upper layers of the city, the finest being Preedian Brothers – for in its roof-space is the finest example of a universe expanding telescope. For

a small payment to the right person, it is possible to obtain an inverted view of the nearby town of Anshul Bd, which consists entirely of ancient bathing machines. Visitors to Anshul Tg are advised to avoid speaking to the old men who smoke in the main square. Observe the patterns they exhale by all means. You may see an outline of architecture or a beautiful bird, but under no circumstances make comments on the thin, translucent papers they use. Close inspection, if you dare, will reveal the roll-ups are made from delicately inscribed papers torn from books formerly held in the grand library. Here, amidst the beauty and art, stories from ancient times are being smoked by the elders, and the city's past is disappearing forever.

YENSER – *The Township of Sharpened Knives*
In a prolonged fit of madness, Voldur-Yenari, a master designer of prisons, dealt sudden and violent death to more than one hundred innocent citizens of Yenser. Once tried and convicted the elders held a competition to find a method of incarceration befitting his notoriety, and for the last twenty years the murderer has been held captive by a clever trick of light and geometry. Visitors apply for tickets which admit them to a viewing gallery where they can observe the prisoner moving about his tiny cell. From their privileged vantage point, the audience are able to divine a simple means of escape; a route which nonetheless remains invisible to the murderer. The conceit is somewhat similar to a two-dimensional drawing, which from a certain perspective appears entirely three-dimensional but disintegrates into a mess of lines and planes when viewed from alternative locations. Yenari is thus bound in place by a fabulous optical illusion, which given the nature of his

expertise, is a most satisfying irony. Some commentators say if he can divine the way out, the prisoner is free to leave, but this is an unfounded myth. Monies raised by admission are paid as compensation to the families of his victims, some of whom maintain an armed presence nearby. Here, it is said, you may frequently hear the sound of supplicatory prayers and the slow, deliberate honing of edges.

BUKA-VOR – *City of Clouds*
As a chick, the Lower Plains corvid has powder-blue eyes which turn black during adulthood and become blue again in death. In a similar fashion, perhaps due to the intelligent nature of the birds, Buka-Vor is an ancient city which guards many secrets and vast stores of accreted knowledge. The city's finest scientific minds are unable to explain though why there exists a hush trap of blue-tiled roofs in the market quarter, or provide a reason why light blue gemstones appear to embed themselves in random buildings of quality. The same noble minds are equally at a loss to explain why the city's famous mu-metal domes are year by year changing to match the colour of the sky.

ATHEELON – *City of Dubious Endeavour*
In certain quarters of this strange city may be found great rents in the fabric of reality, phenomena which tend to create a lack of confidence in the principle of cause and effect. A bullet embeds in a wall an hour before the gun is fired. A cannonball hits the ground five minutes before it is thrown from an ancient tower. A thief finds herself imprisoned days before her larceny takes place. In this unsettling environment, the citizens live in constant doubt

about the direction of their lives, wrestling daily with what in their world is real and what comes from the mind.

CORRINX BY THALAZERENE – *City of Slumbering Threat*
The home of Daedal Trinke, grand-master of the Dimensia, a crystal fabrication whose symbolic mathematical root exceeds two hundred. Deep within the confines of tessellating spherical lunes, the transient symbol-glows are knitted by lines of attraction and repulsion into a multi-dimensional network; shapes and linkages representing the tactical powers and strategies which must overcome enemy forces whilst preserving one's own position. The study of the Dimensia is possible by memory alone, as no written work exists to describe its intricacies. Only one such mechanism is known, and it is buried in a leaden bunker far beneath this city. What fools the ancients of this metropolis were to spend such wealth on a mere plaything. Or how clever they were, to leave such a dangerous piece of machinery undocumented and disregarded.

Katz: Leitmotif

Ink on Paper
The Movable City of Aeropi
Strydia 15th day of Culmination
Lately in [D'ni-Corax, D'ni-Hymek]

It's impossible to forget my first impression of those floating circus fragments, even though the vision came after a day lost in a fog of spirit-drinks, hoodoo dancers, fireworks and questionable alchemicals. My head was strumming and banging like a rusty banjo strapped to a Farrakian bass drum; my brain mounted on a spring-loaded pole and punched by an overenthusiastic prize fighter. I was not feeling well, and woke, not because my body deemed itself fit, but thanks to the icy water thrown over me by an irate tramp who wanted his paper-lined tea chest back.

    I should have recognised the legendary city of Aeropi as soon as my eyes agreed to focus, but the eerie silence on the horizon went completely unnoticed. Of course, at the time I was unaware that something was approaching so the silence didn't bother me. I probably thought it was the same silence that belonged to the beauty of the stars and the dark turning wheel of the sky. In any case, I decided to stick around for a while, to see what, if anything, goes on during the day. The answer, my friend, at that particular time of day in the needle-point city of [Anshul Tg], is absolutely nothing.

Unable to find another comfortable tea chest, I found a deserted veranda and slumped into a rocking chair, recalling all the best bits of the previous evening's bacchanal; a stream of bizarre illusions, orgasmic delights and transcendental conversations all wrapped up in the gentlest of hazy memories. I felt reassured that I was leading a great life.

I took a welcome gulp from a hip flask, my gaze eventually wandering to the place on the horizon where the sun, if it was at all interested in going around again, would be rising shortly. Now I'm not over familiar with this particular city, but I've been laying low here for a while, eager to stay out of the way of certain roughnecked acquaintances with a passion for personal violence, and one of the things I've grown accustomed to is the view on that horizon.

At first, I thought my eyes were playing spirit-tricks, but now I'm pretty certain there was no tower silhouetted there yesterday – and no, I'm not imagining the structure, or how it changed shape as I watched. It started as a thin, perpendicular line, then grew into a fat perpendicular line and then became the needle-eye wink of a narrow ellipse which got fatter and fatter and eventually evolved into a perfect circle.

Interesting, I thought. But then the light appeared. Now I know what you must be thinking: "This idiot is waiting for the sun to rise and acts all surprised when a light appears on the horizon?" Maybe so, but my particular light isn't above the land. If I was a navigator or some other scientific type, I'd describe the angle subtended by the line of light and knowing the distance to the horizon I'd perform some magickal calculation involving the cube root of a tangent ... or something. Then I'd take out an envelope and write down the answer, present it with a flourish and ask if this was the number you were thinking of? Luckily, I have a better way of describing it. It's like an invisible giant scooped up a huge bit of land and slowly lifted it, so me and anyone else stupid enough to be awake at this hour could glimpse the light underneath. And the evolution of the shape of the tower? Well, the giant rotates the scooped-up land at the same time, making sure to keep it level of course, so that structures take on a different aspect depending on the angle of view. If you could be so kind as to try and work out that part for yourself, I'd be grateful. In the meantime, I'll be over in the corner being violently ill, while I think about it all over again.

At first, I imagined it was some trick; a light-based illusion or a magickal glamour designed to make a fool of me while everyone is watching and laughing. Then I wondered who'd bother playing such an elaborate prank on a down-on-his-luck historian and translator of ancient texts. Aside from the monobrowed asses who'd like to see my pickled head mounted on a stick, I could think of no one who'd do such a thing, so I decided to wait around and see if the phenomenon was real. An hour later, having witnessed the arrival in the slowest of slow motion approaches and smoking the sweetest of sweet weeds, I had my answer. I watched with unbounded joy as the smallest of the islands, an ornate ticket booth and a cast-iron entrance gate, made gentle contact with the fixed earth.

The circus wasn't just one floating island as it turned out, but eight, all linked by a series of rope bridges. It's not grand enough for mountains, but the main island has a few rolling hills and a deep cut gorge whose river has run its course. There's also a small plain, where the vast green and gold marquee is located. Circling that, armies of smaller tents are home to specialist acts like the Automatic Girl, The Aetherial Mechanisme and The Jaybird who Understands Magick. Surrounding those in turn are the various sideshows, rides, cages, caravans and trailers, all of great age, like they have stepped out of the pages of history. There is also a splendid steam organ and a huge Ferris wheel, which, when viewed side on, looks like a big tower. There, I knew you'd work it out eventually. Welcome to the Movable City of Aeropi.

Ink on Paper
The Movable City of Aeropi
Tryndia 38th day of Cimmerous
Leaving [Yenser]
Translations [Atheelon, Buka-Vor, Corrinx by Thalazerene]

Troband Velliers, you degenerate skulldug, here are the first few translations as per our recent agreement. As I write, the circus is casting off from a town composed solely of dung shovelers, badger fanny sniffers and opium dealers (for the last of which I'm royally grateful), so the work is a welcome distraction. It's a complex task, so I spend many a quiet moment in the peace of the baggage trailer simply inhaling the magnificence of the scrolls. I'm surprised they trusted you with them (who are 'they' by the way?) and equally surprised you in turn trusted me. I wish to marry them, but there are barriers to be overcome, what with me being flesh and they smelling of a thousand years of dust. Trust me, far stranger things happen in the great Cathedral of Wonder and Zebra-Shit. Back to the point. Few examples of old-tongue exist, so it's an honour to handle these. There, I'm grateful, OK? Grovelling over. Time for a reward as we relieve ourselves of this shithole.

Ink on Paper
The Movable City of Aeropi
Faldia 39th day of Cimmerous

The great hubbub of 'they who must be entertained' is gone, the malodourous presence of the audiences replaced by the no-noise of effortless wafting, fields of trampled mud and a haul of lost property which includes a stuffed ostrich, three bicycles and a piston engine. Also left behind is the insistent thud of steam hammers in my head. That crap hole Yenser is well beyond the horizon, otherwise I'd gladly return and perform a little amateur trepanning on my alchemistry supplier. Strange dreams of circuses with feet lapped by oceans and distorted heads gurning away in my shaving mirror. Still, it's an improvement on dreaming about gangsters filling my body with lead. But enough of the self-pity and on with the translations. The putative author of these early records is an elephant arse licker of the first water whose personality is amply demonstrated by his covering letter, also translated here. The missive is different in style, wit, intelligence, courage, gall and in fact every discernible manner from the descriptions of the cities. I will bet your sister's questionable honour that he and the author of the city gazetteer are two entirely different people and unlikely to be contemporaries. But both are ancient. I look forward to seeing to what nefarious purposes you use this.

To the King's Most Sacred Majesty

It was one day, as I was walking in Your Majesty's palace in Kroom-Vrak (where I have sometimes had the honour to refresh myself with the Sight of Your Illustrious Presence, which is the Joy of Your People's Hearts), that a presumptuous ne'er do well emerged from one of the two tunnels close to Vrak Howse and did accost me in the manner of a pickpocket or purloiner of fancies. I shudr'd at the thought of his presence in such a noble playce and made to find a constable. As I did so, the villain broadcast to all he was an honourable map and gazetteer seller and thrust a sample of his wares upon my person. At that moment, sundry ruffians of his undoubted cognisance rushed in and invaded the Court Roomes, Galleries and Playces to such a degree as decent men could hardly distinguish one decent fellow from the other; a deplorable situation, which none could support without manifest inconveniency. But sweetness, like your presence and benevolence, descendeth from strength and a little sweet honey drip'd fortuitously into my thoughts.

Your Majesty is a most knowledgeable lover of Noble Buildings, Gardens, Pictures and all Royal Magnificences, but an enthusiast too of the common and varied tapestrye we are pleas'd to call life. To that end, I dedicate this worke to your Most Sacred

Person, a surveye of the cities and splendid customes of a world in which we are most grateful for your continuing and glorious Reign.

SIR

Your Majesty's Ever Loyal
Subject and Servant

Sherbutt Moncrieff Fountayne

I am so glad that glob of sickness-inducing kangaroo snot ended when it did. What an absolute fucking donkey todger Mister Sherbet Fountain must have been. Anyhow, I trust these few city excerpts meet your requirements. And so to my position, which I beg you reveal to nobody, as per. Carnies are no friends of those who seek me, so it gives them enormous pleasure to conceal my whereabouts. Sadly, I have no exhibit-worthy physical talents and would look ridiculous in a top hat. In short, a circus, even one as large as this, has no need for a translator of ancient texts. If you don't pay up I'll be out on my ear and certain ancient documents will end up being used to wipe tigers' arses.

Yours in loyal servitude (ha-ha!)
Otto Katz

P.S. In answer to your question about the nature of Aeropi, I have eavesdropped, I have asked in a 'roundabout' way (such fun!) and, when that didn't work, I tried full-on confrontation. But the carnival dwellers are not for budging, to the extent that further displays of curiosity might result in the permanent rearrangement of my already challenging facial features – and not in a positive way. Unfortunately, they regard any enquiry as to the magickal history of this place as an affront to their honour or some other superstitious bull-tackle. Granted, if you don't venture near the edge, the place seems almost normal, except for those sheer open horizons. Nobody seems bothered in the slightest that a group of levitating islands exists, and cares even less how they are 'steered' or why they just don't fall out of the sky. Folk seem happy to drift from one place to the next, never giving thought to how (or why) a few million tons of rock does what it does or why there's a circus limpeted to its upper side. And nobody hereabouts remembers a time when it wasn't.

Diary Fragments 1

Holo-stream Fragment – Para 24.11.39
Hrisey, Iceland – January 16 1956
Margret Guðmundsdóttir – Music Teacher

When the world went mad, our little island survived intact, except for the calved northern tip which nonetheless has stayed with us for our entire travelling adventure. The adjunct has no name, but some refer to it as the Piano Isle because of the concert grand which languishes there in the abandoned farmhouse. The instrument refuses to hold its tuning due to freezing temperatures and damp, but this is widely agreed to be a benefit, since we get to hear a different tonality every year. The island is linked to the main homestead by a perilous rope bridge, crossed by the entire population on the anniversary of Inception in order to attend a very special concert. 'The Pearl and the Swan', written by my late husband Einar, is a gut-wrenching composition for piano-forte in minor keys. It represents our steadfast nature and symbolises our struggle. It is an anthem for a shattered world.

Holo-stream Fragment – Para 13.03.47
Brooklyn, NYC – June 3 1968
Bruce Chaka – Photographer

I'm sitting in a diner in Brooklyn. I got a window seat with a view of the East River, and I'm waiting for a guy from the garment district who has a whole bunch of tattoos. I'm hoping he'll fit the book I'm doing, *The Illustrated City*, which is basically the boroughs showing off their tats. When he walks in, we engage in small talk, but I can't keep my eyes off of his face, his neck, his arms. The guy is like a walking art gallery and straightaway I'm thinking of putting him in the park with the bridge as a backdrop. We talk some more over coffee while he admires my camera and then we make our way there. As I line him up for the first shot there's the roar of a motorcycle behind me. Tat man runs at me like I'm in danger, but grabs the camera out of my hands as the rider scoops up my bag. What a pair of shits. They're burning rubber and fifty yards away before I see the full picture. The one that says, "You've been robbed, sucker".

Ten minutes later I'm leaning on the railings cursing my own stupidity when I see the bridge pedestal move a couple of inches into the air and drop back a second or so later. The shock when it lands creates a shallow wave in the river, so I know I'm not imagining it, but I look around and the city seemed to, well, miss it. There's a yellow cab driver inviting traffic to get the fuck out of his way, a European peasant shouldering a side of beef and a rail of knockoff plastic-wrapped leather jackets clattering by. In an otherwise deserted alley, a mob guy rolls a kid for dough and further along a dealer exchanges a wrap for hard cash as an Irish cop looks the other way. That's New York for you – "If it didn't happen to me, buster, then it probably didn't happen". Only I'm pretty sure it did. I have a nose for this kind of thing, which is how a lot of my stuff gets – got – used on the front page of the *Herald-Tribune*, God rest its mortal soul. The old press photographers' mantra is 1/60th at f8 and "be there". It's a great guideline, but I guess in an ideal world it means "be there" with a bastarding camera, not "be there" when your gear is on its way to a hock shop in Harlem. I'm sitting here on the picture story of a lifetime, perhaps literally, so I decide to give myself a well-deserved beating. I slap my forehead again and again for getting relieved of my camera at the most inopportune moment.

I only stop the abuse when I see the bridge pedestal lift again.

Hannah: Establishing Shot

Holo-stream Clip
New York, NY – August 21 2083

In a world where everything is broken or bent out of shape the seamless expanse of sky visible from the observation dome is a constant source of wonder. Above me there's a hypnotic arch of cirrostratus clamping the opposing horizons, but tomorrow it might be piles of goose down cumulus, the towering threat of thunderheads or perhaps even a clear blue yonder. These natural gifts are sometimes joined by other phenomena, and it's the thought of discovering more of these sky-borne mysteries that keep me going day after day. Fewer than twenty-four hours ago I spotted a faint suggestion of rolling hills or farmland. A sliver of pale blue hinting at a lake. The image in the telescope was unsteady though and a bank of cloud swallowed the mirage before I could be sure I wasn't dreaming.

As I turn and smile at the child, I decide not to log it until there's a positive sighting. The boy we found cowering in a drain is reserved and slow to engage, but a new slab would invite a frenzy of sketch-making and note-taking, an unbearable enthusiasm that might make his relationship with the rest of the group even rockier.

He's quiet now as we approach the end of our shift. We're watching skyscrapers in the north, where pale fingers of steel and glass grasp at swirling mists. Further beyond those lonely wrecks there's a vague hint of green. It could be the park or even a distant jungle if I squint and use some imagination.

'Hannah?' says the boy.

As he fixes me with those pale blue eyes, I smile and wonder how much longer we can protect his innocence.

'Yes?'

'I'm really, really hungry.'

'I know you are,' I return gently, 'and I promise we'll find food soon.'

'You said that last time,' he whines.

'Uh-huh,' I say, aching to be fed myself. 'Well, I guess we'll just have to be patient.'

My heart aches at the sight of him. He's starving like everyone else, but those angular features and loose clothes look far worse on a child than they do on any of us. I guess if I ever wanted a baby brother then dragging a seven-year-old from a storm drain probably wouldn't be the way I'd go about it, especially since I sometimes feel I did it to make me feel better about myself. Dumb-ass Hannah and her stupid sidekick, weighing us down, costing us nourishment, breathing our air. I know what they think, but what's done is done, and his presence is just about tolerated. Alex christened him 'drain boy' but I changed the moniker to Deeby. It seems to have stuck.

'Hannah?'

'Yes, Deeby?'

'Are you still my new big sister?'

My heart swells with pride at the thought.

'Oh, you poor thing,' I say, gathering him up in my arms. 'Why on earth would you ask such a thing?'

'Because Aunt Pia said my family were probably all dead.'

'I'm sure she didn't mean it,' I say, furious at Pia for gobbing off. 'You probably just misheard.'

'I don't like dead people,' he whispers. 'Their eyes are so still, and glassy and—'

'Shall we fill in the log book?' I ask.

It's an attempt to intercept the thoughts before they surface and swamp him. The poor kid is usually as locked as a rusted safe, but I sense a darkness forming in him.

'Yes, please,' he replies quietly. 'I like doing that.'

I try to make him feel useful, so he doesn't seem like a drain on our limited resources, but the truth is he needs looking after and, as his rescuer, the task quite rightly falls to me. Accurate logs are always helpful though and, if we're lucky, those produced by Deeby might help us to track down an alternative home. Then all we have to do is find a way to get off the island. I give the boy a reassuring cuddle and we move to the south side of the dome; that's only south as far as the island's original ground position is concerned though, since Manhattan as a whole is headed west.

The view over Battery Park is my favourite; I could gaze for hours over the prow of our island sky-ship where cannon once protected the newly established city of New Amsterdam. In a world where the future is so uncertain, the proximity of the past is a welcoming comfort; an inhabitable space that can't be taken away.

Deeby rests his log on the map shelf and opens it to today's page, proudly displaying his work. The writing is neat and legible and uses a vocabulary for which we'd all love to claim credit but can't. As Alex says: 'The kid came kicking and screaming out of that drain, pre-taught and ready to go.'

'Did you do log books when you were young?' Deeby asks.

'Of course,' I say truthfully. 'Every kid does, otherwise how would we know where we are and what we've seen? It's important to keep a record, so one day—'[2]

'One day what?'

'It doesn't matter,' I say. I like to believe there'll be a day when everything is right again, but there's no point in getting the kid's hopes up.

'Can I have a look at your logs?'

'Sorry. I can't remember where I put them.'

'Please?'

'I said no. I don't know where they are.'

Actually, I do.

The books I filled with tiny handwriting and pencil sketches are on the island, but like the mother who helped me write them – and the twin sister who pointedly didn't – they are currently well out of reach.

Deeby sulks, but it won't stop him showing off his handiwork.

'We're here,' he says moodily, indicating our coordinates in his own log. 'And here's what I've seen.'

I scan the entries, spotting the slabs which have been in the vicinity for a few days. There are a couple of new arrivals and some older entries logged as more distant than they should be.

'Are you sure about all this?' I ask gently.

'I checked it carefully.'

Like most of the slabs in our group, we sit in a regular east to west orbit around sixty-five degrees of latitude, so the view over the edge is mainly frozen tundra or freezing seas speckled with ice floes. But Deeby has entered just over sixty-seven degrees of latitude in his log, which, if true, is a cause for some concern.[3]

'Of course,' I say, 'if you checked it, then it must be right.'

I leaf back through the pages. The slabs listed are the usual sparse rocks and tracts of farmland punctuated with an occasional item of interest. Deeby's favourite, the Las Vegas strip, is underlined in red ink. Aside from the wrecked casinos and remains of the Strat, what makes that particular rock so special is its sheer speed and wild instability. The strip and part of the surrounding city tumbles end over end every ten minutes or so, like a crazy fairground ride for the extremely brave. I sometimes have nightmares about it running us down in the night.

'Wow, look at that one,' yells Deeby.

He's forgotten to maintain his sulk, pointing excitedly at the view overhead, visible through a vast plexiglass dome.

The observatory wraps a pair of occupants in leather clad luxury, providing a panoramic view of the super-cruisers plying in and out of the old yacht basin terminal. Overhead, watchers are treated to close encounters with strato-planes on their final approach to the mega strip in New Jersey. Or at least they did; the world of technology got buried by the advancing Phage and only partially rescued by the Inception of Manhattan.

Many believed once the island was in the air, we'd be safe, but blind panic, cholera and typhoid wiped out many more in the years that followed.[4]

'It's a radical,' I say, 'and travelling at speed.'

Deeby scribbles feverishly in his notebook, attempting to capture a likeness of the slab before it disappears, perhaps forever.

'This is exciting,' he gabbles. 'My first radical ever.'

Seconds later the concrete and iron monster has sailed from view and I get a feeling of loss, as though the slab has slipped out of existence and been usurped by its own likeness.

'Hannah, why do the radicals fly north to south when everything else flies east to west?'

'I have no idea,' I mumble.

I'm still distracted by the thought of the slab falling into history.

'There's probably some scientific reason that nobody understands anymore. Did you finish making the log entry? It'll be good to have something to show the others.'

'I'll finish it later, because, umm, because…'

'What is it sweet cheeks?'

'I don't want to say. You'll be disappointed.'

'No, I won't,' I say, thrown by his suddenly serious tone. 'I promise.'

Deeby shuffles his feet nervously.

'I'm really sorry, Hannah. I watched carefully like you asked, but I didn't see the lights in the north today.'

'Hey, don't worry,' I say, utterly relieved, 'it's not your fault they didn't appear.'

I pull him close for a hug, wondering if I imagined what might have been Morse code sent by Mom, even if neither of us knows our dots from our dashes. I might as well have fabricated mysterious carrier pigeons or electrical transmitters or messages folded up to make huge paper aeroplanes, such is my desperation.

'Daniel is coming up the ladder,' says Deeby, his tension dissolving.

I sigh, wishing I could dismiss my own thoughts so easily; I'd spend the days wrapped in a stress-free cloud of cotton wool.

Moments later, a clatter from below signals the end of our four-hour watch.

'You have good hearing,' I say, mentally extinguishing my imaginary lights.

'It's not the sound he makes,' says Deeby. 'I just know when he's close.'

The submarine hatch set in the floor of the dome room gives a little squeal as the wheel rotates. It clangs open to reveal the smiling face of Daniel, who's standing on the ladder below.

'Ben just got in with food.'

'That's great,' I say quietly. 'Deeby needs to eat.'

'OK then, fracture girl,' teases Daniel as he climbs into the dome. 'Time you two weren't here.'

He has blond hair and freckles — which I share — cracked spectacles and a missing tooth — which I don't. I also lack his nose for edible treasure, a skill that has helped keep our group alive since the chasm opened up and survival became even less assured.

'Thanks for not mentioning the food out loud,' I whisper.

'No problem. But don't get too excited. He didn't exactly bring back a picnic basket.'

'Anything is better than nothing,' I say, glancing at Deeby. His face is gaunt and I can hear his stomach churning from where I stand. 'Any thoughts about what we discussed the other day?'

'Teaming up with another crew or getting off the island?' says Daniel.

'Whichever you like,' I reply. 'And in any order.'

'Finding a better crew will be difficult,' says Daniel. 'There's the trust thing for one. And as for getting off the island, it's been tried before. Some idiot sees a slab passing underneath, grabs some dirty bed linen and a few seconds after jumping realises that's not how parachutes work.'

'I was considering a plan with a little more finesse. It's just so frustrating to watch all those prime plots floating by, like birthday presents you'll never be able to unwrap.'

'I hear you.' Daniel smiles. 'It'd be nice to find some place of our own, maybe start planning for the future instead of reacting to the present.'

I nod and consider the idyll. We might even fall for each other at some point given the chance. Daniel has a good heart though, and it might be wasted on me.

'Why don't you go and relax,' he says, 'maybe think up a magical escape plan while I take care of the boy.'

Before Daniel finishes speaking Deeby is already jumping up and down on the spot, getting excited at the thought of staying on watch.

'That would be great,' I say, squeezing his hand in appreciation. 'I love the kid to bits, but I could certainly use some time alone.'

'Knock yourself out,' says Daniel.

'Do you really love me to bits?' whispers Deeby.

'Of course,' I say, 'and Daniel loves you too.'

'You bet,' says Daniel, 'you're the champ.'

'Why do you call Hannah fracture girl?'

'It's a joke,' says Daniel. 'Sometimes when you like someone you give them a different name.'

'Like Deeby?' he says.

'Sure, just like that.'

'But why fracture girl?' asks Deeby.

I decide to stick around, just to see where Daniel takes it.

'Ok, what do we see when we look north?' says Daniel.

'Lots of tall buildings,' says Deeby. 'Almost too many to count.'

'Maybe a few less than that. So, which is the tallest?'

I look towards Central Park where Nordstrom One used to stand. Nearby, on the same footprint that once hosted One57 is the decapitated Nordstrom Two. Even missing the upper half it's still taller than the Freedom Tower. But Deeby is looking beyond that to the northern edge of the park. The majestic building dominating that part of the skyline is a five-thousand-foot monster fabricated entirely from plywood, bamboo and glass.

'The North Woods Needle,' says Deeby. 'The one with the dark green windows.'

'You really know your stuff,' says Daniel, 'so let's find out what you know about things closer to home.'

'Okay,' grins Deeby.

'Right,' says Daniel, 'what about the one shaped like a diamond chandelier?'

'The Fulton Street dome. It was built over the old dome on top of the subway station. Hannah told me that, didn't you, Hannah? The day we saw that factory flying upside down.'

'OK,' says Daniel, 'so you know where the big gap is? Where there are lots of buildings missing?'

'Right there near the station,' says Deeby, pointing out the location.

'Well, that's where the fracture is,' says Daniel. 'It's a really big gap between us and the rest of Manhattan. Way before Inception there was a tunnel there and when the crash came it caused a shock wave and the island broke apart along the line of the excavation. But Hannah can tell you more about it, if you like. She was there when it happened, weren't you, Hannah?'

It's not something I'd considered sharing with Deeby in case he got scared, but Daniel has left me no option. I'd been scavenging alone in the financial district, having argued with my sister Lilith earlier in the day. That was the last time I saw her, heading north in a strop, probably to get her side of the argument to Mom first. We were traversing the series of islands which define the north-western passages when a boy not much older than Deeby appeared, gesticulating at the sky behind me. I turned, expecting to see the cloud that had just put us in shadow, and was shocked by a million tons of sub-strata heading towards us on an avenue-wise collision course. It was odd to witness something so massive moving so soundlessly and majestically. It made the experience so much more threatening, as if our final moments were being played out in slow motion.

The boy ran to me in panic, burying his blue-washed face against my chest, but he kept peeking out and, realising we were safe before I did, he ran off shouting abuse and waving the fossilised Krispy bar he'd stolen from my pocket. I considered running after him, but the belly of the incoming slab snagged us north of Pier 86 and demolished quite a few tall buildings in the process. The shock wave of the collision reached me soon after and I woke the next day, bloodied, groggy and laying on a piece of roadway that dangled over a quick-moving blur of forest a couple of miles below.

'Well,' I say, deciding on a simplified version, 'there was a huge collision one day when Manhattan got bumped by another slab and we got broken into two pieces; a big one and a much smaller one.'

Daniel chimes in with a welcome observation.

'It's why we all get so hungry,' he adds. 'Because the smaller part of the island we live on doesn't have enough food for everybody.'

'So, we fight,' says Deeby, 'and people we love end up watching you with glassy eyes.'

Both of us fall silent as we watch the child's mood darken again. Daniel looks at me in shock as I stifle a sob in Deeby's hair, pulling him close and cuddling him so hard he squeals.

Holo-stream Clip
New York, NY – September 6 2083

The place we call the crib is located in what was previously a high-class residential area, which is now a low-class ruin like everywhere else in the city. Even so, the unusual architectural style is at odds with its surroundings, like a stare-eyed baby cuckoo attempting to style it out in a blackbird's nest. There's no real evidence of the building's history, which is sad, but I believe our home was a rich person's folly; an attempt to reclaim and protect an imagined past by embodying it in an impenetrable fortress. I wonder if they lived to witness the levitation of their dream? A genuine castle in the air.

I slide down the ladder to a niche at the next level. There's a hatch here leading to a cloistered landing with access to the outside atmosphere. Sometimes, when the hatch is open it lets in the sound of the wind singing across the ropes, but today, even at eight thousand feet, the silence is absolute – the result of a tailwind matching our progress.

I step to the railing at the edge of the landing, taking in the vast ice fields and frozen lakes which once formed part of the Russian tundra.[5] For a short while, after the second Soviet collapse, they belonged to New Europe, but

Inception came, and like most of the rest of the world, they went back to being just plain old land; exactly the same land as before, but no longer divided by tendrils of hate or the imaginary lines in old men's heads. Now of course the boundaries of our various islands are all too real.

With Deeby's sad observation still fresh in my mind, I'm in no hurry to go below so I distract myself by imagining what the island will look like a hundred years from now. Maybe we'll be a jungle ghost ship carrying the bodies of the starved on an endless journey. Maybe the city will get rebuilt like in the picture books, or perhaps it'll be buried in a mountainside somewhere. Or perhaps I'm being too pessimistic as usual. Our descendants might find a way to join all the slabs together again and start over, but somehow I don't think that's going to happen. It's people's minds and attitudes that need to be grafted together, not pieces of rock.

I stay a little longer, allowing the cold wind to bite my face as I consider how few words Deeby needed to paint such a harrowing image of death. It's like he can reach inside and determine the simplest way to communicate an emotion, which to me felt like the loss of a parent. Or perhaps that was just me, turning it into something personal.

The cold forces me inside. I descend the freezing metal ladder and, at the lowest level, step over a warm ball of fur sniffing at the bottom rung. Pointy is an unkempt mass of grey and off-white studded with odd coloured eyes and an over-active tongue. He's also quite possibly the last dog in the city, maybe the entire world.

I lean down to tickle his protruding hips and ribs and he follows my familiar smell into the mess room. This is the best protected location in the building, with thick metal grates on the windows and a main door that would be more at home on a battleship. In the middle is a massive oak plank table where ten places are laid, despite there being only eight of us left in the group.

Ben snorts as I enter. He's sitting next to the empty seat Adele would normally occupy. Not bothering to enquire what the noise means, I sit next to Alex, a sandy haired, green-eyed kid with a chiselled jaw and a perfectly honed body. He's fine, but a little distrustful of the rest of the group, Ben especially.

'Eleven freaking months of starvation,' whines Ben. 'When the hell is it going to end?'

I know what's eating him and it's not the food situation. He's pining for Adele which, strictly speaking, is Alex's job.

'Haven't you learned anything?' I ask. 'Even Deeby complains less than you do.'

'Yeah, well there's another thing,' says Ben. 'What happens if we hit another slab?'

I can see it now, my preferred solution. Ben is standing on a chess table in Washington Square Park. He's doing his badly-informed but self-proclaimed expert thing when someone emerges from the crowd with an old-fashioned electric clothes iron. They're whirling it around their head like a giant bolus, approaching Ben with great stealth until finally it's too late. Ben turns and notices the flying appliance just in time to see the pointed end embed itself in his forehead.

'Yeah,' he continues, 'so the next time we get clobbered it's every man for himself; I don't want some seven-year-old dead-weight dragging me down. I say we put the kid and his mongrel dog back where we found them.'

'Fortunately,' I say, smiling at the image in my head, 'nobody is asking you.'

'I vote for stuffing them back in the drain,' grins Alex, clearly taking the piss. 'Maybe they belonged to someone who lives in the next drain over. Or maybe there's a reward?'

'Yeah,' says Ben. 'Or we could trade the kid for food. Maybe even eat him. He's young so probably nice and tender.'

Silence. Nobody has ever heard of it happening, but if food gets any scarcer it's a distinct possibility.

Alex senses the conversation has hit a barrier so he reaches into his pocket and pulls out a penny whistle. He manages a few tuneless notes and I'm just about to complain when I notice it's a piece of candy.

'My last solo recce,' he grins. 'I was saving them for a rainy day, but it seems to be raining now.'

'Hilarious,' says Ben weakly.

I think he knows he overstepped the mark.

Alex silences the cacophony by sliding a whistle across the table.

Ben's attitude fades from storm to moderate gale. At least on the surface. I can see a time in the not-too-distant future when we'll fight amongst ourselves for food. And with the exception of Pia – smart but frail – the group are all bigger and stronger than me.

Alex sends another whistle in my direction, so I snap it in half and give one piece to Pointy who's waiting patiently beside me. I suck slowly, savouring the taste and wishing it would last forever. Pointy bites, crunches, gulps his share, oblivious but grateful. Ben gives me the scowl accompanied by the usual rant.

'What's the point of giving half your rations to a stupid dog? We could eat for weeks from that skinny carcase. Just think how all that protein would build your muscle mass, Hannah. It'd keep you out of trouble when you climb.'

I scowl back at Ben, motioning for Pointy to jump into my lap.

'My rations. My rules.'

Pointy licks my face.

It's true though. I slipped last time I climbed. We were laying a hazardous new route when I lost my footing and, by pure luck, was saved by a safety harness I generally never wear. I barely had the strength to get myself upright and would probably have died from suspension trauma if Alex hadn't hauled me up.

'Do we actually care if Hannah falls?' Pia makes her entrance, her footsteps barely audible despite the horrific leg injury she received falling through a window in a burned out garage. She takes her place on the other side of Alex, glancing briefly at the two empty settings at the head of the table. Her almost whisper hones the knife. 'She's only here on sufferance, and if she kills herself out on the net there'll be more rations to go around.'

She leans forward and looks down the table at me and Pointy with that superior smile of hers.

'He is not going to end up on a plate.'

'There's no need for you to argue the point,' she says, 'the sheer logic of necessity will eventually do it for us.'

And then she gives me that 'I'm smarter and older than you' smile, which I find faintly hilarious.

I glance at Alex for support. He's missing Adele who's out on a scavenge and would ordinarily sit opposite him. Today, she's paired up with Raoul – Pia's idea. She reckons we need to feel comfortable climbing with every member of the group and not just our regular partners. I agree, but not to her face. Her sense of superiority is bad enough.

Pia herself will be aching for Raoul to return and take his place opposite her. They aren't doing it to the best of my knowledge, but there's a definite bond between them which goes beyond mere friendship. In fact, there are bonds of differing strength between all of them – not us – a complicated cat's cradle of dependency and trust.

Then there's me, Deeby and Pointy, sitting in the middle like that damned cuckoo again, only this time in a starving eagle's nest.

'Time for the share out,' announces Pia, with her self-appointed air of authority.

We reach into our pockets and spread out the day's findings. This is difficult for me, and I know the others feel it too. When I've worked hard to bring an item to the table it's difficult to let it go to someone who hasn't been out. And if I haven't been scavenging myself or haven't found anything, I feel guilty taking my share. When I was younger and there was more food around I'd have thought this incomprehensible, but these days we live like animals, existing only to stoke our bellies. I wonder how we can ever value ourselves in the circumstances.

Alex throws four bone-shaped dog biscuits onto the table followed by a packet of birdseed he found in a pet store. Pia takes charge of the sorting as Ben chucks in a strip of beef jerky. I slide in a petrified chocolate bar I found lodged beneath an emptied vending machine. I also chuck in a recently dead rat on Daniel's behalf.

'Is that it?' says Pia distrustfully, as if we might be holding back.

She's not scavenging because of her injury, but presents a crow's wing from Raoul and a packet of solidified gravy mix from Adele. Then she takes a hunting knife and divides the spoils, taking care to place shares in Daniel's, Raoul's and Adele's places.

'Shouldn't Raoul and Addie be back by now?' I ask, as she weighs out the birdseed.

Pia glances at the head of the table and I know she's

imagining the worst, even though they're only a couple of hours late.

I guess sharing mutual pain and helplessness is one of the deepest and darkest experiences, and this group has had its share. We're wrapped in a kind of mental bindweed; the empty settings at the head of the table signifying only the most recent losses. Jamie and Britta went missing a year ago just before I joined, but they were preceded by others, which explains the seventeen names carved into the middle plank of the table. It's a family built not on love or trust but the need to survive.

'They aren't coming back,' says Pia.

She's muttering under her breath now. I know she's struggling to imagine a world without Raoul in it.

'Calm down,' I say, 'they'll be here soon, you'll see.'

Pia stands and limps around the table towards me. I think she's about to unleash some of her favourite cuss words but her bad leg collapses and she falls against me. Pointy yelps as he's knocked to the floor but I manage to cushion Pia's fall. Which is when I smell the state of her wound.

'You need to get that dressed,' I say. 'And we need antibiotics. It's festering.'

Pia picks herself up in an ungainly fashion. Her mask of confidence is slipping.

'Yeah, well if your mother was here maybe she could wish up some medicine for us,' she says. 'Or perhaps you can have a go at fixing it? The gift gets passed down through the family, right? So, what do we think, are antibiotics going to magically appear?'

I bite my tongue, mainly because this is my own stupid fault. We stumbled across a stash of alcohol a while back and Pia decided to throw a party. And while we were all stinking drunk, I let slip my mother, Rachel, was tried as a wish caster when I was a kid. They didn't believe me, of course, which makes Pia's jibe all the more difficult to bear. The ability to make the world conform to your wishes by pure mental effort is not one that's popular, or even believed in by the majority. But those who want to punish others for the tiniest of differences don't let logic get in the way of their physical or verbal attacks.

'You know what Pia?' I say, 'sometimes you make it really difficult for people to feel sorry for you.'

I flick her a one fingered salute and get up, eager to breathe air which hasn't been in her feeble lungs. As I leave there's a sound of retching and I turn to see her puking like an old cat.

The mechanical latches on the door are complex and it takes me a while to open it and reveal the intermediate lobby. Once I'm inside, and Pointy safe beside me, I close the inner door and unlatch the external door. It leads onto a fortified roof that overlooks the dome. On the other side of the glass, Daniel is studying the eastern skies through binoculars. Deeby spots me and gives a cursory wave before returning to his log book. Watching them, I feel a sudden wash of joy, as if keeping him safe insulates me from the horror of our broken world. I wave back unobserved and crack open the submarine hatch which is set into reinforced concrete. There's a rush of stale air from below as I lift it and, for a moment, I'm startled by the olive-skinned face staring up at me from the access tube.

'Raoul,' I say, stuttering in surprise, 'thank God you're safe. Pia was worried sick. We all were.'

Raoul gives me a broad smile, then shouts down the ladder to the indistinct shape below him.

'Hear that, Addie? They were fretting over us.'

'How touching,' says a muffled Adele. 'Now can we please get inside? I'm starving.'

My heart leaps with joy at their survival. Our survival. All of us. And as each of them comes off the ladder, I give them a hug. It's funny but, even though I've lived alongside them for almost a year, I hadn't realised I cared about them until just now.

Immutable Cities 2

HAV – *City of Glorious Silence*
A closed city, and generally considered not to be worth the journey. Naught is known of what goes on inside its massive stone walls, except for an ancient text which reveals: 'A city of spies and ubiquitous subterfuge. Many have possession of crowes which are sended upon errands to distant playces. They return at intervals bearing messages learned by rote or clutching reeds or symbols inscribed upon vellum. Arrowes have oftentimes brought these skanky creatures from the sky, but the tongue they employ is foreign, the reeds nothing more than they appear, the scripts blurred by the raines or rendered up in complexe cypher.'

KARSE-BEREK – *The Inhospitable Backwater*
A former ice station and research facility in the region of Borelia, closed in accordance with the conditions of the Nova-Mundii anti-proliferation treaty. The sole structure remaining above ground was never a part of the science

station, but an unlikely four-storey house with a single room on each floor. It was encouraged into its current position by starry-eyed fisher folk who sledged it across the ice from an inland location. Today it is jammed into a sandy inlet and protected from the sea, rain and ice-bound freezing winds by a wall of slate. The original house had windows, but is swallowed now by layers of walls. Today the house possesses five outer skins, all heavily tarred and insulated. It's thought the original intention was to guard against residual magick, although it's well known now that wooden structures offer no such protection. There is no greater pleasure though than being inside the structure, feeling safe from the elements, the multiple walls doing much to add to the occupants' feeling of well-being. Light is piped into the cosy interior through tulip ropes, whereas smoke is extracted by an ingenious one-way chimney. If ever you come this way, enjoy the immense sense of immunity from the inhospitable weather and sign the visitors' book before you leave. Avoid the subterranean laboratories where magick is still active, though, and please be sure to leave the pen for the convenience of other travellers.

FARAD-CAPACITO – *The Gathering of Gentle Harbours*
A group of feral coastal cities twisted back to primitive roots, their identities reclaimed by pirates and criminal gangs which overran them. Previously prosperous, they had traded in spices, precious metals, gemstones and exotic fabrics but, since their fall, the sole item of exchange is captured ships and the lives of their crews, both ransomed for vast sums. Imagine the adventure involved in visiting such a place. At night the cities are cloaked in a black

velvet hood and operate under strict curfew. Surrounded by militia of varying loyalties, they are as well-armed as any two of their opposing factions and, since the enemy refuse to combine forces, the pirates are protected by simple arithmetic. This equation of imbalance is reinforced by hundreds of armed and heavily protected compounds forming the perimeter. If you ever find yourself in Farad-Capacito, and it is recommended you do not, then you will eventually find yourself captive. In that case, the best course of action is to appeal to the better nature of the Matron Qing Shih, who runs the fiercest and most profitable outfit. A former lady of the night who worked in a floating brothel, Qing Shih also controls the local stock exchange and profits handsomely from the actions of the other outfits. She is difficult to find, not least because there is a vast price on her head, but a likely location is the Haz-Mirak, which lies a mile or so offshore. The Mirak is built from seven large ships bound together to form a huge metal heptagon, the outer defence surrounding three smaller ships arranged as a triangle; the whole affair linked by perilous mesh walkways. The entire construction resembles an arena for physical trial, and it's hard not to imagine the bravest of travellers testing their mettle here. Moored at the centre of the inner ships, is a former lightboat whose tower is equipped with gas burner lights used for signalling. It is also used as a gibbet, upon which are hung those whose ransoms remain unpaid.

ARALIA, SEA OF ISLANDS – *The Lost Ocean*
This place was once a vast inland ocean, teeming with fish and surrounded by forests and abundant wildlife. Now there is only desert, the waters redirected for irrigation

purposes and leaving a shoreline littered with deserted fish canneries, docks and derelict boat yards. The arid sandscape is criss-crossed by great dunes; home to the skeletal remains of wooden boats and the rusting hulks of steel trawlers, a sad tableau completed by winds from the barren wastes to the east. When the last drop of water evaporated, just a single person remained, anchored in place by her father's grave. When they found Zuber Erethal's emaciated body it was seated and dried of tears, her perfectly preserved head cupped in bony hands.

OLEANNA – *The Shining Diaspora*

A city of spires built upon towering sky-reachers which lies in the path of the prevailing wind. Once every dozen or so years, the winds grow to titanic proportions and the aerodynamic pods lift from their moorings, borne aloft on the maelstrom. In this way, the city has grown downwind for hundreds of miles, scattering its distinctive technology, art and music to random skies. Sometimes, perhaps once in a century, the winds blow in unpredictable ways, and cities like Atlantea are fashioned, a sprawling artistic metropolis built at sea. Atlantea sits upon the ruins of earlier spore-landings, piled up in the millennia since the blind benevolence of the diaspora began. In other directions and birthed by other winds, the lawless cities of Palacinka and Nostroov also owe their existence to the sporadic outpourings of their lofty parent and, like other children of Oleanna, are much more famous than their progenitor.

The foremost of Oleanna's descendants is the city of Pyrrh, the sapphire jewel of the plains. In the Pyrrhean dialect, there are forty-seven words for the colour blue and another thirteen which provide material for constant argument. Pyrrh is home to the infamous Gadron Tharoc, a possession fetishist who reclines like a toad in a reinforced bunker. In perfect safety, and insulated from the opinions of his fellow citizens, Gadron the Greedy directs the actions of agents who scour the ruined world searching for rare artefacts to fill his famed cabinet of curiosities. It is not possible to visit the treasure house or even approach the environs of the bunker, but the distended gut of the collector may sometimes be observed wobbling on stick thin legs towards the exclusive restaurant known by locals as the Gluttonous Eyes in the Rotten Potato.

BURABON – *The Glimpse of Futurity*
Erected at the intersection of temporal fault lines, it is composed of three distinct regions which nonetheless occupy the same physical space. Aryul is the polluted city of the present, Pretania the city of the ancient past and Pharox the same city in an inexplicably prosperous future. The citizens of these times and this place are abnormally incurious, which is fortunate, given the potential for calamity if they were otherwise. Instead, the good folk of Burabon continue to conduct their daily lives whilst completely ignoring the outsiders who gather at the observation points to watch what has been, what is and what will be.

MAGGADIN – *The Execrable One*
Beware of all who return from the city of Maggadin lest you incur their displeasure with a misplaced gesture or a contrary opinion, as it's possible they will have in their possession some hateful trinket. An amulet perhaps, containing a seagull heart pierced by copper pins; a desiccated

bullfrog in a cotton bag; or any one of a number of similar abominations which may be purchased in the market between the tall eaves. The famed composer of sear-songs, Jannu-Mera died when a curse doll was left beneath the floorboards of her bedchamber. A note pinned to the doll's breast described the method of her painful death with frightening precision. The cursive strokes of the script have been recognised as those of a well-known Maggadin witch.

LAKE BEKAT-NEL-TORSH – *The Suspended One*

During the region's typically harsh winters, the frozen surface of Bekat-Nel-Torsh resembles a shattered mirror reflecting some ancient tragedy. This vast expanse of water is deeper than any other lake and holds more than half of the world's freshwater reserve. In the northern sector, sixteen metallic needles known as the Towers in the Lake mark the position of the battleship Krusnsk, frozen in time by the kind of rough magick which prompted construction of the shield wall. The vessel is classed as a war grave, but fear, not decorum, is what keeps the curious at bay, although for a substantial fee it is possible to hire the only ferryman willing to approach the monument. The waters around the needles smell of peach blossom, cinnamon and bitter almonds, and the air tastes of burnt sugar, all symptomatic of a massive magickal deployment. Those foolhardy enough to board the ship report seeing members of the crew frozen in agonised postures, suggesting a brutal and drawn-out demise. Some believe the crew are still alive and make repeated calls for efforts to free them from their bonds. Saddest of all is the copulating couple in cabin number nine, who have suffered irreverent graffiti carved into their naked forms.

DYO-KYA – *The Mother of the Seas*

The nearest stretch of coast is more than two thousand miles distant, but there is a strong naval tradition in the land-locked city of Dyo-Kya. On the first night of each full moon the citizens gather in the piazza to witness a unique naval battle. Those locals rich enough to afford it are decked in blue and silver silks, each of them wearing an ornate hat which supports a miniature sailing ship equipped with live cannon. Due to the inherent danger, ultra-rich enthusiasts have been known to press gang their servants into the role, many of whom have died in the service of their masters' ambitions. The navies move according to a strict set of rules across a sea of undulating blue silk – the glorious sight of ships giving battle in the moonlight should on no account be missed. Although frowned upon, gambling on the outcome of the battle is common, as is betting on the number and identities of those who might lose an eye or suffer facial disfigurement from gunfire. Silks are now fireproofed following the conflagration of the fleet which occurred some years ago and which none survived, save for Entuso the famed battle choreographer.

Katz: The Fourth Wall

Ink on Paper
The Movable City of Aeropi
Haksdia 47th day of Cimmerous
Translations [Hav, Karse-Berek]

Dear friend Velliers,

My new home is bearable but, more importantly, safe. It's also relatively worry-free, as long as my special tincture of poppies holds out. One of the conditions of residence is bird clearance, so I spent this morning in the company of Ludmilla the Fire Artist, picking up the carcases of creatures unfortunate enough to wander across our flight path. It seems we emanate a field of influence which birds (and perhaps other creatures) cannot abide. In more interesting news, I've enclosed a description of the Wandering Towne of [Aeropi], which appears to be an early reference to our own canvas-clad metropolis. I have absolutely no idea how it's possible for this to appear in a thousand-year-old document. Until now, I'd half-wondered if I was part of some elaborate spoof, or the places mentioned in these documents were fabrications or exaggerations. Now I'm only slightly doubtful of your intent. The description sounds like it was culled from a publicity poster, but even so, what a terrific glimpse into our past! I get the sense when translating that I know these far-off places, even though they're so madly displaced in time. They are like a shimmering mirage, present even when I close my eyes.

Next stop on the tour is [Farad-Capacito], which, like many of those we visit, has seen its share of plague and fire, drought and pestilence. These days the pirates have it, but the rubes need us more now than ever. Something to distract them as they mourn the loss of magick, wake for a brief interlude of light, then await our leaving so they can return to fitful slumber. Sadly, the freak show is no longer with us, so we're only half as interesting as we used to be.

What other treasure awaits us in the untranslated pile?

Such joy, but there must be more to life than hiding from mobsters in a circus trailer.

Otto Katz

P.S. After penning the above I had a confidential conversation – or at least I thought so – with one of the side-acts I've been getting to know. I mentioned to Cassandra the prophet I'd heard of some acts from way back in the day and it was like tossing a frog on a skillet. She went from pink to red to purple and then screamed loud enough to bring a dozen rousties down on top of me. One of them, with fists like hams, decided I'd taken advantage of the lady and he and the rest of the goons proceeded to beat the shit out of me. So much for beginning to fit in.

P.P.S.   Much needed payment should be dispatched without delay to the next but one city on the tour – the roiling cesspit and former bejewelled ocean which is [Aralia].

P.P.P.S.   I have refixed the mezuzah which fell down some weeks ago. Perhaps it's why my poor face resembles a plate of mince.

Ink on Paper
The Movable City of Aeropi
Strydia 5th day of Allegiance
En-route to [Oleanna]

Travelling north, the next place on the grand circuit is one of the many we refer to as 'tennies' – a location where ten percent of the population loves us and the remaining nine tenths would take the greatest pleasure in tearing us apart. In case you're the slightest bit concerned, I'm still bruised black, blue and purple. The general feeling is that I didn't deserve to get mashed to a pulp for failing to molest Cassandra, but probably deserved a lesser licking for asking questions about things I ought not to know. Overall, I think I've been taught a valuable lesson – although I'm not sure exactly what it is.

Now, onto the translations. I have ignored entirely the superfluous rectum-locutions from that self-oscillating lick-spittle this time, not least because the script is difficult to parse. If you insist, I'll provide the words of the venerable Sir Tosspot Fuckwit under separate contract, but it's just more of the same self-aggrandising crap and will cost money you could use to pay me. Better you spend time analysing the actual texts, where I sense a network of connections that run deeper than words; something of the dark world, I think.

I'm still trying to find out about the old circus, but being far more careful about who I talk to now. A minor snake charmer claims to be of [Burabonese] descent and Prem the clown hails from the city of [Maggadin] but I dare not enquire further about his home town in case I end up horribly dead, which is probably not the optimum outcome. Viewed from the safety of the ropes, Prem's act was joyful, but even so I noticed an amulet in the form of a golem attached to his cape. I swear as soon as I laid eyes on the protective figure, he fixed me directly with a look of abject fear. I'm now wondering if the circus might be as good a hiding place as I imagined. Why, for instance, does he believe it necessary to protect himself against occult forces? A night cloaked beneath the poppy haze is most definitely in order. The mezuzah is still in place. I double checked.

dung, hay, boiled nuts and broken ribs,
Shalom Aleikhem
Otto Katz

P.S. As we crossed [Lake Bekat] I spotted a pod of soophers floating in the shallows. They are shy mammals that sleep in water, joining tentacles to avoid drifting apart while unconscious. I don't know if the two are connected, but we recently acquired a gigantic wooden octopus from a travelling theatre. The creature appears to serve no purpose at all, except to provoke daily arguments over what colour it should be painted.

P.P.S. I have an old folding camera which I'm using to create heliographs of the performers. There is something timeless about this place, as if history passes but the place itself never moves. There's a dreadful sense of loss too, which makes me want to record the inhabitants of Aeropi to protect them from the ravages of time. I'm a preservationist by nature and can't resist committing those ancient faces to eternity.

Ink on Paper
The Movable City of Aeropi
Faldia 19th day of Allegiance
Heading away from Dhoka, lately [Dyo-Kya]

Troband, a curse on your tight-fisted balls. Yes, I will mix metaphor and simile any way I choose. The bruises are mending and the ribs strapped, so I can't complain (too much). We were in the region of Bonar-Vell recently, close to the modern city of Dhoka, known in ancient times as Dyo-Kya. After the shock of translating the Old Aeropi segment and recognising its special place in time, the idea of visiting Dhoka was too much of a temptation, so I threw any thought of resistance out of a window I don't possess. You could say I was drawn to the place.

    I couldn't afford passage on what was left of the meagre pittance you doled out last time – less than half the agreed amount – so I was obliged to get Hannu the Mesmerist to hypnotise a monorail guard while I concealed myself in the baggage car. Stray magick be damned! The occult leakage gave me a shitter of a headache but for twenty wondrous minutes or so I could see ten seconds into the future and made a bet over two raindrops running down a window-glass. I now have enough money to eat for a week. This does not excuse what you owe me, especially since I'm low on my special substances.

On arrival in Dhoka, I was desperate to see how much they've improved that magnificent naval battle and prayed this would be one of the days it was enacted. In short, they thought I was mad. Quote from street hawker: 'You bain't see no sea here d'you boy?' Fucking cheek. 'You'm a freppin muffin, an no mistake.' By which you might guess they had never heard of the famous ceremony and were prepared to punch the lights out of anyone who said otherwise. I felt completely let down by the lack of spectacle, so it didn't help when the same delightful gentleman announced that: 'We don't like your freppin trousers and we don't like you neither'. He was, however, still happy enough to charge me double for a portion of his wretched grasshopper wing and pink cheese pie.

A boy overheard my enquiry and tugged me to one side. He had light blue eyes, brown rat-nest hair and a sly look that warned me to keep a hand on my valuables at all times. It's strange, but I had no recollection of him being there moments before. He dragged me by the hand and I sensed immediately that it was safe to follow him through a network of alleyways and back streets until we came to a decrepit warehouse decorated with carvings of the various constellations. Finest of all of these was a beautiful rendering of 'The Mathematician', with superb representations of the equations.

We gained access through a rotting window frame and, once inside, the kid showed me a multitude of hats with model sailing ships attached and all manner of ancient naval apparel. Judging by the number of medals these uniforms sported, they must have been worn by some very brave admirals. True, we had to break open a few boxes to find all this; it wasn't just laying around waiting to be examined.

Asked how he could possibly know, the boy gave me drivel about predicting that I was going to decide for some unfathomable reason to stay in the city and search every building until we found evidence. He said he had predicted where we would discover the loot so took me straight there. Complete bollocks, of course – unlike my ten-second glimpse – but an entertaining side track. I'm ashamed to admit we opened more of the boxes and found a fine bronze statue of a wolf which, sadly, was too heavy to carry. On the other hand, after breaking open a few cabinets, I liberated some top quality dream nectar, a leather-bound writing book and a rather pretty pair of satin slippers. Awful, I know, but if you'd pay me on time I wouldn't be forced into this life of crime.

Your reluctant partner in filching and expropriation,
Otto Katz

P.S. The boy escorted me to the monorail and begged to accompany me. When I refused, he ran off with the writing book and slippers. Bloody little thief. Worse though, I had to barter away most of the opium for a third-class ticket and spent the journey trying to avoid the gaze of a woman I swear was reading my thoughts. I like to think that man is a universe unto himself, but the crone's stare eventually forced me to admit otherwise. Eventually, we are forced into contact with others and must acknowledge their existence. One party always receives suffering and the other inflicts it.

Ink on Paper
The Movable City of Aeropi
Haksdia 27th day of Allegiance

Something about the boy troubled me, but an entire week went by before the answer leeched into my pathetic brain. I was sitting in the mess tent, attempting not to gag on the injurious slop they insist is edible, when I realised he'd used my name, even though I failed to introduce myself. I share a trailer (chicken-shack on wheels) with Kal Barando, a clown-cum-mind reader who has never threatened a bar of soap in his life. Kal's act is pure bunkum, but when the campfires are lit and alcohol flows the carnies are always drawn in by his tales of the circus going back centuries.

I mentioned the boy to him one night, about feeling as if I already knew him even though our paths had never crossed; about the connection I felt as soon as we met and how it tore me apart to leave him stranded in that dismal place. I had stored the emotion inside, but framing it in words brought it bubbling to the surface, which pleased Barando no end. From there it was an easy decision to go back and rescue the boy, an idea which registered on Kal's face as an overpowering joy, as if some great disaster had been avoided, or at least postponed.

Ink on Paper
City of Dhoka
Date Unrecorded

Even after receiving your payment (feel free to continue acting out of character), I returned to Dhoka as a stowaway on the monorail again, eager to see what temporary power the drive-system would grant. The journey was longer this time because the show had moved further away from Dhoka, so the headache turned into an entire day of serious vomiting, visions of migrating geese in flames and waking the next day in a brothel with empty balls and a full wallet. I left a hearty tip, as I had expected it to be the other way around. Importantly, my pleasuring room had a partition of blue silk, burn-marked, ripped and holed, and clearly once a part of that man-powered ocean. What else have these people lost or thrown away? The city is squandering its past.

I found the boy at the junction of Throttled Larynx Street and Boulevard of the Seven Wrestlers. More accurately, I found a ruckus sounding like three wildebeest trying to open a refrigerator with chopsticks. At the centre of this furore was the boy, cowering, dust-covered, and taking blows from an assemblage who, incredibly, had formed an orderly queue. When I say taking blows, it's more like he was managing them. At the last moment, he'd twist aside so the fist intended for him pounded into rock or brick but never on flesh. He knew where the impact would be in every case. My arrival gave his attackers the excuse they needed to retire with bloodied knuckles. I dragged the child to the monorail station in a hurry and, though it pains me to say it, paid for two real tickets. During our journey to link up with the circus, the boy stared at the desert most of the time, meeting my questions with grunts and monosyllabic answers. What was his name? Where was he from? Why was he in Dhoka? It wasn't until he fell asleep and started talking in his dreams that I began to regret my actions and reached for my pleasure pipe. Even through the pleasing layer of drug-induced insulation, a disturbing fact insisted on making itself known. The kid was not from these parts. From the little I could make out, his family were fishermen or maybe sailors; definitely something to with ropes and nets, maybe even a circus act, which would be handy. Unless, of course, he ran away from the circus in the first place.

Looking over my shoulder,
Otto Katz

Diary Fragments 2

Holo-stream Fragment – Para 10.04.17
Charter Flight BX07 – May 6 2069
Texielle Brandt – Cabin Crew

In my dream, I fly on gossamer wings over wind-drummed tents and out over the desert towards the source of ethereal music. We leave behind the clouds of dust, garbage heaps and polluted drilling farms and make our way towards the distant horizon. This is where the promise of the city lies, its tall buildings serried like crones' teeth, punctuated by gaps.

When I wake up, I'm strung beneath a vast hydrogen balloon, marooned in the sky with a bunch of over-privileged, over-entitled, mouth-breathing oxygen wasters. Luckily for us, they squeezed an extra twenty on board at the last minute, as if the job of serving champagne in a confined space isn't difficult enough already.

The trip was marketed as the Celebration of the World Breaking Apart flight, known to the over-privileged passengers as the 'Goodbye to All That Trip'.

It's great to know the towering intellects of these diamond encrusted passengers will be preserved, so visitors to museums of the future will be able to wonder at what the disaster has wrought, and what the rest of us must have been like, if these idiots were the ones we chose to save.

Yesterday we had a tiny problem when all the passengers ran to the windows on the same side – despite a warning this would destabilise the gondola. For all their immense wealth, they were eager to first of all see and then covet the wanderer passing below us. It had a lake with an island in the middle, a house and fishing boat, all surrounded by a deciduous forest, mainly oak, I think. What a wonderful life.

We were quickly overtaken by the island though and thoughts turned to yet another sumptuous meal in the Restaurant at the Edge of the World. The drinks and nibbles service went smoothly until I was cornered by Lydia Strax, a woman who's as beautiful as she is intelligent – and not in a good way. She has a plan for a – I believe fictional – city where the citizens will be able to interact with whatever they see reflected in their magic mirrors; fragments she tells me of the great mirror of Kladesh which was supposedly some great scientific achievement associated with drawing power from the rays of the sun.

Usually, citizens will not share their visions, each believing they have some unique secret to protect. Instead, seldom eating, playing or sleeping, they wander aimlessly in worship of their reflective mirror-god, eager for the approval of others like them. She's welcome to a place like that, and I'm sure she and her money belt will be very happy there. Tomorrow we change course and head north. I can't wait to breathe that cold, fresh air.

Holo-stream Fragment – Para 10.04.17
Kroken, Norway – May 6 2069
Torbjorn Aho – Destitute Mayor

I have an entire town to myself, so you couldn't really call me homeless. It must simply be habit that makes me sleep under the stars; a desperate imitation of my freezing childhood perhaps, which was spent in a wooden cabin at the back end of a mountain road. I recall ice crystalising on the inside of my bedroom window, the sight of my breath forming above the frozen pillow and the geometrical pattern on the cheap curtains which, when viewed side on, looked like a cartoon duck who's also a sea captain.

They reckon scientists were (or are) working on evidence of an external influence which 'informs' the universe, something they're calling Dark Information. What I want to know is if it affects ordinary mugs like me, and whether my balls will still feel like frozen cow eyes this time next week. If there are parallel universes like they say, is there one where a wandering slab gets close enough for me to be rescued or do I die in every possible world? If so, then why me? Why am I the only poor sucker who gets to die everywhere and everywhen? Why am I bothering to record this? Oh, and yes, while I remember, does everybody on the ill-fated hydrogen balloon get to die every time? Even the good-looking servant girlie who got ripped in two? It crashed about a kilometre away and, although I just about burst a lung to get there quickly, they were all dead. The passengers were all bronze skins, glint-white teeth, and watches for telling the time on Mars. And they all had champagne flutes in their hands. I mean, what the hell is that all about? I set fire to the wreck a week later, once I'd found the girl's bottom half and given her a decent burial. I think she deserved that. Life has meaning, however short.

Holo-stream Fragment – Para 08.44.19
Fleetwood, England – July 14 1967
Roberta Barnum – Holidaymaker and Poet

I can only tell you the same story I gave the reporter from the Fleetwood Chronicle. I was walking along the sea front past the pier amusements towards the model boating lake. And there he was, Professor Aubrey Winston Grey, a wizened owl in wire framed spectacles, engaged as usual in his life-long search for gullible souls. Clad in a black cape and mortar board he stood a foot higher than everyone, courtesy of a tatty trunk. He had his back turned to the bay. It was as calm as I'd ever seen it. Too calm, in fact. As if it was lying in wait, deep and patient. A passing schoolboy bid him good morning and enquired how the numbers were going.

'Bishmullah Cushtibump, it's money for old rope,' the professor yelled, much to the boy's delight.

A young couple passed by moments later, 'See Emily Play' squeezing its way out of their tinny transistor radio. Identifying his intended victim, he invited the girl to rub the Buddha's belly for luck. As she touched the statuette, the professor drew out an envelope, allegedly containing the scores for tomorrow's football matches. But he hesitated, as if he'd sensed the awful event just moments before it happened. Perhaps he really was a seer?

I remember the Sun made a sudden movement, deep purple clouds came down and the air filled with the sound of rushing water. Not like a stream or a river, but the thunderous percussion of an entire sea running away.

The professor went white as he turned around to face the waters of Morecambe Bay – the only time I'd ever seen him looking in that direction. None of us spoke as the full-tide waters drained in minutes, revealing the mudflats all the way to the fire-ravaged remains of the Wyre Light.

Holo-stream Fragment – Para 37.37.33
Lyon, France – December 12 2273
Pascale Despres – Professional Chess Player

The first suggestion we were under attack was the glass jar containing a dolphin foetus that crashed onto the cobbled pavement behind me. I twisted and glanced up in one movement, but there was no explanation, either for the appearance of that particular specimen or the other examples of pickled marine life which followed. But the strange phenomenon was almost certainly linked with what happened next. Why was Presqu'île no longer a peninsula but an island? Why was the earth coming apart?

Holo-stream Fragment – Para 03.00.17
Bombay, India – June 3 1888
Unidentified Boy – The Street Food Pedlar
with Impossible Blue Eyes

I never wanted to fight, but my parents are poor and knew I was quick and strong. They made money from my first fight and, ever since then, it's all I hear. Every time I win, there's a new tattoo to mark the victory, a progression of shamanic symbols crawling from ankle to groin like a poisonous twisting vine. Every night, I find myself praying to the girl in the mirror that time will twist and the fighting will stop.

Hannah: Persistence of Vision

Holo-stream Clip
New York, NY – September 11 2083

I was happy when Raoul and Adele came back safely, but clearly not as much as Pia, who decided we should celebrate in style. Raoul and Daniel are out scavenging though and Adele is on dome watch, so the celebration is not quite as big as she would like it to be.

Alex, half-amused, half-shocked, sits alongside me in the wood-panelled library as Pia and Ben render themselves stupefyingly drunk and turn the celebration into a train wreck. Pia loses her wafer-thin veneer of modesty and swears the air blue while Ben rips books from the shelves and pokes fun at anything he doesn't understand. Which is pretty much all of it.

'You have absolutely no sense of how to behave,' I say. 'These books are precious.'

'That's right,' laughs Ben, 'they'll keep us warm when winter comes.'

He tears out a page, screws it up, and throws it at me. Then he takes another swig. I pick up the balled paper and flatten it out again, reading the badly creased page with some difficulty. It's a series of horse pictures I remember from being a kid. Mom found a plastic projector with a continuous strip of film and if you held the thing up to the sun and cranked the handle it looked like the horse was galloping. It was all the more amazing since we'd never seen a horse in the flesh, although it's possible we ate part of one in those early days.

'That's an encyclopaedia you're demolishing,' I complain. 'One day soon you might need to rebuild an engine or calculate a trajectory or do something else to help us put the world back together.'

Ben grabs the page back.

'Yeah? Well, a page about horses isn't going to help much in a horse-free world, is it?'

'The principle's the same,' I say. 'Some day you'll need the wisdom in those books.'

'I think writing must be like frozen talking,' says Deeby.

We stop and stare at the child.

'That's clever,' I say. 'Who taught you that?'

'I just made it up,' he replies.

I examine the child closely; he's a picture of pure innocence, but that's not the way seven-year-olds talk.

'Yeah, and books are icy lakes filled with words,' says Ben, tearing another page, 'so be careful you don't drown beneath the ice.'

In some ways I pity Ben. When Inception came and the island took to the air the surviving population was pretty confused. The old life didn't mean much anymore. A lot of them decided we didn't need education or any of the other stuff that defines civilisation. I was lucky –

Mom taught me rigorously – but Ben drew the short straw. All he knows about the world is the wreckage he sees in the present. It doesn't necessarily make him a bad person, but it sure makes him difficult to live with.

Raoul and Adele are late back because they'd climbed to a penthouse. It had taken them just over an hour to scale the outside of the building and only a bit less to get back down. Considering the effort involved, it's not surprising the place was untouched. In fact, it was so well-preserved Adele was prepared to stay there forever and enjoy the marvellous views of the sky. It was what they came back with that interests Pia though: four bottles of single malt whisky with an impossible name and a taste of iodine, dark earth and seaweed.

After a few shots each, Pia and Ben decide to breach the study, one of the rooms I'd quietly tried to barricade. Inside were more of the little personal touches we'd grown accustomed to finding elsewhere. Like the hand-blown glass figurines, the memorabilia from the opera and the exquisite scale models of da Vinci inventions.

Ben is now systematically destroying them.

'Please don't do that,' I say, in my most reasonable voice.

'Why not? History is dead, isn't it? We started again at Inception, didn't we?'

I feel myself sinking into quicksand, anticipating another argument that goes around in circles. We've had quite a few recently, and I wonder if it's a sign of increasing desperation.

'You might have started again,' says Alex, supporting me for once, 'but most of us count the years the old way. We didn't restart history just because the island took off.'

'Doesn't matter what year it is,' says Ben. 'This stuff is still junk.'

'And what about when the world recovers?' I ask. 'What do we tell our children? "Sorry but we burned or smashed what was left of your ancestors"?'

'The world isn't going to recover,' says Pia, ever the cynic. 'Take a look around. We're stuck with this crappy setup, so you'd better learn to live with it.'

In my heart I know she's right. We're in a fix and that's the way it'll stay unless there's a miracle. And none of us believes in those. I just wish Pia would use her intellect to keep things together instead of trying to blow us apart.

'Please don't talk like that in front of Deeby,' I offer weakly.

'Sorry,' says Ben. 'I forgot you want the little man to be the next ambassador to, er, nowhere.'

'I don't mind the cussing,' says Deeby, 'but surely elegant language would serve you better?'

Ben is stunned into silence. For a moment anyway.

'Swallow a dictionary, did you?'

'I don't have one,' says Deeby politely. 'I do have a little diary though.'

He takes out a tiny leather journal I have never seen before.

'Where did you get that, honey?' I ask gently.

'I was in a house once, searching for food when I discovered this. It was placed very deliberately on the mantelpiece, like an object of veneration.'

'Sodom and Gomorrah,' says Ben. 'What age is this kid again?'

Deeby passes me the journal and there's a familiar tingle, like a little charge of electricity. As a kid I used to collect abandoned diaries from all over the neighbourhood, stashing them in a basement only I knew about. Or so I thought.

I knew it was wrong to intrude on those poor people's lives, but I'd devour their thoughts whenever I could. I imagined myself as a mad conservator immersing myself in lost time, enjoying their triumphs and shrinking from their fears. Then my beautiful twin sister found the hoard, and put an end to my guilty pleasure. I can still remember most of them though, and when I bring them to mind it seems like a little act of remembrance.

With two shining seas to guard us, we believed we were safe. The government walled up the borders with Mexico and Canada and declared, without exception, nobody was permitted to enter. Approaching aircraft were shot down, ships were turned back or sunk by submarines – no matter how valuable their cargo – and armed guards protected every inch of coastline.

We should have taken our lesson from history though because a fortress, no matter how strong, always has a point of weakness. The eyes of the country were turned to major threats, so nobody noticed a tiny raft from Haiti finding refuge in the creeks and mudflats of the Louisiana bayou. And nobody noticed when the young boy who survived the trip made his way into a small town and got taken in by a homeless shelter. What they did notice, however, was the emergence of the Phage in that same area. Some say it was even welcomed by the rapturists who went about spreading it deliberately in the name of their notably absent saviour.[6]

'Hey,' says Pia. 'Do you remember what happened last time we got drunk?'

'Yeah, Hannah told us some interesting stuff,' giggles Ben.

'But this time I'm sober,' I say, 'and you're the ones putting on the show.'

'Sorry,' says Pia. She takes another slug of whisky, but sounds contrite.

'Apology accepted,' says Ben.

'She wasn't apologising to you, you great lump.'

I'm watching Pia closely. She's mulling something over while I'm doing my best to think positively about her. After all, we're in this together.

'I love Raoul with all my heart,' says Pia quite suddenly. 'You all know it, I just never got around to saying it.

'So why mention it now?' I ask, somewhat taken aback by her frankness.

'It's a game of truth or consequences,' giggles Pia. 'Who's next?'

'I don't like Adele as much as she likes me,' Alex says eventually, 'and Pia, maybe now you've told us, you should think about telling Raoul how you feel about him?'

Ben looks pleased with Alex's revelation and smiles as he reveals his own truth.

'I once ate a whole packet of beef jerky,' he says. 'All except for one strip – I handed that in for sharing.'

'I knew it,' I say. 'How long have you been stealing food from us?'

'Long enough to watch you and the stupid mongrel shrivel. Your turn.'

Pia gives Ben one of her looks. He's been marked down for a serious talking to.

'Come on, Hannah,' encourages Pia. 'Let's hear something from you.'

I shrug. They've already heard my deepest secret, but they don't believe it.

'Oh, wait, I know. Does anybody know Morse code?' I ask with sudden inspiration. 'Because I saw someone signalling from the other side of the chasm and kept it to myself.'

'Maybe it was your mother,' says Ben, 'sending over a few choice items from her spell book.'

'Perhaps,' I say, gritting my teeth, 'but we've all had a turn, so the game's over.'

'Not quite,' says Pia. 'What about Deeby?'

'No,' I insist, 'you're not dragging him into this stupidity.'

'Please, Hannah?' says Deeby.

'Yes, "Puh-leeze, Hannah?"' mocks Ben.

'Tell us a secret little boy,' says Pia.

'Please don't do this, Pia,' I beg, 'he's just a—'

'But I want to,' says Deeby.

'See?' grins Ben. 'The child genius wants to play.'

'Stop this right now,' I say, fearing what Deeby might come out with.

'It's alright, Hannah,' he says.

'There you go,' says Ben. 'He's dying to tell us. Come on kid, we're all ears.'

He doesn't speak straight away. Instead, he looks around the group, like he's looking into our souls. The tension is palpable.

'I gave one of the bad men glassy eyes,' says Deeby.

My intake of breath feels like it will never end.

'What's he talking about?'

'Huh?'

'He's telling you he killed someone,' I say, eventually. 'Are you satisfied now?'

'Bullshit,' says Ben. 'What did he do? Beat the guy to death with a teddy bear?

'The big boy told me how to do it,' says Deeby.

'And then he ran off?'

Ben finds this highly amusing.

'He doesn't run anywhere, stupid. He's in my head. He said the man deserved it for hurting my mummy.'

'Jesus,' hisses Ben, 'the kid's a fucking psycho.'

Deeby's face is a storm of crows that threaten my sanity. My stomach twists into a knot the shape of which I have no name for. It's a pain connected directly to my childhood; something that demands to be feared. The boy is on the edge of a precipice, breathing hard.

'That's enough for now,' I say. 'Shall we go for a lie down?'

'Don't think so,' says Ben, gripping my wrist. 'I want to hear his other secrets.'

'That's not part of the game, is it? One truth, remember?'

'Please don't touch Hannah like that,' says Deeby, breathless.

'Get lost kid,' says Ben. 'I'll break what I like and touch who I like.'

Deeby's frown deepens and my instinct tells me I need to put an immediate stop to this. I wrench my wrist out of Ben's grip and turn to Deeby. I've seen that same look in other people's eyes before now and it didn't end well.

'Let's not do anything we might regret,' I whisper. 'Why don't we go and join Adele in the dome and help her to check the sky for new slabs?'

Deeby nods and takes my hand as we turn towards the door, but we've only gone a few paces when Raoul and Daniel appear and block our exit.

Daniel seems shocked, his gaze apologetic.

'We have a problem,' says Raoul, his voice wavering. 'The aquifer is poisoned, which means our security is breached.'

'So?' says Ben.

'We secure the building,' snaps Pia, 'or sleep with "kill me now" signs tied around our necks.'

'How do you know for sure the water is poisoned?' I ask, grateful for the support from Pia.

'Trust me, you really don't want to know,' whispers Daniel.

He glances at Deeby, obviously concerned at the boy's agitation.

'Pointy is dead, isn't he?' says the boy.

Daniel nods. Like the rest of us, he's surprised at Deeby's intuition.

'Jeez,' smirks Ben, 'lucky it wasn't one of us.'

'I don't like you,' says Deeby, looking thunderously at Ben.

'The feeling is mutual,' sneers Ben. 'And I don't like your new big sister either. The sooner you stop stealing our rations and find somewhere else to live the better.'

'I bring in as much food as you,' I say. 'And you've already confessed to being a ration thief, so get back in your box, creep.'

I thought we'd finished with the whole grabbing thing but he's on me again. This time there's no doubting his strength. He traps my arms and, although I try to remain quiet, the pain forces a scream from my lips. Daniel tries to intervene but he's not a fighter and backs off when Ben kicks out at him and increases his grip on me. I shake my head, encouraging him to stay back. I don't want him getting hurt on my account.

'Get your hands off Hannah,' breathes Deeby.

I try to wrest my arms free, if only to reduce Daniel's obvious anguish, but Ben is wise to my moves. He twirls me round and slams me against Deeby, who screams as he's knocked to the floor. When he gets up to face Ben there's a menacing quality to his body language. The child moves like a small but deadly predator.

'Let her go,' he says quietly.

Ben falters for a moment, realising there's more threat in Deeby's whisper than his scream. For someone who thinks mostly with his fists, he seems to have realised that the boy's formerly placid mind could become a source of threat. I see the fear disappear though, as if he's managed to refute the logic, and he hurls me aside, intent on doing Deeby some harm.

I feel detached, as if I'm watching from a distance, and for a moment the world feels less solid as gravity slips from my shoulders like a falling shawl. When I return from my reverie there's a fizzing on the backs of my hands, as if a nearby storm has charged the skies.

I lift my head from the floor and see Deeby, his gaze fixed on Ben as an unholy wet crackling sound fills the air. Ben's hand goes up to his nose but there's too much blood to staunch and it drip-drip-drips onto the wooden floor; star-edged craters on the surface of Mars.

From the look on Pia's face and the tingling on my skin, I know what Deeby has done.

'Deeby, no. You mustn't do that. Ever.'

I grab his shoulders and shake him. Hard. As his head lolls comically from side to side, I know I've overacted. He rolls back in bruised terror, surprised I've turned on him. I reach out to pacify him, to explain, but he's moving towards the door.

Pia leaps to her feet, angry but ill prepared for her booze-induced unsteadiness.

'Get that wish casting freak out of my sight,' she screams, pointing an accusing finger at Deeby. 'I don't ever want to lay eyes on him again.'

Despite the slightly comical wobbling, I'm shocked by her rage and don't wait to be told twice. The anger in the room is palpable, and not just from Pia. Ben is wild and drenched in blood and Alex is looking daggers. I don't want to think about what might happen if we stay.

Although desperate to remain with him, I signal to Daniel that he should stay put and I run after Deeby. For his own sake, I need to explain why I shouted or he'll remember it forever like a scolded puppy with me in the part of Cruella. That person is not me, even though the cold guilt is pouring into my heart as I run.

The rain-soaked roof is silent except for the sobbing coming from the ventilator he's crouching behind. He makes a dispirited run but I grab an arm and, despite fierce wriggling, I manage to hold on. The poor kid needs to hear the truth, even if he'll hate me for it.

'Deeby,' I say, struggling to control my mental maelstrom. 'I need to tell you something important about wishing.'

'It's bad, isn't it?' he says.

'Yes, it is, because people can get hurt. Or worse.' I pause, realising I'm the one doing the hurting. 'Me and my sister made a stupid wish once and, in order to protect us from some horrible people, my mother took the blame for it.'

'Blame?'

'People are frightened of things they don't understand,' I explain. 'So, people who know how to make wishes usually keep very quiet about it.'

'And when others find out they get jealous?'

'Not really,' I say. 'They get violent.'

'Is that what happened to your mother?'

The rain lashes our faces. It's the perfect setting to bring out my darkest secret and lay it to rest.

'She was taken and punished in a terrible way,' I confess. 'My sister and I were forced to watch her suffer and it was something I'll never forget for as long as I live.'

Deeby's face drops as he analyses what I've said.

'So, if wishing is bad,' he says, 'it means I'm bad too.'[7]

'No, you're not bad, not…'

As the boy's tears well up and begin to flow, I sense I've laid a lifelong guilt on his young head like a poisoned garland.

Deeby wriggles out of my grip and sprints across the roof to the submarine hatch. Before I've even moved, the hatch is open and he's on the ladder, dropping from view. I give chase, making my way through the maze of ladders and walkways leading to the aquifer in the basement, all the while considering the magnitude of the mistake I've made. It might have been simpler to let Deeby find out the consequences of wish casting for himself.

Touching down in the basement, Deeby is way ahead of me and I stand in horror as he squeezes into a tiny ventilation shaft that's too small for me to follow. And by the time I find out where the shaft leads, he'll be well gone.

It's then I spot Pointy's pathetic corpse. My heart freezes. I run over to stroke him, even though he won't feel it, and find his poor tongue hanging out like a strip of leather. Deeby's diary is lying next to the body, so I pick it up and brush the warm book against my cheek, unable to escape the feeling that this is a goodbye token. I was supposed to be the kid's guardian, but instead I've exposed him to something I always intended to hide. When I think back to how it went when Mom gave us the lecture, it was the gentlest possible introduction to the subject; a complete contrast to the way I just bludgeoned the information into the poor kid's head and expected him to absorb it. I sink to my knees, cursing my incompetence and hoping Deeby will make sense of what's happened and return. After a while, the sounds of the night begin and there's no sign of the boy, so I simply pray that he can find somewhere safe to sleep.

I eventually decide to climb up and relieve whoever is on duty in the dome so I can watch the night clouds roll by. Having bid goodnight to Adele, I close the hatch and settle into the chair, fixing my gaze on the approaching skies. Soon, I start to make out dark shapes in front of and below us and, when cloud cover permits, I see pinpricks of light, like stars in a moving picture show.

I'm about to fetch the binoculars to investigate when the hatch wheel rotates and the cover lifts. I wonder if it's Deeby. Relief turns to massive disappointment, and finally to guilt, when Pia, despite her injuries, climbs through the hatch and stands before me like a solemn Egyptian statue. She wants rid of Deeby as much as Ben does, but it won't stop her making a song and dance about it.

So, I just wait for the salvo of accusations.

First of all, she gives a little sigh and pauses, presumably for dramatic effect, before unleashing the words I know will give her great pleasure.

'You're absolutely useless, Hannah. You had one simple thing to do, look after the stupid kid, and you can't even get that right.'

I nod, blinking salty tears which fuse together the distant pinpricks of light; I'm thinking that, for once in her life, Pia might just be right.

Diary Fragments 3

> Holo-stream Fragment – Para 08.44.19
> Blackpool, England – July 14 1967
> Alice Ball – Civil Servant

I'm not really sure how long a chicken lives. Even worse, I'm not certain how long they keep on producing eggs. I guess you could say I'm curious. Maybe even dying to find out. I certainly will be once the eggs stop coming since they are what's keeping me alive.

They said that what happened to the world was a judgement. Something about magic, or alchemy, or perpetual motion – or none of them. All I remember was the darkening sky, purple and black. I knew for certain something was wrong when that inky bank of cloud draped itself over the rollercoaster and proceeded to swallow the pleasure beach. Not so much pleasure to be had there now; not that many are around to enjoy it. Almost everyone has died or left, thanks to a violent impact the year after we lifted off. I did see the mayor once though. He was dressed in the formal robes of his office and carrying the ceremonial mace; mumbling like a madman as he patrolled the rotting boards of the south pier. I remember the town when it was full of holidaymakers, but the only sign of them now are the wet fizzings in my brain. There's nothing physical to show they ever existed, except for the saucy postcards that litter the esplanade and the ketchup bottles visible through the windows of the boarding houses. I used to enjoy getting the tram up the coast to Fleetwood, but it's no longer possible. Even if the electricity returned, the tracks end in a twisted knot where the little fishing town and its pier snapped off and floated away.

The same thing happened to the section of promenade where the famous tower used to stand. I watched in awe as Woolworths and the Tower Ballroom broke away, taking the great iron beast along with it. The whole massive assemblage tottered off towards the Isle of Man, but only got a few hundred yards before its centre of gravity flipped and the tower ended up pointing at the waves. I watched people tumble out of the shop and fall five hundred feet into an impassive sea.

I don't understand any of it. Things have changed, but not my memory. I know things are different but can't work out how. Can *you* tell me how long a chicken lives?

Holo-stream Fragment – Para 23.57.09
Chicago, Illinois – July 12 1934
Paulo Hernandez – Foundry Worker

I already told the other doctors, but this one makes me go through the whole thing again. I tell him I'm not crazy, and this time I don't shout, which seems to work better.

He makes a note in the file and asks me to carry on. I tell him how I went to work that morning, same as ever, except my Camaro is playing up and I have to leave the choke pulled out all the way over to the mill. He writes that down. So, I tell him how I slotted my sweet baby into the first space I could find in the car park and set off to the sign-in shack. I'm pretty proud of the chrome-work on my rig so I turn back for a parting glance. And that's when there's this huge noise in the sky, like two planes crashing together. I duck down behind a pickup. I guess taking cover is the best thing when you're under attack.

'Ex-military?' he asks.

'Yeah,' I say, 'two tours in Vietnam'.

He writes that down too and underlines it.

So, I tell him that I get up and there's no debris, which is weird. He writes that down and looks interested when I tell him about the car. He's scribbling away like a rat in a tin can. My car is gone and in its place there's an old straight eight. It looks like something from a gangster movie. I never saw such an old car in such good condition. Then it hit me, I tell him, all the other cars are from around the same period. Twenties and thirties. Nothing newer than a thirty-four Buick sedan. So, the doctor asks what's so unusual. 'Plenty of steel workers can afford a brand new Buick,' he tells me. And so, I'm losing my cool again. Eventually he tells me it's 1934 and I say: 'I wasn't even born then.' I'm screaming it though, because I can't believe this doofus is trying to con me, or why he'd even bother. And this guy does not like me screaming. So, I get taken back to the padded cell again where they're playing Fred Astaire and Ethel Waters records just to mess me up. I caught a look at the notes on the way out though. He'd written, 'A delicious confection, the result of an unstable mind,' which is a pretty strange thing to say. There ain't nothin' delicious about this place.

Holo-stream Fragment – Para 07.07.02
Kaunas, Lithuania – January 16 2056
Victoria Seilis – Survivor

'Vicky?' he says eventually.

'Uh-huh?'

'If you could have just one wish, what would it be?'

I think for a moment, recalling the stories my dad told me about the world before.

'That's an easy one,' I reply. 'I'd put the world back the way it is in the book.'

'You're far too attached to that old thing,' grins Tomaz. 'It's not healthy, but go ahead and read me the one about the first levitation.'

I smile and flip through the grubby pages of the diary I found in a derelict pet store.

Eventually I find the childish thumbnail sketch which identifies the entry I'm looking for. It's like a memorial to the old world.

Nobody knew how old Mrs Goldstein did it, but as kids we'd invented this story about the anti-gravity device she'd built in the basement of her brick-built haberdashery store. I don't think anyone seriously believed it, it was just a bit of fun, but it's one hell of a coincidence when you think of all the stuff that happened around that time. The story goes that one day she invited some friends – and quite a few enemies – over for tea. It was when she'd finished playing her Grieg piano concerto that she made the surprise announcement.

She wasn't going to wait for the Phage to surround her, she said. No sirree, she intended to take her store and start up a whole new life somewhere in China.

Some of those present took great pleasure in pointing out the logical flaws in her plan. First of all, and most importantly, the idea was proof that she was crazy; she needed to be locked up someplace where they didn't have keys. Secondly, there was this whole China thing; a country more than six thousand kilometres to the east, which probably already had a means of supplying its haberdashery requirements. Also – and this was a real doozy – her store weighed thirty tonnes, give or take, and was more or less permanently fixed to the earth. No one understood how she couldn't see that these so-called 'minor obstacles' were a significant barrier. A week later though, a crack appeared in the sidewalk outside her store, which must have made her feel pretty damned good. It widened and lengthened throughout the day and, by sundown, had encircled the entire store, the ground within the circle floating an entire metre higher than its surroundings. As night fell the gas mains ruptured and the lights went out. In the void below the store, which was now almost four metres deep, electricity cables sparked and sputtered and putrid waste spurted out in an unholy fountain of shit...

'That's so cool,' says Tomaz. 'I'd love to know what happened to the old girl.'

I fight back tears for a woman I never knew. He seemed happy for her, so I told him the rest was unreadable, which wasn't exactly true. The pages after this were noticeably smudged, but if you concentrated hard the letters were still legible.

> *... but her miracle ended just a few seconds after take-off when she opened the front door of the store and stepped off the threshold into the street. Almost immediately, the building dropped out of the sky and crushed her. Nobody thought so at the time, but the haberdasher was one of the lucky ones.*

> Holo-stream Fragment – Para 17.76.04
> Covin, Alabama – April 23 1972
> Gloria Miller – Retired Physics Teacher

I was walking Dillinger, my Labrador, when Inception began – I think that's what they're calling it. We were out along the dirt road where Highway 96 diverges and the railway sidings join up with the line to Fayette. My dog howled like an old wolf moments before it happened, like that intruder thing he used to do with the postman back in the good old days when we had post. Moments later, we were cowering beneath an old ore wagon as the planet ripped itself apart in a demonstration of our insignificance.

We don't have power these days but I did manage to find an old radio set in a barn. It's one of those really old ones where you have to poke around on the crystal with a cat's whisker. Whenever I think I can stomach it, I give the news transmissions a go, but they never have anything good to say. They keep repeating how the mantle elevated and broke into so-called slabs, but I can see that for myself. What I can't see – so don't yet believe – is this idea of time slips they're talking about. I can't imagine how they would know such a thing had happened, or indeed how it would even look. I guess you'd need an external observer to look at two or more slabs and perform a relativistic comparison. Or maybe just look to see what style of clothes people are wearing.

Observation, hypothesis, experiment, analysis, conclusion. Now that's a guaranteed method which can't be beat. And that is why I started to keep a log.

Hannah: Jump Cut

Holo-stream Clip
New York, NY – September 18 2083

For what feels like minutes – but is probably just seconds – my chalk covered fingertips hold my entire bodyweight; toes searching the moulded glass-work for a viable foothold. It helps that I'm nothing but skin and bone, but my grip will fail if I can't relieve the strain soon. We're six floors above the street at Broadway and Liberty, nose to nose with the forbidding spire known as the Zuccotti Pinnacle. I'm exploring the complex surface of the beast, looking for the outcrops, dents and channels that decorate its vitreous skin and breathing the kind of ecstasy that only height can bring. This is where we fight to survive, a life of rock shoes, open-finger gloves and the vast tangle of aerial roadways that helps to keep us aloft; a drunken spider-creation of wires, cables, ropes, pulleys, nets; anything we can use to traverse the city in search of food.

'You OK down there?' says Daniel.

He's free-climbing right above me and his words have a strange echoless quality, as if the glassy patterns have the ability to absorb certain frequencies.

'Sure,' I answer.

I shouldn't have said it because I don't have a foothold, but as I catch sight of the flattened remains of Trinity Church I locate the support I need and my tortured knuckles can finally rest. The church is not getting the credit for that though.

If it was up to me, I'd climb alone and search on my own terms, endangering nobody but myself. Pia insists we climb in pairs though, and while she's not my favourite person, I know she's right about this. Daniel is my first choice for a partner because he understands the twist and writhe of ropes better than anyone. He's also the only one apart from me who's remotely interested in finding Deeby.

The poor kid has been missing for a week now, and it's nobody's fault but mine. Meet Hannah Keter, the stupid girl who can't even babysit a seven-year-old.

'Hannah.'

Daniel pulls me out of my trance with a forced whisper, motioning for me to look down through the tribal layers.

The storey below is run by the Shades, and the two beneath that are controlled by Lurkers, after which it's a drop into the wild zone if you're tired of living. Above us, all the way to the thirtieth storey region, are the Altos, once described by Pia as half circus acrobat, half lunatic and half bird.

My mouth dries when I see what Daniel's looking at. Far below us, gang members are emerging from a burned-out store. I marvel at the way their breath forms a group of tiny clouds. We're directly overhead so it's hard to distinguish body marks and judge how they might react.

The Maoris keep pretty much to themselves. The Woads are harmless too, but their blue-painted faces are a rare sight these days; they are nearly extinct from hunting. Their hunters are almost certainly the Fratelli Boys, mindless psychopaths who'd mutilate and possibly kill for a sniff of a Hershey bar.[8]

'Cranks,' whispers Daniel. 'Might be friendly. Depends when they last ate.'

'And whether they know it was us who stole their water,' I hiss.

Daniel's foot slips and he dislodges a delicately moulded surface detail, which I fail to catch. To my relief, the eventual impact on the street goes unnoticed.

There's real tension in the air; people know the food is nearly exhausted. So far, pretty much everyone has respected the loose tribal boundaries, but a few more days of hunger will turn Cranks into killers if our own situation is anything to go by. It wasn't deliberate, but we caused the death of a neighbour last year in our eagerness to reach a supply of canned goods. Every so often, we take something to his former mate, but recently we haven't been able to do even that. There are far fewer places we can get to these days. Buildings which hosted rope-ends have generally been sealed to stop people coming up from ground level, but some of those seals have been breached, compromising safety. Previously accessible windows are barred, ropes frayed or cut and deadly sharp-traps appear overnight, complicating previously direct routes and limiting the number of places we can search for food. The whole district feels like a dormant firecracker itching for a light, and I'm not certain what'll happen to us if it explodes.

Below us, a gang member spots a shadowy figure in the distance. The unwitting target carries a heavy sling bag and walks with a pronounced limp, so the mob, always eager for an easy victim, move to pursue him.

'Shake a leg, Hannah,' calls Daniel. 'We need to get off this building before anyone else shows up.'

'I'm right behind you.'

We complete our ascent and traverse hand-over-hand on a line which terminates at a steel and glass office block. My hands sting from supporting my weight as we swung across, the after impression of the wire biting just a fraction more than the cold. The building is painted with a cross to show it's cleaned out, but it'll give much-needed cover. Also, we need to check everywhere if we want to find Deeby. Crosswinds are strengthening and the cold is biting, and thicker gloves will limit our choice of route.

Daniel transfers from the rope to a ledge, side-walking his way to a broken window. Inside, there's a battalion of filing cabinets standing like metal sentries, their contents strewn across a burned up wooden floor. I'm shivering. It seems colder in here than outside.

'We can start another fire if it gets bad,' he suggests, kicking paper about.

'Or keep moving and find something to eat,' I say.

My fingertips show blood through the chalk and my biceps won't stop twitching. As I unhitch my backpack to get water, Daniel kicks an antiquated phone book. It lands open on electricians. The irony is not lost on us. There's a bunch of tech stuff piled up in here, haptic pads, communicators and flex-screens mainly, and, rather inexplicably, an ancient keyboard and a museum-grade mainframe. It seems someone planned to build a wall with all this stuff in order to keep out the cold. No use for anything else, I guess. Alex once pointed out that a magnet moving inside a coil no longer induces a current, which was a long-winded way of saying electricity is screwed. I prefer the message I saw scrawled on a wall once somewhere up on 27th street[9]: *Wot, no power? That's another fine mess you've gotten me into.*

I catch sight of my reflection in armour plate glass. My hair looks like a bird should be incubating eggs in it. My left eye is still closed from a fall two days ago and the jump suit I liberated from a dollar-store smells like it needs to be taken out and shot. Water is too precious to waste on personal hygiene.

I prepare to move on, but Daniel has other ideas.

'Rest,' he insists. 'It's dangerous to climb when your mind isn't on the job.'

'I know,' I snap back. 'I spent my entire childhood dangling from cornices and walking taut wires.'

'Then you know why we need to stop.'

I finally nod, too tired to argue, let alone climb. We started before dawn and have been in and out of every building we came across since, praying in each location that we'd find some sign of Deeby. As we settle down to rest, my stomach gurgles and I think of him complaining of hunger that last night. The waxy skin on the backs of my hands resembles parchment and, as I doze off, I find myself wondering what might happen if I became fully transparent.

Daniel shakes me awake and, after a quick look in my eyes, pronounces me fit to climb.

'Hey,' I say, still sleepy. 'What time is it?'

'Coming up to eleven.'

We keep track of the time by judging the sun's position in relation to buildings, so it's not particularly accurate. It still indicates, however, that it's time to put the last bit of my 'find Deeby' plan into action. First though, I have a confession to make.

Daniel is not going to like it.

'I need to be at the New Nihon bank,' I say. 'At noon.'

'Are you planning on meeting someone?' grins Daniel.

'Maybe. It depends if anyone saw the messages I left and if they've seen Deeby.'

Daniel looks worried, angry even, and I begin to question my wisdom, if that's what you could call it. I'm starting to think it might have been pretty stupid, but it's done now, so no turning back.

'What the hell?' he spits. 'You left messages? When did that happen?'

'I've been climbing at night,' I admit. 'I dropped notes at the major intersections asking for news of Deeby. And I offered food to get him back.'

'Are you out of your mind?' yells Daniel. 'What if some gang of maniacs finds out? And how the hell are you going to hand over a ransom without getting killed?'

It's a valid point, and I can't believe I didn't consider it.

'I'm sorry Daniel. I was just so desperate to find Deeby and make him safe.'

In the time since Deeby disappeared, we've sucked on half a frozen lemon we found in a drain, devoured a packet of baby food solidified into a massive biscuit and shared a rotting tulip bulb which had made its home in a coffee pot. It's not great cuisine, but a definite step up from licking the glue from peeling wallpaper.

'We are not going to meet with a bunch of psychopaths who may or may not have found Deeby,' yells Daniel.

'But we have to,' I plead.

'Just take a moment to think, will you? They know

where you intend to be and when. And they know you'll be carrying food.'

'It's a chance I'm willing to take for Deeby's sake,' I say.

Before Daniel can stop me, I'm running topside, heading for the rope system leading to the meeting place. I bound up the stairs two at a time and make it to the roof before him. I'm looking down on Broadway again and take a nervous glance to my left. A couple of blocks in that direction is the chasm; even a distant glimpse of it makes me queasy.

From here, the net spreads four ways. There's a sharp wire heading north; a perilous route that'll wear out thick gloves in a single crossing. There's a safe four-cable traverse to a high balcony, but the family living at the end of the route is unpredictable. The third option is a sloping highwire which needs a balancing pole and benevolent winds.

I make my way to the fourth option which I hope will take me to Deeby. It's a pair of blue nylon twines traversing Broadway and crossing to the New Nihon building. I'm on the ropes before Daniel can grab me, pausing to let a slab-quake subside then sprinting the final section.

I make it to the other side while Daniel is still halfway.

He's not pleased, but he can't stop me now. I climb through a shattered window and step inside the bank, waiting for him to catch up. Then I see the angry look on his face. I break into a run again, heading for the vault and hoping nobody has found the rope I hid on my earlier visit. As I run deeper into the building I consider how badly I've let Daniel down. This is crazy, even by my standards, involving him in my stupidity without a thought for the consequences. I only hope he'll find it in his heart to forgive me. I couldn't bear to be in his bad books.

I make it to the vault room just before Daniel. In front of me is a circular door – the kind a missile wouldn't penetrate – the same door I decided to tie myself to if Daniel didn't like my plan. That's pretty much a given now, so I wrap the rope through a grab handle and twice around my torso so he can't pull me away. As I do so I realise that it's a pointless activity, which Daniel soon points out.

'Great,' he says, breathing hard. 'So, when the crazies arrive, you'll be tied down as well? You really are making the job far too easy for them.'

Stupid, Hannah, stupid, stupid. I am so fucking stupid. But I'm not giving up now.

'You know how much I want Deeby back,' I snap, 'Why is this such a surprise?'

'It's not,' says Daniel. 'I knew you'd try something. I just wish it had been a little safer.'

And so, we sit and wait in silence, me tied to my door and Daniel clearly fretting about who might turn up. He occasionally glances at me and shakes his head slowly. After an hour or so, he breaks the hush, not to tell me how stupid I am – which I've been waiting for – but with a question I'd also once considered.

'We live in this urban environment, right?'

He does the thing where people stick their fingers together and make steeples.

'Uh-huh.'

'But a city isn't a self-supporting organism,' he says, 'it's just a bubble with no way of supporting itself. So how did we survive for this long? Before Inception they'd bring food and supplies from the mainland every day. We were like a floating hotel fed by New Jersey. Now all that's history and Manhattan has been in the air for sixteen years, yet somehow we didn't all die of starvation. How does that stack up?'

'I don't know. Maybe there is a God after all?'

I give him a serious look that I hope says don't question me.

'Or perhaps magick is real?' I offer. I know he won't go for that, so I feel pretty safe suggesting it.

Daniel gives me a wry smile then glances at the sun-clock buildings. It's way past the meeting time and nobody has showed up.

'So, where's the food you were going to use as the reward?' he asks.

I unwrap myself from the rope and pull at the massive door, which is closed but not locked. It's a struggle but eventually we're able to survey the contents. Stacked inside on massive iron shelves are a hundred or so gold bricks.

'I don't think anyone accepts precious metals as currency these days,' says Daniel.

I enter the vault and reach behind a brick. I pull out a tin of tuna I hid the previous night and present it to Daniel with a curtsy.

'Since nobody's coming, we may as well eat it,' I suggest. 'Shall we take it up to the roof for a feast?'

Daniel is so keen to get started on the fish he sprints up the stairs without checking for traps or ambushes, but we get lucky and arrive safely on the chill-scape of the roof. There's a battered leather sofa on the helicopter pad so we seat ourselves royally and survey the kingdom. As Daniel cuts open the tin with his knife, I look around for possible trouble. It's not likely this high up, but you never know. Daniel smiles as he folds back the lid and offers the fish to me.

'I think I'd like to see the whole city from a distance one day,' I announce, savouring each tiny flake like a Russian princess eating caviar. 'With all the ropes and nets, it'll look like giant spiders came in the night and wrapped the city in a thousand webs.'

There's a silence filled only by the sound of Daniel chewing.

'Hannah?' he says eventually.

'Uh-huh?'

'If you could have just one wish, aside from getting Deeby back, what would it be?'

I'm so happy in this moment I consider showing him the holo, but I change my mind. I'm not ready for him yet.

'Easy,' I reply. 'I want Pia to give it a rest with the jibes. But mostly I want to find Deeby and my mother. In that order. Mom can take care of herself, but we owe it to Deeby to take care of him.'

Daniel gives a sympathetic smile which ignites a certain warmth in me.

'I'll have a word,' he says.

'And I'm quite sure Pia will listen.'

'Is it true what she says though?' says Daniel, looking thoughtful. 'All that stuff about wish casting?'

'Of course,' I say. 'I thought you were the only one who realised.'

'I do now,' says Daniel, sounding uncomfortable. 'So that stuff Deeby did. You can do that?'

'Sometimes, yes. It's complicated.'

'I see,' he mumbles.

He looks shocked, scared even, a reaction I've seen often, but this time I look away instead of facing up to the questioner. It's like he's embarrassed by our sudden inequality. I want to explain this thing is a burden, not something anyone should want, but those childhood memories of repression and punishment bubble back to the surface and I suddenly feel the need to scratch an old and badly infected wound.

Holo-stream Clip
New York, NY – September 19 2083

I lay back into the sofa and close my eyes, forcing those dark thoughts into a casket at the back of my mind and shutting it with a violent but reassuring click. If I'm to deal with the past then I must pacify the present, so I pull in a lungful of cold air and consider our position. Deeby and Mom in that order. But to help either of them we need to stay alive. Another problem, once again thanks to yours truly. We're exposed out here, overlooked by dozens of higher buildings and vulnerable to attack, so first we need to get somewhere safe. It's a simple plan, and those are usually the most effective, but when I open my eyes my heart gives a double beat. There's an unfamiliar face grinning at us through a smashed panel in the Zucotti Pinnacle. He's pointing at us. No, he's pointing behind us. And laughing.

'Daniel?' I whisper.

There's a whirr of movement at the limit of my peripheral vision. Still seated, I turn my head slowly, but the look on Daniel's face tells me everything. Standing behind us with a grin like a starving hyena is a boy, seventeen or so, his tanned face split by an ugly vertical scar. He's stocky, strong looking, which tells me he's well fed, which in turn tells me he's a force to be reckoned with. He slaps a broad machete on his thigh, an ugly weapon that identifies him as Chang, a psychopath we have so far managed to avoid. We get to our feet uncertainly, Daniel moving to protect me as the aggressor walks around the sofa and faces us.

'Kick the food over here,' he spits.

I put the tin on the floor and slide it towards him with a toe. Chang eyes us as he finishes the tuna and tosses the empty tin back at my face. As I catch it, the lid cuts my thumb.

'More fish,' he says, moving towards us. 'You've got plenty stashed some place.'

We shake our heads, backing up to the northern edge of the roof, trying to formulate a plan without speaking. Chang *swish-swish-swishes* the air with his blade.

He once belonged to a gang of lunatics called the Impervious Ducks who appeared the day the chasm formed. I laughed when I first heard the name, but the amusement soon evaporated as they overran the neighbourhood. They'd kidnap and ransom for food and, if payment wasn't forthcoming, victims were tortured out in the open and sometimes thrown over the edge.

'I hear you got thrown out of the Ducks,' says Daniel, playing for time.

'They kept me hungry,' says Chang, 'so I knifed three of them when they fell asleep.'

'Nice work,' I say, 'but we only just found the tuna.'

Daniel looks hard at me, moving his eyes deliberately so I'll follow the line of his gaze. About twenty yards to our left there's a pile of debris from a forgotten construction project. Behind it, partially visible, is a sign.

TRASH CHUTE

Chang advances and I know from his eyes he won't hesitate to use the machete. He'll slice one of us to begin with, to encourage the other to hand over the food.

He's close. I can smell the body-stink on him. Smoked meat and stale sweat.

'I know where you live,' he grins.

'No, you don't,' I yell, realising I sound like a fractious child.

'The building with the dome,' he smirks. 'I didn't know

it was in use but, once I did, it was easy to figure out a way in.'

'There's no way you made it inside,' says Daniel. 'It's too well defended. And there are only ever two of us out at a time.'

'Yeah, right,' grins Chang, 'so I spoke to this guy who poisoned your water? Dude had been watching you for quite a while. Had your strengths and weaknesses all mapped out. If I hadn't come along, he'd have turned you over himself.'

'I don't believe you,' says Daniel.

I'm not so sure now. It's starting to feel like less of a coincidence him finding us here. Like we're playing a board game and he's three tosses of the dice in front of us.

'You want proof? OK, so your little girlie here, she argued with the kid on the roof. Dude watched her run after him in a panic. And she didn't close the hatch.'

It's like being punched. I can't deny it. I was in such a hurry I chased Deeby down the ladder without spinning the lock wheel.

'Dude snuck down there pronto and flipped the safety,' crows Chang, 'so every time you locked it after that the hatch was still open. Like when you came out on this little expedition. You were two bodies light, so I just couldn't resist going for a look-see.'

Daniel steals a glance at me. There's accusation in his eyes, but fear too. In my belly there's nothing but burning ice, and a quick hatred fuelled by Chang's gloating.

'I cut them,' he whispers, making us strain to hear the words. 'All your little friends back at the playhouse.'

I hope I've misheard, but he repeats himself, and this time he pulls a silk square from inside his shirt. The same creamy fabric I last saw on Pia is stained a deep crimson.

'The cripple girl begged me to finish her in the end,' grins Chang. 'But only once I'd dealt with this guy.'

He chucks down Raoul's thumb ring, and I realise I have been holding my breath since he first spoke.

'Reckoned he could beat me,' he continues, 'but it turns out he wasn't as fast as he thought. Didn't kill him straight away though. Hacked off bits of him one by one, gave him time to take it all in, piece by bloody piece.'

I try to swallow. It's like there's a rock in my throat.

'And looky here,' he sneers, showing me the blood-stained flat of the blade. 'All of their pathetic, whimpering little lives mixed together. The two who were love's gift, the pair who didn't need each other and the gutless creep with the encyclopaedia. He wanted to die when he saw what I did to the others, and I guess he was right. Once a picture gets inside your head there's no wiping it away.'

Like I need to be told.

I try to swallow the bile rising in my throat. I try to think of a way to undo it all, but my heart and brain freeze; the shock of an ice water plunge. I look back at Daniel. His eyes are red, flooded with tears which refuse to run onto his cheeks. Instead, they form a pool reflecting not sorrow, but a deep, inexpressible anger.

The moment lasts just long enough for an uncomfortable silence to descend. Chang enjoys the delay; lets us feel the hopelessness of our situation.

'We'll mourn them later,' I whisper, glancing at our possible way out.

Daniel's eyes flicker like paper lanterns. He is completely demolished.

'Can you actually do the mourning thing when you're dead yourself?' grins Chang.

He slaps the thick blade rhythmically against his thigh,

and I can't help noticing the edge has a nick in it. For a moment, my entire world contains nothing but that tiny metallic irregularity and the signature mark it must have left as it carved its way through the flesh of my friends.

'I'll take the backpack too,' says Chang. 'You won't be needing it.'

I scream at Daniel, who's hesitating, hoping to jolt him into action. Why does it always have to be me pulling the trigger? I throw the tuna tin at Chang, slicing his cheek and catching him off guard for a vital moment as I sprint to the edge of the helipad and glance over the side. The trash chute has slipped in its harness, so the circle of yellow plastic marking its mouth is twenty feet below roof level. At this point I'd like to say I do all my own stunts because humour is supposed to be effective in diffusing fear and I'm scared shitless.

But there's something else. Time is in short supply right now, yet I'm wasting it by making space in my head for whimsical notions. Why is the world such a bizarre place? Why are we not going to school or visiting zoos or lazing on sun drenched beaches and swimming in brilliant blue oceans? Is it just us or are others being punished? And, if so, are all of them being chased by malevolent psychopaths too? What did we do to deserve all this?

Granted, we were screwing up the planet in every way imaginable, but is the proper punishment to have it screwed up even more? And if it is, who decides? I'd like to meet them one day and give them a swift kick in the crotch or trap their head in a vice, maybe even set fire to their hair. Yes, that's what I'll do. If they ever put the earth back together and make a movie of my life, I'm going to play myself so I can beat them to a pulp with a baseball bat.[10]

I glance back at Daniel. He's right behind me and if I don't drop now he's going to barrel into me. I pause on the edge to measure the distance then step off. It's not a clean entry, but I make it feet first into the chute. I push my elbows and knees out to slow my descent and feel Daniel's feet touching my head as my lungs fill with dust. His feet slip down to my shoulders, and then he's gone again as he slows his fall and I let go, plunging faster and faster. I realise we don't know what awaits us at the bottom of the chute and try to brake, tearing the skin from my hands and elbows and burning the flesh on my knees. Daniel's weight presses me again, but I see the chute opening below me. I drop into a pile of concrete dust in a dumpster, rolling aside as Daniel thumps in alongside me. Any other time we'd look like a comedy duo with powdered faces and dusty clown costumes.

Chang is close behind and, as we roll out of the way, another pall of dust announces his arrival.

I don't know how he managed it, but the psycho is still holding the weapon.

'Run,' yells Daniel.

Chang lumbers after us, but we're fitter and faster. He's built for power and we're built for speed and, as the gap between us widens, I begin to feel safe. It feels like we've escaped him, but the joy doesn't last. I steal a glance at Daniel and he knows it too. The streets are deserted for now, but the nu-graffiti tags give it away. Without thinking, we've dropped into the wild zone.

Not thinking things through seems like my new trademark.

We're running and limping, heading north to the end of our world where the chasm beckons us with unnatural gravity. It's like we've always been falling towards it; an unnatural break in the cityscape that creates a feeling of constant instability. Eyes blink at us from alleyways and boarded windows. I try to forget the fairy stories. Like the boy who slipped on a practice climb and fell into the shadow pit near the old pool hall. He screamed for help, but nobody went to his aid. They were about to lower a rope when everyone froze at the sound of a large animal prowling below. In later tellings of the story, this mythical creature became a clattering, scissoring monstrosity known as the 'knitting machine', even though nobody ever laid eyes on it.

We skitter to a halt a few paces from the friable edge of the chasm, lung-burned and gasping. Daniel looks shell-shocked, apparently running on instinct. I move carefully towards the crumbling precipice, testing the solidity of the tarmac and stopping as soon as I can see over the side. Beyond the ragged edge of roadway is sixty yards of clear air down to the mass of twisted girders and pipes which, with the assistance of a ruined subway tunnel and various train tracks, hold the two parts of the island together. Below that, the blue-white of the Arctic Ocean slips idly by.

East, towards the seaport with no sea, or west to seek sanctuary at the WTC memorial. I'm guessing not even Chang would violate the unwritten accord there, but if he's patient he could starve us out.

This is the choice I have to make.

As I dither, a group of masked figures appears, making the seaport the logical choice, but when I glance east there's a group of Impervious Ducks, and other gangs beyond them. The sharks have smelt blood.

There's another choice, of course. I could just step out over the edge and free myself from the grief piling up inside my head. Pia, Alex, Adele, Ben, Raoul, all gone. But I'm determined to make sure my movie doesn't end like that.

Before us lies a mess of pipes, cables, extruded girders and drawn-out sections of subway which emerged when the shock wave hit, and below it is the moving mass of land I'm going to launch myself towards. But maybe killing myself is a coward's option. I should stand up for once. After all, my Mom's waiting on the other side, and there's a run I haven't noticed before. It's a line across the chasm, not quite a rope, but a braided mass of copper phone cables fastened three floors above us in Shades territory.

'It'll be difficult,' says Daniel, clearly feeling better. He gives me a reassuring squeeze as he transfers chalk to my hands. He's warm. And he's right; from where I'm standing, or possibly because of how I'm feeling, the traverse looks impossible.

He reaches high for a grip and makes his first foothold. The building is a brownstone monster with tooth-notch walls signalling an easy climb. I'm not scared, but a slip would prove fatal. Chang is just fifty feet away, and I hear the rumble and chatter of approaching Ducks.

'Go,' I yell. The encouragement is for me, not Daniel, who's already climbing confidently, carefully.

'Come on, rock monkey,' he yells down.

I appreciate the effort he's making, but the idea of Chang shedding our friends' blood has eroded my self-confidence. My progress isn't matching Daniel's and, as Chang starts to climb, the hairs stand up on my neck. I thought he'd be too inexperienced to follow, so it shows how much I know.

'He's coming after us,' I yell. It comes out more like a strangled croak.

'Concentrate on your holds,' Daniel replies.

The chalk does its work, absorbing my sweat and enhancing my grip. I haven't a clue how Chang is holding on, unless it's by sheer brute strength. He's close enough that he taps my ankle, tries to unbalance me. I lift it away and he taps the other as soon as I take a foothold. His face is visible directly below, between me and the wall, so I call to him. I sound braver than I feel.

'Hey, Chang!'

As he looks up, I sprinkle a miniature snowfall of chalk from my fingers. Chang closes his eyes until it settles, then gives a violent shake of his head. It terrifies me; I've made the mistake of assuming because he's violent he's also dumb. Clearly he isn't.

'My blade is hungry for flesh,' he grins, 'and so am I.'

Daniel reaches down and takes my wrist. He hauls me through a window and into a room where the phone braid is tied to an ancient server rack. It's a good belay and will hold fast.

'Go,' says Daniel. 'I'll keep him busy.'

The braid is an unholy mess of thin wires with jagged ends protruding at intervals like a crown of thorns. It's a single span too, not the double or triple we're accustomed to, and doesn't look as though it will hold us both. I climb onto it and monkey-hang, screaming at Daniel to follow. He's at the window where Chang will climb in. I know what I'd do in the same situation but Daniel couldn't hurt a fly, and there's no way he'll summon the courage to push Chang off the wall.

'Can't do it, can you, cissy?' says Chang.

He slices the pointed end of the machete into the window frame and hauls his bulk up into the server room just as Daniel climbs out onto the braid. He slings himself under and within seconds has caught me up, his hands bloodied by the wire-ends.

'As quick as you like,' he hisses.

I reel in shock at the sight of Daniel's hand. Blood is pouring from where two fingers and a thumb should be.

I arch my head back and locate our destination on the far side. The wire terminates at the sixth-floor window of a steel and glass scraper. But there's a hundred feet of braided copper to negotiate first. After the first twenty feet we're over the chasm, so the only thing between us and the distant Phage is a few twists of subway wall. There's a vague tapestry of sage green and ice blue down there, which to the naked eye resembles an earthly paradise.

'For God's sake, hurry,' yells Daniel.

His hand drips a river of blood; he's barely hanging on anymore. I gag at the thought of him caressing my cheek earlier.

Chang hacks at the braid with his machete, the blows pinging along the wire, making my fingers fizz with tiny bolts of pain. I sense every ounce of anger in those impacts, making me even more determined to reach the other side. A quarter of the way across, Chang is still hacking at our lifeline when my heart skips and for a moment threatens to stand still. The braid ahead of me is unravelling.

'Daniel, the braid,' I scream, 'its...'

'Let me look,' he yells.

I shift my weight to allow him see past me. His complexion turns white.

'It's not as strong as I thought,' says Daniel quietly. 'It won't hold us both for long.'

I know what he's thinking, as if the thoughts were my own.

'Let go you whining coward,' screams Chang. 'Save me the trouble of slicing you.'

Daniel lets go with his injured hand and hangs by his legs. I choke on my words of farewell and give a simple guilt-ridden nod instead, which he seems to understand.

'Take care of yourself, Hannah,' he whispers.

Looking me straight in the eyes, Daniel straightens his legs and slips from the wire. My throat tightens and my breath comes in gasps as he falls. Slowly. Ever so slowly, as though his weight has evaporated and gravity has lost its hold. For a moment he's between life and death, occupying a twilight that I struggle to understand. If I had the power I'd stretch that moment into a lifetime and spend it with him. Instead, I scream as he smashes into a wreck of pipes and cables, twitching for a moment then laying perfectly still. For the second time in as many minutes I entertain the idea of ending it all and joining him.

The thought doesn't last long. My miserable life has been bought at a huge cost and I'm damned if I'm going to throw the sacrifice back in Daniel's face.

'Just me and you now,' yells Chang.

The fraying section of cable is just ahead of me. With Chang's blows increasing in strength and frequency, I shuffle quickly over the damaged wire. I'm briefly encouraged by my progress and start to picture a successful crossing but, glancing back, I notice the braid becoming smaller. Then the smaller braid becomes a single wire, and the copper wire stretches and finally snaps and becomes nothing at all.

For a millionth of a second I float, freed from the tyranny of gravity. The wind does not move me, the air does not support me, but I do not fall. Even though my physical body will eventually drop, I vow that my spiritual self will not.

And then a cruel acceleration grips my entrails and wrings them out. It seems Daniel's sacrifice was in vain after all, because I'm swinging to my death. A knife twists in my stomach as I fall, the arc of my descent controlled by the remaining length of cable. Below the wreckage of the subways and pipes I see the earth in great detail, as if the prospect of death amplifies my senses and instructs me to take one last piece of information to my grave. We traversed the skeleton fingers of Norway some time ago, where it's rumoured cities hide from the Phage in the protection of the fjords. Now we're passing over the mid-Atlantic scar; a wound made by a hunting knife, deep and jagged, dividing the frozen witch's tit of Iceland.

It's this image that will define my passing.

Then, with the absolute clarity of someone about to die, the landscape disappears and I fix my gaze on exactly what will kill me. I'm the weight on a pendulum hurtling towards an exposed subterranean garage where rows of personal fliers are turning to rust. And like decaying teeth in a blackened mouth, I know they are going to chew me up and spit me out.

Immutable Cities 3

VORAH AG NASH – *The Monochromatic Jewel*
The region suffers almost constant rainfall, but during the period of greatest precipitation a river pours from the sky, forcing snakes out of the waterlogged ground. The reptiles are believed to be avatars of the dead, who alone have knowledge of a forgotten colour which exists somewhere within the city. No living citizen has a memory of the hue, which is alleged to have been stolen two hundred years after the snakes arrived. The abiding wish of every citizen is to discover the lost colour in a dream and subsequently describe it to their family and friends in an extensive series of melodramas.

KOO – *Resurgam*
An ancient city which grew up around an opera house established on the uninhabited plain between the vast mountain ranges of the Coraks and the Mun-Tisus. It was expected to close in its first season and left for the

winds to devour. Critics were disappointed though when the first of the pilgrimages brought crowds of opera-lovers to the area on their hands and knees. The magnetic attraction was the singer Madeli Tingu, a famous beauty with a great vocal range of vast power who delighted audiences for over fifty years until her much-mourned retirement and subsequent death. It's now rumoured that the unquiet ghost of Madeli Tingu is responsible for several ethereal sightings and grisly murders in the environs of the opera house.

The Arok-Fenix Opera House has burned to the ground and been rebuilt on seven occasions during its two thousand year existence, the most recent being just twenty years ago during a performance of the popular tragedy *Oder-ka-Klemm*.

The climax of the piece is reached during a thunderstorm when the hero kills the faithless heroine, but the thunder machine was so convincing it spooked a pet snake-dragon that had been sneaked in by an audience member. After killing its owner and the occupants of two seats in front, the creature skittered over the heads of others, inflicting many serious scalp wounds before igniting the famed red-silk curtains and escaping into the ornate ceiling.

Since then, audience behaviour has declined further, and it's common for noisy eating, business dealing, arguments and even romantic acts to be performed while the cast attempts to deliver the work. The abuse of substandard singers is prevalent, as is fruit throwing, nut hurling, booing of the antagonist and the repeated jabbing of snorers with sharp weapons – sometimes fatally.

It has been known for rival claques to engage in knife fights. On one occasion, a crowd of drunken sailors burst into the female changing rooms at the end of the show, the ensuing fight soon spilling out onto the streets. Patrons are advised that the nearby drinking house known as the Sack of Bones is no more. Some of the better-off clientele objected to the hostelry's crude appellation, so it has been renamed the Bag of Bleeding Teeth to protect their sensibilities. Travellers in possession of this guide book may take a one hundred percent reduction on their bill on production of a suitably fearsome firearm.

PANDIR-AN-KOOH – *City of Inspirational Algorithms*
A city of twisting spires and vertiginous towers, the famed prominences that mark the Pandir-an-Kooh skyline are wrapped in a permanent blue haze which rises from the chimneys of numerous ecclesiastical computariums. Breathing these fumes often leads to insanity, yet neighbourhoods downwind of these noxious vapours give birth to children with exceptional mathematical ability, a fact not lost on hoteliers who leave their windows open and promote these beneficial fumes in their brochures. The haze above the city is a side effect of complex numerical manipulations performed by alcohol-fuelled mechanical calculators; great ordinating leviathans who ruminate upon the raw data for days. The cud is then passed down to workhouse prodigies (in full view of curious travellers) who visualise the answer in 'n' dimensional swathes of colour, whilst dreaming of a small ship's biscuit and a farthing's portion of water.

XANNIS – *The City of the Pinnacle*
An unremarkable city, save for the red glass tower at its centre that marks the entrance to the abode of the Oracle of

Xannis. The rose pinnacle is reached by a pair of spiral staircases built on the same axis but having opposite phases in the manner of a double screw. Thousands of feet below the surface, a cavern excavated from the living rock joins with an underground lake. Light from the suns is channelled into the void by translucent fibres woven from billions of wild tulips, and there, illuminated by flower-light and seated in a reed boat, is the man who knows everything.

There are many who wish to discredit him, but they are still eager to row out and meet the sage, despite the vast number of purifications and washings demanded of them. Nobody has ever returned from a consultation and claimed to have secured a victory. Always it is the same. The visitor steps onto the raft armed with a confident smile and what they believe to be an impossible question. When they reach the oracle and receive an answer though, the face of the questioner inevitably turns ashen. Many querents will never speak of it again, and those who do speak never tell what they heard.

PNEUMAH – *The City of Lesser Wisdom*
The city is notable for its magnificent observatory which contains the Perpetual Motion Machine. The intricate brass movement of the device is watched over by a sickly native boy whose sole duty is to drip a single drop of oil onto a chain when he believes it necessary. The chain drives a flywheel whose impetus is transferred by a shaft operating a worm gear and, by means of these rotary forces, a pair of baskets is slowly elevated or lowered. One basket contains food, the other a silver-mahogany casket filled with cacodemons. Suspended in an iron cage beneath another wheel is a young girl tasked with taunting the

demons and feeding the boy. The demonic hoard hauls eagerly upon the chain in order to reach her fulsome delights but the oil defeats their desperate grasp. Thus, the motion of the mechanism is kept perpetual by virtue of the physical law known as the Maintenance of Innocence.

XORIFEL – *The Wonderful Arbor*
Beyond the limits of the city, broad-leaved trees transmit chatter to each other via their roots. Saplings that struggle to survive in the suburbs are nourished by their distant ancestors in the suburbs, and standing between two such specimens produces a tingling in one's feet. The pulsing contains no language or code known to man, but the intelligence flowing beneath the soil cannot be denied. Some deny this, insisting the forest is simply a collection of dumb trees, but even the greediest of developers is unwilling to lead an assault on the plantations. Years ago, the forest began to die at one edge of the city, but a green corridor was later observed; a bright trail of growth leading from the decaying region to an abandoned water mill on the edge of the citadel. Here was found the corpse of an arboriculturist who had become the green man of myth; his skin turned to bark, his hair become brilliant moss, his whiskers transmuted into nodes of leaf-bright viridian.

KYRUKK-EN-YAROK – *The Benevolent Mother*
Premier city of the Bloc, Kyrukk is built astride the river Yarok on ninety-seven bridges, which in turn are linked by many thousands of smaller pontoons, the weft to their larger cousins' warp. The ruined pleasure gardens on bridge

seventeen offer proof that citizens of the Bloc know little of joy, save for the fear that someone somewhere is having a better time than they are. They rejected the rusty wheel, shunned the infected goldfish in their polythene bags and stood amused as the carousel organ wheezed its last, condemning the white-painted palisades to a slow, peeling death. The helter-skelter collapsed, the house of mirrors cracked open pathways to the underworld and the once magnificent rollercoaster eventually tumbled into a mildewed heap of timber. Even the ghost train suffered desertion, the departing ghosts presumably convinced that better, more joyless work was to be had behind the desolate factory walls.

In Kyrukk, every citizen enjoys unremitting toil in service of the Bloc, happy to manufacture weapons and various instruments of misery whilst celebrating with an extra potato on feast day. It is not possible to visit the 'golden shimmering citadel of the heroic leader' because it does not officially exist, just as dozens of similar facilities secreted in the surrounding countryside don't exist either. In common with the non-existent cities concealed by the enemy, none of these places appears on any map, and the map they would otherwise have appeared on does not appear on any list of maps.

NIEU CORVO – *City of Ever Curious Custodians*

A city of mass surveillance where unruly gatherings of magpies, crows, jays and ravens watch, wait and, when nobody is looking, submit their reports. To the uninformed traveller, the idea reeks of paranoid madness, but the principle is fully accepted by the native citizens following centuries observing both cause and effect. First comes the seditious word or secret assignment, closely followed by an innocuous gathering of birds. Nothing happens. Nobody saw. Doubts subside as the crime slides into the past, but, just before its disappearance, there comes a knock at the door – a signal of bureaucratic interest. Reasons, explanations, alibis, summonings, oral examinations, noisome questionings and statements. Delay, worry, more delay, more worry and finally the sealing of a fate. Every detail of the procedure is outlined in chapter three of the operations document, *Avian Surveillance in Urban Environments*. No citizen has seen the manual, but its text is settled in the collective consciousness as surely as if it were carved into stone tablets and exhibited in the city square.

BRABAZON – *Citadel of the Cruel*

The city has laboured tirelessly to achieve the utmost quality of violence, superior even to the slaughterhouse city of Branndask or the metropolis of mendicant spies whose name no one dares speak. Brabazon is often depicted on maps as an aquamarine decapus whose tentacles writhe and grasp at the surrounding regions, coveting their wealth, knowledge and peaceful co-existence whilst undermining their infrastructure at every opportunity.

The metropolis is necessarily warlike and possesses a vast array of weapons, both offensive and defensive, and is believed impregnable because of the miniature shield wall surrounding it. Neighbouring cities have attempted and failed to overrun Brabazon and subsequently been destroyed in savage revenge attacks, viz, Lamporia: reduced to a fused mass of glass by an airburst from an unknown weapon; Derellia: bombed into powder and sprayed with a toxic orange goo which never dried; and Canopus: where each inhabitant was burned as the rest of the population listened to their screams. The last Canopian victim was incinerated nearly eleven years after the first.

There is nothing to see in this region with the exception of a remote shed where enthusiasts of the terminological inexactitude gather annually for a boasting, exaggeration and lying convocation. This painted garden storehouse belongs to Tamsin the Abomination, a resident of Canopus who, despite her beautiful name, had the misfortune to be born inside out and was thus spared the torch as an act of compassion.

Katz: Ambient Light

Ink on Paper
The Movable City of Aeropi
Haksdia 42nd day of Allegiance
Moored in [Vorah Ag Nash]
Translations [Koo, Pandir-an-Kooh]

The sun was only half-risen over this potent quagmire of a city when we made our landing. Unlike a land-based circus, our arrival was not marked with the frenetic activity of the setup. We required no pole runners, rope haulers, carousel erectors, sideshow grounders, caravan lashers or tent spikers. Instead, we simply came to rest at a chosen spot and erected a rope bridge between the ticket office island and the nearest high ground.

The boy watched every moment of this activity from the topmost basket on the big wheel and returned to earth with a coat-hanger-in-the-mouth grin. He eats for two, but is always hungry, like some unquenchable furnace burns inside him. Barando refuses to give up his bunk, so the boy sleeps on the floor. What the hell was I thinking, bringing him here? His name is Dina Braid; thrown out of his village due to some superstitious claptrap surrounding his sister. I was inclined to disbelieve the tale, but Barando faintly recollects she was beaten to death for setting fire to crops by witchcraft. Naturally, the rousties got hold of the story and are 'not feggin' happy' to have a source of 'bad juju' in their midst. I mentioned the litany of mangled fingers, broken arms and groin strains which occurred well before he ever joined us and found a festering rat in my slop the next day. From now on I'm keeping my head down.

Some of the rousties claim we should throw Dina over the side, or possibly just give him a scare, but he's never around when they go looking. I wish I had his talent for disappearing. Any talent, really. Not just remembering forgotten languages, but the ability to slide off into a realm of my own where I can sit quietly in a rocking chair and watch the time go by. Sadly, I was doing something similar to that when I first saw the circus, so maybe I don't really know what I want.

Taygorn, the ringmaster, came to see the boy, wanting to know what his act was. Dina wasn't expecting the question but made up some crap about throwing poisoned spears which I would dodge at the last split-second, blindfolded and with my back turned.

'You're not on fire, then?' asks Taygorn.

'No,' says Dina. 'Why would I be?'

'Just checking', the ringmaster says, turning to me. 'And what about you? Are you on fire?'

I grinned like a loon and told him I'd consider it if the price was right. He seemed satisfied and gave us a carny blessing (hands laid on head) then left us in peace. I asked Dina where he got the idea for the poisoned spears, and he told me one of the people in his head knew it, which meant he did too. I'm really starting to worry about this child now, but I'll go along with the lie if it means we get a few extra slices of bacon. Let's just hope we never have to demonstrate our non-existent skills.

I reckon I could do without having to care for a retard, especially if it means not waking up one night with my throat slashed to ribbons and an ironic and wholly age-inappropriate message tattooed on my chest. In the meantime, my strange protege shows an interest in the translations so I'm schooling him in old tongue, using the documents as a primer. Other than that – and confounding the rousties – he spends a lot of time staring at the horizon and talking to himself. Nice work if you can get it.

Slightly concerned and ever-poor,
Otto Katz

P.S. The mezuzah fell down again. It feels like a warning, so this time I fixed it with four nails.

P.P.S. Enclosed is a portrait of Xenobia, the Water Sprite, posing by her glass-walled tank. Tell me if you think those gills are real.

Ink on Paper
The Movable City of Aeropi
Rimdia 16th day of Opposition
En-route to [Xannis]

Noble Friend Velliers, may your loins be thrice blessed

for your continued patronage. The city of [Pneumah] welcomed us with open arms when we arrived, but set fire to the big wheel as a 'please do come again' message and kicked us up the arse as we departed.

Despite the deepening cold, we're mostly happy to be in one piece (or in eight pieces, strictly speaking, which is how many islands we are). In addition to putting out fires, repairing fences and repainting torn or vandalised banners, delays in translation were due to difficulty with the dialect. These are older than we've seen and have something of the fairy-tale about them. Barando showed great interest, despite never having read a book in his life. He wasn't even put off by the lack of pictures. On which score I have been making various heliographs of the cities we pass through. They are modern day, but what about putting them alongside the translations as a reflection of the past? They may not be of such great value now, but the idea of preserving the present for the future appeals to me. If so, what about helping finance the light-sensitive materials? Dina shows great interest in the images and progresses well with reading lessons when he isn't stuffing his face or conversing with imaginary friends. Still, I can't complain. Every time I've woken recently, I'm pleased to report I wasn't killed in the night in a grisly way known only to small boys. We're approaching the northern reaches. If you'll advance the fare, I desperately want to see Karse-Nev or one of the other ice-stations. Just the idea of north fills me with excrement. Sorry, excitement.

Somewhat icily,
Otto Katz

Ink on Paper
The Movable City of Aeropi
Tryndia 38th day of Opposition

You are as tight as a fish's arse, but despite your lack of response I was still able to make the trip. A dirigible heading north landed here for supplies, and although not normally welcome they had acetylene to trade and we needed repairs. I tried to scrounge a lift but the skipper refused. Moments later, with a look from Dina, he'd changed his mind. I worry about that child. He came along for the ride, but I may as well have taken a ship's anchor. I appreciate his imagination and can recommend his company if you like to hear tall tales from the people inside his head, but not if you like to get some sleep every so often. He packs in enough gabble for a dozen.

To be fair he did spot a group of Archads which were once thought to be fictitious creatures. They are huge gaseous bags, sentient herd animals floating on the wind with no permanent home. They were first described by Krenfett Bodubon, who you may remember had rather an overactive imagination when it came to discovering new species. His reputation was destroyed by the press, until one of his more fantastical inventions was discovered living in a tree in [Xorifel]. That sparked a furious hunt for the remaining creatures he'd described, which many believe are still out there. As it happens, so much ice formed on the dirigible we were forced to turn back. An archaeologist and fellow passenger told me how they excavated the thawed-out sites in Cimmerous, but found little evidence the settlements ever existed. He asked a local ice-dweller why they lived in such an inhospitable place when there was a better living further south where it was more habitable. The local took him to see the 'God of Truth', which turned out to be a voice coming from beneath the ice. 'This is why we stay,' he said. 'The voice needs us to keep it company.' My spine froze on hearing it. I bet the archaeologist would kill for a look at our translations, but naught was disclosed, as per.

Penniless and fucking freezing,
Otto Katz

P.S. We were unable to land upon our return due to high winds and were lowered back to the circus like maggots on a fishing line. Dina has begun sketching the cities as I translate them, but his images look nothing like the descriptions. Since we returned from 'north', I've been puking like an owl. Dina thinks it might be the poppies, so I told him to shut the fuck up or I'd snap all his pencils. He is not my mother.

Ink on Paper
The Movable City of Aeropi
Rimdia 51st day of Opposition
The long journey to [Kyrukk-en-Yarok] via [Nieu Corvo]

We're heading south, at last, to a region where the air is warm and many of the natives will never have seen a floating island. On the way, we gained an enormous amount of height to clear a mountain range. I thought it rather risky and took to my bed, but everyone else took it in their stride. I suppose dropping from ten thousand feet isn't much more dangerous than dropping from a thousand, or even a hundred. That latter height, incidentally, is when we let down coloured streamers to attract the rubes' attention. As if mile-wide pieces of rock hanging in thin air weren't enough encouragement. It's considered lucky to grab a streamer as we pass overhead. For the rubes, that is.

Luck is in short supply here and the rousties are on Dina's tail again. I'm keeping him out of the way, but these people have long memories. We recently had a spate of high wire deaths, so everyone is in shock. It's impossible to imagine any of the victims mishandling a rope. The children of aerialists have little pieces of string placed in their hands just seconds out of the womb, yet we had three fatalities in as many days.

It'll be hard for them to get back up there with rumours going around about the ropes being cursed. Once that kind of thinking gets loose it's difficult to contain. I thought it would be hard to shake the memory of those bloodied rags in the sawdust. Even harder was the aerialists' joint grave we dug on the ticket booth island. The sad little memorial was surrounded by the entire circus crew, hats twisted in hands and fear in everyone's eyes as we contemplated both cause and effect.

Distraught,
Otto Katz

P.S. I think Dina senses the increasing stir about him. Recently, he seems more nervous and asked why we appear to be in hiding (he's pretty perceptive) and what might happen to us if we're found. Can't say I disagree with his concern, so I told him about the misunderstanding in [Brabazon] and I think he understands it was an accident. All I did was point out the game was fixed, no surprise there, but they lost a lot of regular customers that night.

Then they were raided by the police. That was nothing to do with me, but the Baem boys don't see it the same way. You can't fart in that town without the Baems taking thirty percent, so please be careful what you say and to whom you say it.

Diary Fragments 4

> Holo-stream Fragment – Para 00.01.77
> Salalah, Sultanate of Oman – February 07 2025
> Mekn-Al-Khamir – Marine Biologist

I was there the day the Great Satan rose up and swallowed the ocean. We had slept on the beach overnight, overlooked by the rocky headland shaped like a donkey's head. Some insisted they saw a gorilla, whereas the boy thought the outline resembled a horse. I first met him when he expressed an interest in seeing the sea turtles climb the steep beach to lay their eggs in the sand. Then he camped outside my office until I gave in.

Now, as we wait for the green-folk to emerge, we lay gazing at the stars.

He asked if there was someone out there, just like him, so I explained the formula for estimating such things. The number of galaxies, the number of stars in each galaxy, the proportion of them possessing planets (which we now know is most of them), the proportion of habitable planets, the chances of life arising. From this, the chances of life evolving intelligence, the entire lifetime of their civilisation, itself a pinprick in the timeline of the universe.

He seized on that last idea and became rather morose, convinced there had been and would be intelligent civilisations but he'd never meet them because their lifespans were so unlikely to overlap. I was impressed he caught on so quickly, but my congratulations were interrupted by the arrival of the first turtles emerging from the sea. I set the cameras rolling to capture the sequence and turned to the boy but he was wading into the ocean, already waist deep. He yelled that everything we had ever been would be lost. Not now, but soon. The ocean, the jebel, the desert. All of it. Lost.

Reaching the point where the beach shelved, he choked on salt water and his head disappeared beneath the waves.

> Holo-stream Fragment – Para 10.70.33
> Lima, Peru – April 23 1957
> Father Dominic – Priest

This is not the action of a knowing and loving God, it is the deranged method of a vandal – or a petulant and uncontrollable child; hence, I no longer believe the stories from a benign age of miracles or the God who wrought them. Rather than believe in nothing though, I choose to believe in anything which exhibits a provable scientific logic. I choose a future of violence and confusion, a future built from unshakable faith and unstoppable force, the same great puissance which changed magic into science, transformed alchemy into chemistry and evolved omnipotent design into natural selection. If I ever fail in my belief and you find me, I ask that you lay my mortal remains to rest beneath a pile of stones.

We cannot outrun death. A monument is the best we can hope for.

> Holo-stream Fragment – Para 23.32.12
> Milan, Italy – July 13 2031
> Carmine Bellagio – Fulfilment Operative

I guess you could call me unlucky. I clocked in at eight as usual, and twenty minutes later we became independent, not just of the company, but our city, our region and, eventually, our country. I didn't bother to clock out because there was no longer a home I could get to without growing a set of wings. If I had, Mama would've been so proud, but after a few hours she'd be nagging me for leaving feathers all over the house. Also, getting the bus would be a problem because of the size of my wings and the height of the doors, so I couldn't go shopping for her. 'You and those blasted wings,' she'd be yelling at me by now. 'Why can't you just be a normal boy and get your mother's groceries? And why do you have three pairs?'

Because I'm a seraph I guess, an angel with smarts. Because when we set down again, Draco will owe me big time thanks to all the overtime. I worked as normal for the first couple of days. Lots of orders to fulfil, sun cream, beach towels, barbecue sets, and not much time to fetch them. Then things started to back up for obvious reasons. We officially decided not to panic, even though there's nothing to do and nowhere to go at night, unless you count the toy shelves. We have everything here. Well, not everything. The company claims 'everything from a pin to a star ship', which is pushing it. Unless the star ships are parked in orbit and only need to come down to get packed into a cardboard box. It's just one of their thousands of little lies, like the free snack machine they told us about at the interview. I'm still looking for it. Perhaps it's next to the 'as much as you can drink for nothing' soda fountain just near the shelves where they park the space rockets. Next to the pool table. If I ever meet one of the 'family' I'll ask them straight out. Why do you promise all those things if you never intend for us to have them? Is taking everything from the little guy what it means to be rich?

Holo-stream Fragment – Para 11.22.44
Inkpie Cove, Antarctica – September 6 2067
Willow Lundqvist – Climatologist

If I'd known I was going to get shot that day I'd have stayed in bed. Problem is, bed in an Antarctic survival hut isn't quite the inviting place it might be at home. I didn't know about the gun when I woke, of course, or even wondered about the identity of the person who'd be wielding it, but when you're one of only two people in an area of twenty thousand square kilometres it's not the sort of thing that first springs to mind.

That morning, my entire thought process was occupied by the idea we'd return to the site where we found the submarine hatch in the ice. Big enough to admit two people side by side, and a complete anomaly. Signs of life in the middle of nowhere. I was sure we'd be heading there, but dad was out early and found a beached whale in the northern cove. That's why we fired up the Sno-Cat, hoping to push the cetacean into deeper water. They say these things happen in threes, but I guess it depends on when you start counting. If six important things happen in one day, do you count the first three? What happens if you get to four? Is it now the most recent three? Why does the first thing become unimportant all of a sudden? Don't even get me started on six things. Honestly, don't. Anyway, while we were preparing to push the whale out with a rubber boom, the situation turned into a Led Zeppelin lyric and part of an island floated by in the freaking-well sky.

A fucking flying island.

I shook my head. Hard. But the gravity defying monstrosity was still there, a terrifying sight with the Corona Australis as a backdrop, like a scene from a sci-fi epic. The line 'I wondered how tomorrow could ever follow today' came to me. It was Robert Plant suggesting maybe something worse was about to happen. And it did. A droning noise alerted us to the presence of a plane which circled twice then landed about a kilometre away. We weren't expecting anyone, but I'm not sure a lack of something could count as the third thing. The pilot got out, donned skis and slung a rifle over his shoulder. Quite athletic, I remember thinking, like an Olympic biathlete, so he was on top of us fairly quickly. I only realised he was a she when the face mask went up.

She unshouldered the weapon, cocked the mechanism and pointed it at my father. Now that really was the third thing. I don't know which of us girls was more surprised when he disappeared into thin air, but I do know what it felt like when the shooter turned the weapon on me and a sharp cracking sound preceded the disintegration of my shoulder and a whole world of pain. The force of the impact knocked me onto my back. I expected to see the girl preparing another shot, but she had turned towards my father, newly re-appeared, who was whistling to catch her attention. As she turned, probably wondering like me where the hell he'd come from, he let loose a harpoon which ripped through her body with devastating effect. The blood is still there on the ice, and if we don't clean it away that's where it'll stay. Sadly, we were unable to save the whale, but it's usually the case with beachings. I always wonder if these intelligent creatures know that when they purposefully drive themselves onto the shore. It's something we need to think about.

Holo-stream Fragment – Para 03.00.17
Bombay, India – June 3 1888
Virrinder Patel – Doctor

The fields where he once worked are gone and I feel obliged to go and tell him. But the circumstances (apart from the obvious fact that the world has gone mad) are difficult. Everyone calls him the decorated fighting man, and decorated he most certainly is. Ink covers his entire body, sometimes clear, sometimes occluded by ageing skin. Last time I visited, those near-black eyes were still bright, but the temple of his body was a crumbling ruin. I remember when we first met. He fetched out a tattered heliochrome taken in his prime. In it, he looked proud, fierce, determined, leaning towards the camera as if nothing could ever move him. He was such a good fighter that, upon retirement, his peers agreed nobody would ever challenge him for the Cup of Lions – he would remain a worthy champion until his death. Now though, in his dotage, a challenge to fight has been received from an ignorant boy in a distant province and since there is nothing but honour in place to prevent it, the challenge must be met. I hear the boy is fit and has many wins under his belt, so I understand why the decorated man is worried. Time is no friend of the aged.

Holo-stream Fragment – Para 13.03.47
Brooklyn, NYC – June 3 1968
Bruce Chaka – Photographer

I finally knocked some sense into my head. There's a camera store a couple of blocks away and the owner is a fan. I sometimes make him a print if there's a big story and he puts it up in the shop. I bust both lungs getting there and barge in like I own the place (a valued tool of every press photographer) and yell for him. He's out back so I yell again and he comes through with the remains of an old Speed Graphic in his hands.

'What's so important it couldn't wait?' he asks.

I'm still breathless but I manage to get it out that I need to borrow some gear. I offer him a signed twenty by sixteen of Rocky Marciano beating out Moore in fifty-five, but he holds out for three prints of the Park Slope airplane tragedy. It's some of my best work, but I still can't look at those images of the wreckage without shuddering. The shock of charred and mutilated bodies lying in the snow alongside Christmas presents kills me every time. The guy wants what he wants though, and after agreeing the deal I get to raid his second-user stock. I pick up a battered Nikon F, because they're built like a tank, but the choice of lenses is limited. There's a compact wide-angle and a short telephoto but they're slow glass, so I take the fifty.

It's the fastest they make. A quick shutter and iris check and then I'm looking for film with a decent turn of speed because the weather is turning nasty. He has a single beautiful roll of Tri-X and another of HP4, a British make I never used before. Jeez, way to go on the stock levels, brother. And then I'm running back, only it feels like ten blocks now, and when I get there, I'm a wheezing, coughing wreck, bent over in the rain. I loaded the first roll of film in the store, so I have thirty-six attempts to capture whatever gets thrown my way before I need to change film with an ocean running down my neck. There's a bum there, searching through the trash; wants to know why I'm taking photographs instead of running. I tell him it's just instinct, and anyway where would we run to? He smiles and offers me a bite of the baloney sandwich he's just found.

> Holo-stream Fragment – Para 17.76.04
> Covin, Alabama – June 23 1972
> Gloria Miller – Retired Physics Teacher

It's fun inventing names for the phenomena I've decided to call meanders, even though the radio calls them slabs. I give them names like the Big Kahuna, Penobscot Minor, Verdant Green and Rusty Trabant, and not forgetting the mysterious Meanies which could be anything really; tempting edges of land just peeking out of the bottoms of the candy-floss clouds. Then there are the identifiable cities, of which I draw pictures (none too proficiently) as they pass. I'm pretty certain I saw London go by once, the unmistakable snaking of the River Isis, obvious even though it was a mud-brown imitation of its former self.

There was maybe a part of Portland too. I went there by air once, and it looked exactly like what I saw when I flew in. Hard to be certain though because my binoculars don't focus properly.

Sometimes, when I'm out looking for food, I call on Vanya Sesostris for a tarot reading. Her pack consists of repurposed baseball and football cards, like the rare Micky Mantle specimen defaced with a scrawled Ace of Wands, and Ty Cobb transformed into a sharp-eyed Hierophant. I got different readings for the same cards once, so I guess my memory is better than hers. It passes the time though, which is something we both have plenty of.

On the way back from the great Major Arcanum guessing game, I usually see old Mrs Gottlieb behind her twitchy lace curtains. She hasn't emerged from her lair since it happened, too busy sitting on that stockpile of food with a shotgun in her lap. One day soon, I may have to pay her grocery store a visit and make a small withdrawal.

> Holo-stream Fragment – Para 10.20.41
> Papakura, New Zealand – January 3 2033
> Emily Southgate – Author

'Renee Zaphisterwash. Magnus Fleabottom. Millicent Bystander. Minesa Beer,' says Kiri.

We're walking home through Kirk's Bush, my children coming up with a seemingly endless list of comical names.

'Florence Trembley Winterbottom, Augustine Trumpsqueak, Lady Honoria Creme Anglaise,' laughs Evan, following up with, 'Pauline Pareto Principle. Kylie Brasshandle-Battenburg.'

'Pathetic,' giggles Kiri. 'Cop a load of these. Rundle-Parts Frogghampton-Nerdly, Portia Parallel Parking and Sir Winkelhorne Parsley Key Fob. Oooh, and just arrived on their motorbike and sidecar, The Honourable Dame Glorinda Putney-Bridge and Sir Paradiddle Parker-Cheese-on-Toast.'

I resist for a while, but eventually can't help asking the obvious question.

'We're listing imaginary victims who perished when their cities crashed,' says Kiri.

I ask if they've ever considered playing a less morbid game.

'Everyone's playing it.'

'But what's the point?' I ask.

'It's a memorial,' replies Evan, 'tombstones for people who never existed.'

As I imagine their horrible slow motion deaths, I begin to see the sense in it. All these people with the weird names had a lucky escape. They never died in agony or of a broken heart, because none of them ever existed.

Holo-stream Fragment – Para 14.12.17
Ghent, Belgium – Jun 17 2027
Julia Maartens – Flower Merchant

I once saw an arrangement of painted stones float by on an otherwise featureless tarmac slab. They spelled out SOS, Emilio and Maria.

Hannah: Unreliable Narrator

Holo-stream Clip
New York, NY – September 19 2083

I'm in a shadowy place, my body twisted into a shape that feels unnatural. Wasps swarm my battered thoughts; eyelids are gummed together with tears and dust and, for a moment, I have no idea where I am. The smell of stale technology fills my senses as I cough, ribs exploding in fiery agony. Sharp flakes of rust find their way to the back of my throat as my one good eye peels open. And then the memory returns, tears flooding my eyes as Daniel's last moments are replayed by a disobedient mind. With every deepening sob, I curse myself for endangering the group and causing their deaths by my recklessness.

I even consider how this is all Deeby's fault. If we hadn't found him. If we hadn't taken him in. If I hadn't upset him. If he hadn't disappeared… if, if, if.

If only I wasn't so all consumingly pathetic.

As my senses gradually return, I detect a sticky goo with my fingertips. I'm lying in a pool of congealed oil and wedged against a wall beneath a rusting automotive hulk, a pre-flyer, gas-powered monster of the kind that used to be bought as an investment. The pendulum has bowled me along a concrete floor; my backpack gone, clothes ripped to shreds and a clear line in the frost marking my trajectory. There's a cramp coming and, unable to straighten myself, I cry out when the contractions begin. My head twists sideways and, through the pain, I first sense and then see movement.

Four pillars of silvery fur that end in massive clawed feet.

There's a soft *click, click, click* of claws and a slow, deliberate placement of paws as a creature approaches. She (somehow, I know it's a she) exudes a dangerous aroma, stealth overlaying sharpness, an elegant pacing that belies her sex. A scarred snout appears an arm's length away and, falling flat to her belly, she pins me with her gaze, the circles of her ice-blue eyes like exotic polar maps. My wonderment is overruled though by an emotional link that connects me to my ancestors.

Fear me. *Wolf.*

My hackles rise. I sense she was born in someone's imagination, but those liquid blue pools stare right into me all the same. The yellowing teeth will rip my flesh and razor claws will gouge my eyes, so it doesn't matter if she's the fulfilment of a wish or a natural born creature. The result will be the same. If she can drag me out from under my refuge, there will be no debate and no escape.

I squash against the wall, watching her evaluate our relative strengths. She, all. Me, none. She belly-crawls towards me, body flattened, claws scratching at concrete to pull her weight forward. Her nose is inches away. I'm about to scream my last when she licks my face and a river of relief washes over me. This creature knows me, and I'm certain she intends me no harm.

'Hey, over here you ugly brute.'

I catch my breath as the voice of a young girl echoes in the distance. The wolf cracks her head on the muffler in her haste to scramble out from beneath the truck.

'Bet you can't catch me, wolfie.'

My bad eye unsticks and the world snaps into stereo vision, albeit limited by my narrow field of view. The wolf is on her feet, turned away from me. The girl keeps up her ridicule, distracting and tempting the creature towards herself.

'No,' I yell. 'Get away from her.'

But what I think of as a yell comes out as a feeble croak from rust-filled lungs.

I flat-swing my arms so they're above my head and dig my fingers into the chassis to drag myself along, shoulder blades exploding with pain. I catch a deep breath as I emerge, twisting onto my hands and knees. My clothes hang in rags. I feel something warm trickling down my back. I can see the wolf clearly now. She's pacing towards the girl, squatting low on her haunches and preparing to burst into a sprint. The girl stands at the exposed edge of the car park where it overhangs the chasm. I try to attract the creature's attention, but my voice is weak and she's fixated on the girl.

'Come on, you stupid mutt,' she mocks. 'Let's see how fast you can run.'

The enraged wolf accelerates towards her; a loping, elegant motion which under any other circumstances would be beautiful to watch but, now that I sense her true nature, the movement begins to feel like an unfolding tragedy.

'Get out of her way,' I scream, the effort a hot knife between my cracked ribs.

The wolf accelerates, but the girl, no more than ten years old, stands her ground. The wolf is in the air now, all four paws clear off the ground in a final leap towards her target. She looks certain to carry the girl over the edge and into oblivion, but a fraction of a second before impact the child steps backwards and out of view. The wolf's momentum is too great for her to stop and now she's airborne above the chasm, limbs flailing in the air. In a mess of pain, I struggle to the edge, expecting to see them both falling and find the girl grinning up at me from a platform just a few feet below. Together we watch the beast fall. She misses the tangled mass where my poor Daniel lies and pirouettes towards the Phage, a tiny shrinking dot against a backdrop of sculptured ice.

I knew her for just a few minutes, but I feel the need to mourn. Again.

The girl, on the other hand, looks up triumphantly, her freckles mimicking my own. She has so many teeth missing her mouth resembles a badly damaged piano.

'You look like you got run over by a truck,' she grins, climbing up and offering a tiny hand.

I shake it without thinking, as I take in the horror of Daniel's twisted remains. Shards of ice form inside me and cut my guts to ribbons.

'I'm Noomi,' she says. 'Lucky I was here to save you from that thing.'

I give a thin smile that I hope hides my disgust; I'm torn apart by the wolf's death and the loss of people I once shared my life with. They were worthy candidates for survival, but fate, whatever that is, chose me.

There's an unstoppable burst of anger when I spot

Chang and instantly dredge up thoughts of retribution from my darkest emotions. He's staring down from the other side of the chasm. He waves the deadly machete at me and yells, but the wind steals his words. I think I can guess his intent, but then I see I'm hopelessly wrong. Slipping the weapon into his belt he beckons a small boy to his side.

It's Deeby.

I stumble back on my heels as if hit by a wrecking ball. Chang located the boy when we couldn't, and it's my fault. Yet again. Ever since we found the child, I sensed our protection of him might fail, and now that possibility has coalesced into uncompromising fact.

Deeby sees me and waves, apparently unaware of the danger. I wonder how he can be so innocent and yet so dangerous at the same time. There's a nagging thought growing inside me that suspects he might be a willing part of their group, but I quickly repress the idea and wave back, hoping to settle him. I'd give my life to protect the kid, but for the moment I can think of nothing I can do to help.

Then, with Chang grinning like he might've lost the battle but won the war, I lower the dredging bucket into the murkiest of memories and realise there might be something I can do after all. I want to do harm to this evil son-of-a-bitch, so I reach down and pick up a shard of glass, suddenly aware that there is no upper limit on what I'm willing to do to him. A dark weight in my head warns me to back away from the intent, but I have no intention of heeding it. I turn away from Noomi and bring the shard against my left forearm, cutting as deep as I dare. I gag as the flesh parts and a river of blood flows between banks further apart than I intended. Feeling faint at the sight of my own blood, I make steeples with my fingers and focus my gaze in the bowl they form. This is where, as a child, I found the mental image of a playing card; all I had to do was visualise the new suit and wish for the change. But the intervening years have messed with my memory or ability or both. Chang stands, completely unharmed, while blood gushes across my wrists and into the useless cat's cradle of my fingers. Maybe it wasn't the dark thoughts stopping me wishing but the fear of complete and utter failure. Maybe I knew I was useless the whole time, like Pia said, but afraid to admit it.

I scream at Chang instead, and with the diminutive Noomi looking on in surprise I scream and scream and keep on screaming, hoping one day the sentiment will kill Chang dead.

Noomi reaches out her hand, but this time I ignore the offer. Instead, unable to stand the pain anymore, I bid farewell to Deeby through a veil of tears, offering a weak wave in his direction. Even at this distance I can see the poor kid struggling to hold it together, and as we turn away to take the stairs to street level I hear him sobbing my name.

The climb is a major effort, and as I push open the door at the top I double up in pain and stumble onto the sidewalk.

'I know somebody who can fix ribs,' says Noomi. Her gaze darts, expectant. 'And arms too.'

'We have to get to the softball park,' I insist. 'Mom will patch me up.'

I turn to go but Noomi drags me back.

'Maybe later,' she says. 'It's too dangerous to go there now.'

Noomi is a giant limpet and, in my present condition, I find it impossible to resist her suction. I'm finding it difficult to maintain focus on distant objects and the blood loss has left me cold and shivery, like I need to vomit. In any case, it's likely Mom has moved from our former base near the Bergtraum park.

'We needn't go far,' says Noomi. 'Then you can get fixed up and rest.'

I agree reluctantly, unable to gather the strength to resist. My entire being aches. My eyelids are weighted with lead. My arms drip blood. And my feet obediently follow hers through the streets, despite my faint distrust.

I spent my childhood in the ropes and nets above this neighbourhood but, after eleven months away, I no longer recognise it. The rotted food sellers have quit their pitches. The soil-trade market is gone, just patches of mud and a few scattered seeds to mark its passing. Only the rat-catcher remains, and even his stock-in-trade is dwindling by the hour. Above us, there's a glimpse of sky amongst the web of cables and wire-crossings.

I see a familiar face at a third storey window but it disappears behind shabby lace. They know me but are scared. Windows are barred, their glass painted out. Doors are barricaded and nailed shut. Ancient dumpsters block alleyways and garbage rusts or rots in every available corner. Every door is a gateway, every window an eye with a ferocious appetite.

NYC will never crash the painted road proclaims in green nu-graffiti.

A boy whose name I forget calls to me from a darkened alley. His skin is translucent. Part of me imagines I can see his internal organs.

'Hey, Hannah.' He smiles weakly. 'I thought you were dead.'

I start towards the ghost, considering letting him lick the tuna scent on my fingers, but a ruby-veined hand fastens over his mouth and wrenches him back into the shadows. My own mouth is dry. Daniel and the others stand at the edge of my thoughts waiting to be mourned, but the primal reflex that keeps me alive won't allow me the time. It's pressing me for action, demanding concentration and vigilance and driving me with bodily chemicals over which I have no control.

The neighbourhood was never quite this bleak or fearful. And there's a hollowed out feeling in my abdomen suggesting that if I stay at ground level I'll end up getting smothered. What I need is to get up onto the net, let my fingers wrap themselves in rope and feel my muscles tauten as they take my weight. Then I can take stock of the situation in safety and make plans to locate Mom. And my sister too, I guess.

I clamp a hand over my gashed arm and lift my eyes to the complex net running above the streets. Many of the old familiar routes are gone, broken down by weather maybe or cut with rot or fraying, but replacements have sprung up in their place. I'd climb if I thought my wrecked body could manage it, but I'm obliged by immense pain and stupid self-harm to stick to the ground like a slug and risk my neck in the wild zone.

'Wish-scum,' screams Noomi, jolting me from my self-pity. 'Look, up there.'

Noomi points at the main clamber net which covers three city blocks. There's a warm memory of running here as children, matching our songs to the rhythm of the rope spacing, but the memory freezes over as two tiny figures hurry across the weave. Running ten seconds or so behind them, three older kids and a man are in hot pursuit. And my first terrible thought identifies the chasers as cannibals.

'Get them,' hisses Noomi. 'Drag them in for punishment, the rotten, filthy stinking little wish-spawn.'

The pursuers gain ground on their prey but there's still four or five seconds between them as the quarry leaves the clamber net and makes the short jump to a suspension bridge. From there, if memory serves, there's a multi-block ropeway that takes them to the remains of the Flatiron building if they want.

'Slit their stinking throats,' yells Noomi, spraying bile on the air.

There's a ruined world reflected in her words. Just like everyone else, she needs someone to blame. The pursuers don't follow. Instead, the man kneels and launches a projectile which explodes in a cloud of steam just ahead of the fugitives. One of them, a boy I think, stumbles and clutches his face, screaming but still running. Noomi is still screaming for evisceration but my heart warms as the youngsters make their escape by cutting down the flimsy rope bridge they just crossed.

I shiver, but it's not the children's fate or Noomi's glee chilling me. It's getting distinctly colder. I limp after my child guide, continuing at ground level under darkening skies, hugging walls and using deepening shadows for cover. All the while, I'm keeping careful watch, hoping to find a backpack and replace the hunting knife and other essentials that were lost when I crashed. Judging by the burned-out husks of the stores we're passing though, there's little chance of replacing such hard won items.

'This will do for now,' says Noomi, indicating a row of ruined shops.

I recognise our surroundings as safe territory, so there's some relief, but I know we're being watched from all quarters. I catch sight of myself in the window of Mr. Katz's shop. Aside from a long crack in the glass, it's the same surface that reflected moments from my childhood. Now it shows someone I hardly know. Her hair is matted. Her face grimy and bloodied. More than that though, she wears a look of despair. I need to find a place to lick my wounds.

Noomi whispers, but I don't catch what she says. I watch as a snowflake descends in slow motion and balances on her eyelashes. Soon it's followed by a dozen more, then a thousand as darkening clouds empty onto our heads. The cold is extreme now, there's hail mixed in with the snow and soon we're dodging pieces of ice the size of marbles.

'Let's get inside,' urges Noomi. 'This will be a bad one.'

I consider sitting in the freezing snow to soothe my pain, maybe even stay there and wait to be covered up. For the moment though, I'm temporarily buoyed by simple curiosity. I want to see what's happened since I left and I'm eager to discover what drives the child who keeps asking for my trust.

We stumble through the shop door and set off the tinkle-bell. I call out from habit, but old man Katz doesn't answer. The mezuzah[11] has been hacked from the door frame and lays twisted out of shape on the wooden floor. I recall he had difficulty getting it to stay in place, so eventually resorted to nails. Shelves are either toppled and ransacked or burned. Torn and rat-chewed manuscript pages litter the floor. An old leather chair sits empty, a dent in the dark green cushion echoing the bookseller's absent shape.

'What happened to Mr Katz?' I ask, jamming the door closed behind us.

There's no answer, just a shrug from my guide. I flatten the tinplate mezuzah and pocket it, hoping for more luck than it brought the previous owner.

'Maybe he got arrested by the better households' police,' observes Noomi.

I have to agree. The mahogany counter, once proudly polished, is hacked to pieces, as is the big leather-bound book surrounded by its satellite volumes, their pages flipped and spines broken. The miniature clay golem who once guarded the till lays shattered. I let out an involuntary sigh. Old man Katz would be horrified by all this disorder.

He was a kindly gentleman who would invite kids for 'tea and tefillin', which was his idea of a joke. He'd scare us with stories about how the golem was brought to life by the Hebrew symbols written on its forehead, and how the little clay monster prowled the shop at night. Best of all though, he liked to reminisce about the good times before Inception, when you could get Nova lox and bagels and cream cheese and combine them in a salty kind of fishy heaven. I can't even begin to imagine how good that might have tasted – unless it was like the tuna I shared less than an hour ago.

It was always a surprise to me how much time Katz had for us kids, especially given the amount of time he spent studying old texts and making translations. It was like he used our youthful energy to inspire his thoughts and mystic visions, which he delighted telling us about. All those fabulous cities of the imagination and the people who lived in them. It was like visiting a different world for a while, where we could forget the daily squalor in which we lived. Our favourite story of all was the one about Rabbi Loew and the Golem of Prague which was created to save the people of the ghetto from expulsion or death by order of the Holy Roman Emperor. I think that was the day I decided to ignore God.

I sink into the leather chair with a sigh and, in the comparative safety of the shop, thoughts of Daniel soon return to haunt me. Eventually, he's joined by the others. I think of Deeby, of our group dying at Chang's hands and the sight of children being hunted as prey. I can't imagine how those hunters justify their actions with adults, never mind children. I guess if they're ever called upon to explain the inexplicable they'll claim they were only following orders, like so many violent foot soldiers before them. I don't care what anyone says, that kind of thing has to be inside you to begin with, it's not just a question of abandoning morals and obeying your superior whatever the command. Flaying children alive to make lampshades from their skin is not a matter of obedience, it's a moral defect.

'Weather's coming in,' says Noomi.

She scowls at me as if it's my fault that we're penned like sheep in a gale.

'It feels like a wish-storm,' she says. 'Those stinking little fugitives must have brought it down on us.'

I think we just flew into bad weather but don't bother to contradict. Mom's mantra when it came to wishes was neither confirm nor deny, but it's difficult to resist correcting a mind filled with such vitriol. I also don't want to think about it too much, having attempted to execute a wish and failed miserably.

The hail pelts against the window as Noomi locks the outer door and sets fire to a Hebrew script in the cast iron grate. I wince. The hand-written scroll looks valuable, but I guess the demand for mystical Jewish texts[12] has gone through the floor since we all went crazy. Maybe Ben was right. The only use for history is to keep us warm.

'I know where to get food,' says Noomi. 'There's a ton of it in a warehouse near the Brooklyn bridge stump. And there are fields uptown growing wheat. I can show you, if you like.'

Hail falls down the chimney and hisses in the meagre flames. I doubt Noomi's stories, but say nothing, if only to avoid lighting her fuse, which I imagine is quite short.

We lived in a farming co-operative in Central Park in the early days. Then it was taken over by a gang who eventually figured out you had to work at growing food, you couldn't just threaten it. Noomi can sense I don't believe her; she's become nervy and distracted.

'My Mommy saw Prague once,' she says. 'It passed close enough she could count the arches in the big bridge. And old Mr Wong reckons he once saw the Taj Mahal go by, but nobody believed him. The week after, he tried to escape from the city with helium balloons. It was the craziest thing anyone had ever heard.'

Hissing in the grate, the old texts throw up blue and green flames as ancient inks are consumed by fire. Noomi pulls at her hair and gazes into the middle distance like my sister Lilith does when she's lying.

'If I could escape from this place,' she continues, 'I'd have my own little island where I could sit in a lighthouse for days and never see another soul. We'd only see other slabs by accident because we'd keep clear for our own safety. Not so far north that we freeze, but far enough to keep out of people's way. And close enough to the equator so we get sunshine for the crops. And there'd be a little estuary with some water trapped behind a dam, and a sailboat I can use for fishing. And there'll be no wind at the edge of the slab, so I can sit out at sunset and dangle my legs over the sky.'

'You don't want much, do you?' I ask.

The flames in the grate are snuffed by a sudden gust and a falling clump of snow.

'What about you?' she asks.

I hesitate, thinking about my only material possession. Ever since the chasm opened up, the picture has occupied a place of safety, kept reassuringly next to my skin. I want to take it out now, not because of this girl but because I'm close to Mom and it's only a matter of time before I find her. I can't believe I want to bring it out now when I hesitated with Daniel earlier, but I reach inside my bra and retrieve the crumpled treasure. It's a clammy white square with a glossy window, behind which there's a three-dimensional picture. I think they called them Holaroids.[13]

'These are my parents,' I say, passing it to Noomi. 'It was taken in Coney Island.'

'Never heard of it.'

'It was part of New York. In the days before Manhattan moved to the skies.'

'Is that what they call a carousel?'

I nod, surprised she recognises what my parents are sitting on.

'You can make out the sea in the background,' I say.

'So, you want to live in the three-dee? Because the world inside it is in one piece and everyone is happy?'

She surprises me again. There's some kind of cruel intelligence at work here.

'There's a boy I need to find first, but yes, it would be good to stand alongside them on the boardwalk,' I admit.

What I don't mention is the hallucinations I have after eating rotten food. I've seen other places within the confines of that Holaroid frame, strange, anomalous cities, and sometimes wonder if I might prefer to be there instead.

'I don't know anything about your father,' says Noomi, examining the image closely, 'but there's a lot of hurt coming from this picture.'

She would benefit from a hurtful slap in the face, but I resist the temptation. Instead, I snatch the thing back and stow it, all the time aware of the pull it exerts, like mental gravity.

'I don't know anything about him,' I say. 'Mom came to live in Manhattan when she discovered she was pregnant with us.'

The fire burns down and Noomi's brow furrows as if she's thinking things through. I was going to tell her about Mom and Lilith getting stranded on the opposite side of the chasm; how Mom showed up and waved to me the next day and how it was the last time I saw her. But somehow, I think she'll twist the story into something spite-filled and ugly.

Noomi gives a nervous laugh as she glances at the door. I hear the crunch of snowy footsteps outside and all too late realise the girl has taken my short-lived belief in the kindness of human spirit and shot it through the heart. There are deep, urgent-sounding voices out there, muffled by the deepening snow, and lanterns throwing dappled light onto the ceiling.

'Noomi?' I ask. 'What's going on?'

Noomi avoids my gaze, confirming my fears.

A shattering crack splinters the frame, blasting the door inwards. In the vacated space stands something half-human, half-mammoth, spindrift circling his massive head like an unworthy halo.

'Snake got your message,' he grunts at Noomi. 'He says you better have them goods you was sent out to get, otherwise you is one dead girl chile.'

Katz: Shutter Speed

Ink on Paper
The Movable City of Aeropi
Haksdia 27th day of Caltination
Passing over [Berganax] and [Anlashock]
Translations [Narak-Tih-Kurr, Porah-Ardexia]

Daggers at you, Velliers, you odious tripe-hound. Pay what you owe or I swear my pen will run dry. The boy continues his studies and now has a basic grasp of Ingulesh old tongue. I'm impressed by his uncanny intelligence but dismayed by the lack of empathy. He's also far too self-involved for my liking; he still talks to himself under his breath. I can just about live with that, but the people walking around inside his head could do with taking a long walk off a short pier.

In desperation, I made the mistake of asking a trapeze artist and amateur herbalist if she could make up something to calm him down but the potion made him even more edgy. And now, thanks to her capacious mouth, there are whispers about Dina talking to ghosts. Not only that, the odorous slop she sold me for night terrors was as much use as a flying weasel turd.

With your record of tardy payments, you don't really deserve to be hearing any bonus detail, but folk are pondering the recent outing of our only airship, which many believed incapable of flight due to its dilapidated state. Moving away into the evening gloom, it looked like an injured firefly dragging its legs and looking for somewhere to die. But we soon found out the reason for the trip. Our elders and betters had been out visiting the competition.

On the day the rival outfit returned the compliment by visiting us, the bearded lady told me how her husband was creating a map of the worlds in their tiny caravan. At the time I heard 'world' in the singular, but now I'm not so sure, because later in the afternoon she told me about a circus that travels between alternate realities. She is off her bewhiskered nut I suspect, and I pretty much forgot about the idea of these fanciful 'elsewheres' when a cry went up that the Narjuk Collective were coming.

From a distance they resembled a group of schoolchildren towing toy balloons on strings; an impression which changed rapidly as they approached, the collapsing perspective revealing a massive collection of airships, tethered dirigibles and floating islands. Having descended to match our own altitude and coming to a halt a mere hundred yards away, they simply hung silent, apparently awaiting our hail.

Judging by the way their performers lined up against us like an army of spangled dragonflies, I recalled the rumour that sometimes when they visit a small town there is nothing left when they move on, the circus oh-so-slighter fatter around the waist. I remember my uncle

Zeb spinning this story to me as a six-year-old – the ravenous travelling circus that eats towns. It was all the more terrifying since it came on the eve of our visit to the Narjuk Circus, a treat to take my mind off the recent loss of Zeb's sister, my mother Trilla.

As a child I recall the freak show in frightening detail, but I imagine much has changed since then, either in the show itself or my ability to comprehend the strange and terrible. In any case, I imagine their purpose here has nothing to do with me. But the boy perhaps?

Living in a travelling show, I get to see unusual things; legerdemain that confuses the quickest eye, tricks of the light that confound and confuse; physical abilities that baffle and amaze. I'm familiar with the entangled notebook scam, the belly-flash rollover, the lemon-drop and even the high-walking face trick, but the arrival of the Narjuk is more worrying, more baffling and more threatening than any artificial trick or performance. There's a feeling in my gut, and I think in everyone else's too, that this isn't a simple meeting of minds, but a point of inflection in history; a time when one significant thing ends and another even more terrifying thing begins. I really hoped the management knew what they were doing, unable to understand why one circus would visit another, when they both chase the same dwindling audiences year upon year. Well, the answer was quickly provided when one of the Narjuk's airships overflew us and dropped a line. A rigger attached it to the hoist point on the gilded caravan and our management were transported to the other side like a scene from a fairy-tale. Lord and Lady Sarsa-Parilla stepped out on the Narjuk side and shook hands with someone presumably high up, judging by his fabulous plumage. I didn't know what to expect when he took up the megaphone, and going by their reactions neither did anyone else.

> *Travellers, performers, friends, family. We assemble to mourn the passing of our brothers and sisters in unnatural and reprehensible acts. Lovers of the open skies, stand and remember them, and keep their names forever in your hearts. Liu Liu Tang, avian artist and angelic presence. Gregia Sloss and her performing dogs. Presker Nooay the strongwoman. Fenny Parooni the flying mermaid and aerial choreographer. Badooni the animal hypnotist. The Teenah sisters, equilibrists and mirror walkers. Voltaro the Nubivagain dart. Bebe Tireah the wolf girl. Treanna Stryke, aerialist and whip handler. Megana Froyt, distinguished mistress of the ring.*

There was a deadly silence, backed only by the sound of a mournful breeze. I don't know the circumstances of these deaths, and was too afraid to ask, lest I formed any kind of link between meeting Dina and the arrival of the Narjuk.

No time for levity,
Otto Katz

Ink on Paper
The Movable City of Aeropi::Narjuk
Tryndia 28th day of Caltination
Passing over [Andevhorr]

Remember how your favourite toy transported you to a future where you were full grown? Yet now, if you still had the thing, it might transport you once again, only this time back to your childhood. You'd feel safe, living in a modest packet of time fixed firmly in the past. I always imagined a roaring fire, festive snow falling outside and a living room floor cleared to permit the laying of rails and the running of tin-plate locomotives and coaches with lights on the inside. After last night though I'm not sure I could bear to experience that moment of absolute joy without the presence of a darker counterpoint.

Everyone gathered in Le Grande Chapiteau this morning, eager to find out why the Narjuk came a-calling, well aware it wasn't just to announce the dead. Taygorn, the Aeropi ringmaster gave us a pep talk, during which he recalled the time when our outfit and the Narjuk were one and the same. This was eleven hundred years ago. I'd like to say I laughed it off, but a chill in the tent set my spine on edge, and I just knew it was true. It must have been quite a split to drive them apart in the first place, but the question on everyone's lips now must be what need has brought them together again and whether it's something we should fear. The trigger for the reunion must surely be the unknown force behind the deaths, but there's no explanation from management, perhaps to keep us from panicking. I feel a strange potential growing nearby, like the power generated by Tesla's earthquaking machine but with a magickal charge taking place of electricity.

It might be that imaginary power driving my paranoia, but in addition there's all the extra attention being paid to 'the boy who talks to ghosts', who, for all I know, has blabbed all sorts of stuff that could get us into trouble. That might even be why some of the Narjuk acts have taken to hanging around our trailer. Lady Vyper, in particular, seems to regard me as a pane of glass put there for the sole purpose of staring through. I dread to think of her seeing the real me cowering in my shell. I'll continue to supply translations as long as possible, but none of us can make promises which depend on such an uncertain future.

Safety in numbers,
Otto Katz

Ink on Paper
The Movable City of Aeropi::Narjuk
Rimdia 51st day of Caltination
Passing over [Narukh and Valderirah], approaching [Hir-Diab]

It has been like a pair of wild beasts circling each other, but the circus factions are gradually blending together along the lines of their specialities, clowns with clowns for instance, as if nothing could keep them apart. I still wonder at the motive though, or more accurately I worry about it now that we're a bigger target. It's strange catching sight of the Narjuk balloons and airships out of the corner of an eye, but stranger still seeing new performers about the place. The freak show is as wondrous to behold as you can imagine. I think I saw your mother there at one point (two invoices are overdue!). Thinking back to the translation of Old Aeropi, if Taygorn is right then it's at least eleven hundred years since we had a sideshow, which gives you a latest date marker for that particular document. Oh, almost forgot, Dina has a crush on the daughter of an illusionist and psychokineticist who arrived with the Narjuk. The girl thought he was cute to begin with but his attentions became, uh, how do I put this, inappropriate for a child. He said one of the boys in his head made him do it, which didn't go down well. Anyway, she warned him off so let's hope that's an end to it. I don't want her making him vanish now he's making progress with the language. It's a shame, as I'd like him to have more freedom in that respect, but he reminds me of my younger self and my own equally ineffective approaches to the opposite sex.

Reduced to Onanism,
Otto Katz

P.S.   I gave up on the heliographs. A clown with a passion for malice spread a rumour about how cameras work by magick and that was that. Considering their extensive relationship with time and tradition I'm surprised they aren't more interested in its preservation.

P.P.S.   I just had word about the murders. The artistes I mentioned were slaughtered in their beds, all on the same night. Carnies are not easily spooked but losing people like that would have anyone on edge. There is a tension in the air like a razor wire singing in a breeze.

Ink on Paper
The Movable City of Aeropi::Narjuk
Faldia 59th day of Caltination
Moored in [Ocka Julce], lately passed over [Darkenteria]

According to Barando, the circus never visited Ocka Julce before due to the city's reputation for violence and unfair dealing. This time round it's said we stopped to show the enemy we weren't afraid to look them in the face. Consequently, nobody was that keen to step out into the city, but a group of us were anxious to replenish supplies and an apothecary of ill repute was mentioned. That's how me and Dina ended up in Swain Parok's tiny shop along with Marisa, the cooch dancer, and Barath, the man with the barbed wire face. The plan was that Marisa's beautifully sculpted form and Barath's horrendous visage would distract potential assailants long enough for us to escape, but we encountered none of the sort of street-rough trouble we'd been promised.

Instead, we got the kind of trouble none of us had expected.

Parok's eyes were narrowed to such a degree it was impossible to detect even a sliver of decency. There was, however, a small flicker of recognition when he laid eyes on Dina. I should've known he was a bad 'un, but the urge for bliss was strong and my colleagues were at my back, blocking the only exit from the shop. It was around seven feet square and stank of sweat, sulphur, piss and vinegar, the floor sprinkled with bright metal fragments and shards of coloured glass, like an explosion in a cathedral. The apothecary sat perched on a tall wooden stool, his wiry frame wrapped in a harlequin suit of mixed provenance. He was bleeding a red-throated lizard into a glass beaker. I caught a look of pleading in the creature's eyes and turned away in shame. As a distraction, I picked up a treatise on the intelligence of octopuses. Hoping to engage Parok in conversation and perhaps spare the lizard at the same time, I enquired why someone would wish to eat an intelligent creature.

'I know,' he replied, continuing to drain the reptile. 'It's pure barbarism, but you didn't come here to discuss the sentience of cephalopods or how good they taste when fried in a little butter, did you? Some family trouble, perhaps? A relation suffering from inconvenient longevity? A business partner suddenly obsessed with the number six?'

'I think you know what we're looking for,' said Marisa.

'Yes,' said Parok, returning his gaze to Dina. 'You wish to know if the child with the elaborate tattoo means you harm.'

'No, we don't,' choked Marisa, 'we just want some…'

The temperature dropped and chilled my nerves and those of my companions who exhaled in shock at the intensity of Parok's magickal onslaught. I ran my eyes along the bottles behind Parok: antimony, bismuth and arsenium, phlogiston, oak galls, squid ink, but absolutely no sign of my sweet opium, just an increasing darkness, like the approach of jet-black birds in a child's nightmare. When Parok began that unsettling chant, I sensed consciousness slipping away and fought to force my eyes open again. To my horror the beaker was brimming with blood – the lizard was assuredly not. I turned to run, but my way was blocked by a shell-shocked Dina. Either side of him stood Marisa and Barath, their pale eyes staring back at me from drained, bloodless faces.

I cannot stand to write any more,
Otto Katz

Immutable Cities 4

BERGANAX – *City of Unresting Spirit*
Take care not to leave the city without visiting the House of Glossolalia. This is no ordinary dwelling, but an intricate prison at the centre of which lies a demon of great strength and unusual clairvoyant powers. She is known as Serena Pillaka, the demon girl. This innocent beauty was convinced a coiled serpent slept at the base of her spine and, by parts, became fearful at the thought of awakening the creature. Due to psychotropic trance induction and other procedures, she underwent a collapse of the mind, speaking in strange tongues at one time and weeping and screaming with unnatural laughter at another. Day and night she would scream, 'Zina naludy bratika speka gollagolla tretika galuda', which no one could comprehend beyond the physical impact of the words themselves. Fearful of the violence she might visit upon them, her guardians entombed her in a bronze coffin, leaving just two essential apertures. And so, with the entrapment complete and their mortal fears allayed, they sought reward

from those eager to see the wonder they had wrought. Gaze into the upper aperture for an entirely reasonable fee, or for three times that amount slide back the lower curtain and witness the fundamental nature of the demoness.

ANLASHOCK – *City of Eternal Clamour*

Sitting in the mountain pass between Ven-Dura and Ven-Borador, Anlashock is a city engaged exclusively in the construction of vast machines. Hangars are hewn from the mountainside, the rock so thin in places that light shines through, illuminating spaces so vast it is difficult to imagine what they were created to contain.

The hangars are surrounded in turn by herds of grabbers and carriers that carry raw materials into the construction complexes. The air surrounding them thick with the incessant thrum of machinery, the smell of wood and leather and doped tissue pervade the air. It is lit by a sparkling sea of lights and reverberates incessantly to the clang of metal on metal, all of which signifies some great mysterious industry.

It is impossible to gain access to the assembly areas so we must imagine what the squadrons of flying automata are protecting from our gaze. What we can say, however, is that every two years in the spring, there emerges a ship so vast it is impossible to believe it might fly. What mighty engines power these leviathans we can only speculate, but those who have witnessed these insect-like beasts emerge from their lair say they move as though alive, their motion in the air accompanied by a gentle liquid whirr which becomes inaudible as the craft gains altitude. The only clue then to the passage of these cathedrals of flight is the movement of their shadows across the land, when they invariably head north through the mountains and are never seen again. The cities of the north are known to be warlike but the leviathans show no external evidence of weaponry or offensive capability and, despite their size, they do not appear to be designed for the shipment of cargo. Equally strange, therefore, is their apparent lack of passenger accommodation.

Their insectile appearance is fearsome in the extreme, and it is not difficult to imagine those of a feeble constitution suffering a mental breakdown or perhaps even a total collapse upon seeing the fiends. Whether these machines were primarily designed to instil fear or their horrific features are the result of some evolution of purpose, we do not know, and the author of this pamphlet does not wish to find out.

The purpose of these giants remains unclear and all attempts to extract an explanation from shipyard workers have met with failure. It is impossible to follow the ships to the frozen regions on foot or by mechanised ground transport and there is no other airship which can match the speed of these leather-backed leviathans. Only one in twenty travellers to the city ever returns. Not recommended for visitation.

NARAK-TIH-KURR – *City of Architectural Benevolence*
The joint seat of the noble Tih and Kurr dynasties is the most ancient inhabited city in modern Cyrusia, and a truly dangerous place to visit. The immeasurably beautiful architecture comes under frequent aerial bombardment from an unknown aggressor. No warning is ever given, nor responsibility ever claimed. The chance of death is not as great as in other conventionally violent cities, but the

prospect of witnessing the devastation of an architectural gem is in many eyes a greater and much more serious risk. Discretion advised.

PORAH-ARDEXIA – *The Merciless Treadmill*

A city of hapless minions in the employ of a faceless regime, Porah consists of myriad drab offices charged with the management of an entire backward region. Endless corridors stink of floor and brass polish, each one challenging the curious eye to comprehend their distant perspective. Thousands upon thousands of stale rooms dull the imagination, being filled with dust, candles, pneumatic message tubes and stainless steel nibs. Each tiny work-cell is characterised by the smell of sepia ink and an accumulation of yellowing papers, a dismal drone-scape of dim lighting, window draughts and hardened sealing wax. But there exists an unnoticed dynamic. Amidst the roto-file machines and rusting cabinets, data accretion occurs on either side of an arbitrary line, each mass of information gathering a differing electrical charge. An accidental spark in these offices, therefore, has the potential to annihilate millions of citizens in fiery death, whilst sending a modest tax refund to others.

ANDEVHORR – *The Remote Mystery*

There is no city here, only a magnificent cathedral marooned in the great dusty plain. Where did all the faithful come from, and if they ever did come, where did they all go? And who was responsible for placing the ancient prognosticating machine at the foot of the marble altar?

NARUKH AND VELDERIRAH – *The Cities of Forgotten Hurt*
The twin cities of Narukh and Velderirah began as remote settlements established by feuding families whose names have been deliberately forgotten. Also disappeared from memory is the reason for the warring, but a great animosity still exists between the two cities. Between them lays a wall, a gargantuan structure soaked in foreboding and melancholy which began as a line of twigs in the dirt to mark the limits of the disagreement. Deaths on either side were marked by the addition of more twigs, then branches, stones and eventually bricks taken from the homes of the slaughtered. Today, painted upon many millions of those bricks is a mural describing the network of tunnels and pipes beneath the cities, a warren of channels which were excavated for the sole purpose of inflicting hurt on the other side.

HIR-DIAB – *The Village of Ignoble Pursuit*
At the confluence of two mountain gorges lies the village of Hir-Diab, famed for its triple-storey bridge which crosses a pair of swift flowing rivers at the point where they join to form a single tumult. A span of brick covers a much older arch of rough stone which in turn protects the trunks of ancient trees persuaded over countless years to grow horizontally and form supporting spars. The crossing is only passable on foot, the cobblestone path providing access to a clapperboard warehouse; the place is dedicated to the movement of anonymous brown-paper packages. Each mysterious gift is tied with a length of coloured string and carried into the warehouse by trusted couriers. And each eventually makes its way back into a trusting world by the same means.

OCKA JULCE – *Practitioners of Glass*

In a rude and rough painted shed on the outskirts of the city may be found the mechanysme who sitteth all alone, parts of him flesh, bone and sinew and parts of him cogs, springs and balances. It is impossible to fathom if he is a machine made human or a man transformed by dark magick into mechanical form. His metallic parts will calculate irrational numbers to the utmost accuracy and, if the suns are smiling, he may also be persuaded to determine the longitudes. Such precision suggests he is mechanisme pure and simple, but the mouth parts may also hold a conversation if he is so inclined. Oftentimes his talk is puerile or evasive, but the maybe-soul at the heart of the thing has at some junctures discoursed on pretty matters of politic or disclosed scientific intelligence previously unexplored by the great scholars.

DARKENTERIA – *The City Formerly Known as Angelus*

A perplexing city which has defeated all scientific attempts to analyse the phenomena which occur within its massive stone walls. The only means of entry is by one of three pneumatic sled portals which pierce the barricade hundreds of feet from the ground. Those in the north and east are entirely safe, but the southern access should be used only by those aware of the risks. Known as the Gate of Introspection, those entering the city by this route are viewed with suspicion and are often the subject of violent assault. Perpetration of such an attack is believed by the citizens to be unlucky, especially if their victim has already caught sight of his future self in one of the many public mirrors. It is positively dangerous to make an attack if the victim has contrived to observe his dark inner-self in one of the four privately owned looking glasses.

Diary Fragments 5

Holo-stream Fragment – Para 11.12.87
Barnum, Colorado – May 7 2060
Morris Minor – Slab Jockey

I can remember it in every detail, the day I first fell from the sky. Strictly speaking, it wasn't me who did the falling but the town I was riding at the time – a former railroad head featured in precisely zero good eating guides and only ever named in print on the map of its former position in Colorado. The Swedish scavenging crew who rescued me from the wreckage turned out to be mostly friendly, but it took a while. At the moment of impact, they were anything but, which I guess is understandable when your home seems about to be crushed by three million tons of stuff you don't want landing on your head. The stuff in question was the greater part of Barnum. The town's current location is right here in the former financial district of Gothenburg, where it slowly but surely tore up a few hundred yards of prime real-estate, finally coming to rest only when thirty-five boxcars and a disused chicken farm took up residence in the lower reaches of a former banking headquarters. I can see my former home now from our lookout. It has long since been picked clean by other scavengers and largely ignored by crews who prefer to prowl the desolation further uptown. I used to get homesick just looking at it, but not so much anymore. It was the last of many such backwaters and no-places my Mom dragged me through.

Holo-stream Fragment – Para 23.57.09
Chicago, Illinois – July 24 1934
Paulo Hernandez – Foundry Worker

I get their interest by telling them how the nineteen thirty-four baseball season unfolds. I start out with Babe Ruth hitting his seven hundredth home run off of Tommy Bridges, but they're not impressed because the papers have been predicting it for months. So, I move onto details, day after day, batting, pitching and fielding statistics. And suddenly, when the numbers start to match, they listen. But the clincher is my upcoming birthday. I was born exactly twenty years after Dillinger was shot, July 23 1934, so I give them all the details the day before it happens. I really believed it would do the trick, but a couple of days later they move me to a secure cell. Now I don't see nobody no more.

Holo-stream Fragment – Para 03.00.17
Bombay, India – June 3 1902
Oliver Delapole – Tea Merchant

I bought the carved memorial for a few thousand rupees from a fellow who most probably stole it. Not to worry, it's safely stowed now and will be on its way back to Blighty at the end of the month, when I hope to accompany it. I know you'll be thrilled with this little present. The epitaphs are engraved in Hindi but there are wonderfully reproduced portraits of the fighters replete with their tattoos. The first is the brave old man who died during the fight, the other is the boy who perished a few days later. The vendor-thief said the child died from a broken heart, but others say he was poisoned. No matter though. It will look simply divine in the orangery.

Holo-stream Fragment – Para 22.12.26
New Caracas, Venezuela – June 4 2020
Mario Aquila – City Official

I sometimes try to imagine what I want from this disaster and my answer is the feeling you get when lazing in bed and you realise it's an hour earlier than you thought. Such, I imagine, is the feeling one gets when spending a day in New Caracas, a city where all the abandoned poetry goes. A place where rustling leaves are lost letters and the wind is created by the exhalation of regretted words.

Holo-stream Fragment – Para 00.12.07
Gowdray Bluff, Scotland – October 9 1923
Strathern – Lord of the Realm

My Dear Treves,

I woke this morning to find the perishing deer park had parted company with the rest of the estate. Gone, too, is the better part of the orchard and, as far as I can fathom, the entire grouse moor. This is jolly inconvenient I don't mind saying, but until the bally land comes back, I don't see what we can do. Kindly inform shooting parties we may well be indisposed this season, there's a good fellow.

Strathern

Holo-stream Fragment – Para 60.04.68
Split, Croatia – May 1 1823
Tuana Berivo – Snakeskin Woman

Those shite-arses left me here to perish, so why should I worry what happened to them? We have our own place now, our own notion of time and brand-new names for all the days. If things go well enough, I might even start a circus of my own.

Holo-stream Fragment – Para 33.22.80
Midland, Texas – June 1 1982
Pastor Leffe Couber – Preacher

Brothers and sisters, you know the advice. You know what the government wants you to do in the event of a confounded crust-breakage. It's the same advice they gave you in the event of a nuclear attack. Run away! If you see an edge forming, run in the opposite direction. Run away, do I hear? Run away? Well, that ain't the way we do things here in Texas, no sir. If you see an edge forming, run toward it, brothers and sisters. Take an advantage when it's offered to you. Tread on a new horizon unsullied by the feet of sinners. Trust in the Lord. Pray. Pray. Pray to the Lord. Trust in him and ye shall be saved. Make no mistake, brothers and sisters, this judgement, this planet-wide vengeance was sent down by God to punish the faithless. And the world's best scientists agree. Those fellers call it 'spooky action at a distance', and I guarantee to you such a thing could not happen except by the fulsome and forgiving grace of God. Brothers and sisters, I know this to be true, because on the very same day His vengeance struck, there occurred the greatest miracle of my life.

Holo-stream Fragment – Para 19.41.23
Uluru, Northern Territories, Australia – June 3 1927
Maali – Tribal Elder

As a last resort, I presented the boy with my grandmother's musical box. Obsidian, malachite, copper and bronze decorations, and inset with spheres that glow with pinpricks of light on the surface. Deeper within them, oceans wash the skies, gentle winds caress the crops and the spirits of forests bury their feet in welcoming soil. He refused the gift. Nothing, he told me, would ever be right with the world again. Uluru was broken like a giant pebble and the dreaming tracks were fractured beyond repair. How could he ever stay in a world where the land would no longer sing?

> Holo-stream Fragment – Para 33.22.80
> Midland, Texas – June 1 1982
> Pastor Leffe Couber – Preacher

So, what was the nature of my miracle brothers and sisters? Well, I'm here to tell you all the Lord God himself came to me in a vision. Yes, brothers and sisters, the Lord God brought me a message. He laid it out plain so even a poor preacher like me could understand His meaning. I was given the task of remembering just three simple numbers, two and three and nine. And you know, I thought long and hard about what it could mean, and brethren, the answer did not come. But I prayed again to the Lord, and again and again, and on my final time of trying he told me what to do. He told me to use my God given talents to enrich the faithful. And brethren, again I did not understand, so I prayed and I prayed and I prayed, and eventually He showed me. The Lord God told me to use my financial talents to improve the lot of my fellow man. So, here's what I decided to do. I'd take a small seed and plant it, and watch it grow. I took two hundred and thirty-nine dollars and invested it in the stock market and the investment was fruitful. Brothers and sisters, that little seed of faith multiplied tenfold in a matter of weeks. So, I said to my good lady wife, 'We can't keep this to ourselves. We have to share our good fortune with the poor and the downtrodden and the needy.'

So, here's what I need you to do. Send two hundred and thirty-nine dollars today and turn your life around. Don't delay brothers and sisters. Do. Not. Delay. Send the exact amount decreed by the Lord, and the seed you plant will return to you hundred-fold.

God Bless you All.

Hannah: Deep Focus

Holo-stream Clip
New York, NY – September 19 2083

Our route through the city streets is a map of noisome smells that describe the decay of nobility. The damp, the rats, the stench of shit and rotting corpses; but there's something else; a chemical perfume overlaying everything, like the scent of hopelessness. It's like we're inhaling people's desperation. These citizens have given up, resolved to spend the rest of their days in a midden. Am I any different though? Allowing myself to be propelled towards an uncertain fate?

The man-mammoth stumbles on behind, jabbing my kidneys with something hard, possibly a gun. There are still plenty around, ammunition too, so I decide not to run unless there's a clear route freedom. I keep my head down, watching my step on the icy sidewalk, cursing myself for losing Deeby and trusting Noomi. Maybe I should leave the next needy kid I find to rot in the gutter. Only, I know that won't happen. I'll step in to help as usual and the kid will knife me with a sharpened toothbrush or sell me to a meat market. Maybe even turn me over to a mammoth, who'll march me towards an unknown fate.

Seems like I will never learn.

A torn poster urges us to visit the Zanzibar club, marking the beginning of a waist deep wall of trash that another jab signals me to climb. On the other side of the stinking barrier there's a family restaurant with the windows punched in. Next to that is a narrow alley where rusting flyers are parked both sides beneath windows protected with steel mesh. The doors are heavily barred steel and covered in nu-graffiti, like we're visiting a secret art gallery; every new step taking us deeper into private territory.

In the confined space of the alley, the wind accelerates as the storm presses harder. And it's dark now; night has finally caught up with us. Mammoth jabs me forward and I stumble as we emerge from the alley between burned out ground-huggers and permanent barricades. Oil drum fires burn toxic plastic, the flames stoked by crazy people, most of whom are heavily tattooed with gang marks. Some wear flu masks, plague zealots who refuse to believe the city is disease free.

Above us on the comfortingly familiar net, harpooners lay in wait but recognise our escort and allow us to pass.

There's a quiet here, which Mom used to call the 'deafening silence'. No engine noise, no sirens, no radio, no television, no voices. Just the whip of the wind and the scuff of our footsteps as we move cautiously to God knows where.

I crunch diamonds of broken window beneath my feet, imagining it's Noomi's bones as I mouth a silent obscenity in her direction. The little shit ignores me though and trills a silly little song that must sound better in her head than it does in mine. Music is one sound we do still get to hear – but only if it doesn't signal your position to the enemy.

'Shut it,' I hiss. 'I've had enough of your noise for one day.'

Noomi is about to make some smart remark, but the man-mammoth steals her thunder.

'Down here,' he grunts.

He jabs me hard in the back but I hardly notice the extra pain. Although my bones all feel like they're in one piece, the rest of me is a single bloodied mass of hurt.

At the corner of an alley there's a billboard advertising cosmetic surgery and, next to it, a narrow door and tiny window belonging to a former money exchange. The glass is tinted and dirty, but there's something moving inside.

Mammoth nods as we pass the outer sentry. Spindrift whirls in the claustrophobic space between high brick walls. A carpet of ghost scorpions parts in waves as we pass a taxi repair shop and head to the end of a blind alley. Mammoth jabs me again, crunching the arachnids beneath his boots.

'That's the sound of your dumb head getting crushed,' he chuckles.

I consider the irony for a moment. If brains were nitroglycerine, he wouldn't have enough... no, I'm not having that, so I turn quickly and catch him by surprise, kicking him in the crotch with all the strength I can muster. I know I'm going to pay for it, but whatever he doles out now is going to be repaid later when I get my proper revenge.

The neanderthal grunts, disappointingly quietly, as if his nervous system hasn't woken up yet. And then he punches me hard in the chest, knocking me flat on my back and bouncing my head off the floor. I take my time getting up, as if it was a choice, noticing that we appear to have arrived at our destination. I realise now I might have overcooked it with Mammoth. My chest is on fire and I suspect at least one rib is cracked, but at least I'm alive. Still, I consider not provoking him again.

I expected a heavily fortified hideaway, but what looked like the end of the alley turns out to be canvas screens painted with clever perspective. Even from twenty yards away it looks like the alley is empty, and that worries me. They don't care if I know their secret. Behind the canvases is a heavy green door decorated with brass studs, like the entrance to a Chinese temple. I'm thinking it may have been a restaurant, but after a complex sequence of knocks, the doors squeal open and we're admitted into an ornate but dilapidated hotel lobby. The vast space is dominated by massive chandeliers and a pair of staircases winding in opposite directions. Luxury is everywhere, but replaced by its decaying equivalent. Ironic that a place designed for the rich and famous is now home to the worst society has to offer.

One of the staircases has fallen through, but the other leads up to a mezzanine where we find another lobby. The carpets are worn, the wallpaper is peeling and there's a check-in desk with hundreds of room keys on hooks. Seated in front of them is an aged concierge who's reading an old Hollywood starlet magazine.

I ding the old brass bell and Mammoth jabs me again. The concierge smiles sweetly, as if getting rabbit punched happens to all the guests.

'Best if you just cooperate,' she whispers.

She hands Mammoth a key and gets back to reading about Clara Bow as we make our way past private telephone booths and the gaping mouths of elevator shafts.

Seven rib-aching flights of stairs later, we emerge in a door-lined corridor. Although I've tried to second-guess the reason for my capture on the climb up, I've failed to come up with an answer. I notice the doors here all bear the same number,[14] and I'm about to mention it when Mammoth pushes me face first into one of them. Blood spouts from my battered nose as I fall onto my knees and catch first sight of the horror within. Mammoth grabs my hair and yanks me back, forcing my eyes open and making sure I face the thing he's brought me to see. I manage to close my eyes a little, but it's not enough to avoid the vision.

A chill wind cuts in from a blown-out window, and through a veil of sticky tears I make out naked corpses dangling head down, swinging. I can't stop looking but I don't want to see those bodies, so I try to divert my attention from their unclothed forms to the ropes from which they're suspended. Some are smooth, some hairy, some skin mauling or painfully thin or spider twine.

But when that inventory is done my sight is drawn back, inevitably, irresistibly, to the inverted faces, dangling hair and arms raised in futile surrender.

Mammoth chuckles and whispers under his breath.

'This is what happens when we decide not to like you.'

He grins as I'm dragged to my feet and pushed toward the open window where I puke onto the fire escape. We step outside, our climb setting up a dissonant ring of rusting metal. There are no viable web routes at this level, so they're safe from attack, which means there's no way to escape. There's a sisal rope thick enough for a tugboat though and it's tied to the railing right in front of me.

It's too good an opportunity to ignore.

I perform a swan dive over the edge, praying to any God who's listening – because we're a long way up. I keep the dive shallow, no more than a foot from the brick, so I can grab the rope. But it ends sooner than I expect and I only manage to grab it with one hand and twist awkwardly towards the building, lurching from side to side.

I kick against the wall, pushing myself out, and swing towards the fire escape two floors down. It's badly rusted and the fencing gives way on impact, allowing me to crash gracelessly into the wall and scramble through the window. It's a film-worthy escape that would have audiences on their feet.[15]

The room must've been white once upon a time but is heavily mildewed now. A wardrobe gapes, displaying a few twisted wire hangers. Alongside, there's a washstand and mirror and, opposite, is a rickety bed cradling an old man. The mattress is bare and almost as filthy as his clothes. His head rests on a striped pillow, eyes fixed on a glass of water just out of reach.

I don't have the time, but he's clearly distressed and the water seems important to him. It'll take just a second, so I grab the glass and offer it. The old man's head rises slightly as a bony hand fastens round my wrist like a claw, his rheumy eyes meeting mine as he struggles to form words. Somewhat hesitantly, I move an ear close to his mouth and listen to the liquid gurglings.

'If you can get there, you can get back,' he says, struggling for breath.

I put the glass to his lips and let him sip, wondering where 'there' is, when the door caves in. Standing in the corridor with his arms crossed is Mammoth, clearly faster than I gave him credit for. He pulls me away from the bedside and throws me against the wall before driving a fist into my belly. Then, making sure the old man can see what's happening, he lets me scream for a full minute before dragging me back up the stairs to the tugboat rope.

Freedom becomes an even more distant prospect as he ties the rope around my neck. I follow him meekly up the staircase to a windy roof-scape. Noomi stands there wearing a treacherous smile.

It's cold on the flat tarmac surface where they're collecting rainwater in a hundred different types and sizes of receptacle. Beyond the roof's edge, there's a moonlit view of shattered wharves and the barley twists of the FDR Drive, where cars cling miraculously to the roadway. A sliver of safety barrier is all that keeps them from slipping over the side.

Mammoth pushes me past the water farm to a raised area, on which sits an old, wooden cabin. It's sheathed in polythene and glowing dimly from within. A bright metal smokestack puffs smoke into the night sky.

'Welcome to the alibi club,' he grunts.

A stink of chemicals hits me as I'm pushed inside. There are candles, by whose light I make out a bald-headed figure on a sofa facing away from us. The sound of his breath is amplified by a syrinx, an artificial voice box buried in his throat.

'We call it the alibi,' he wheezes, 'because we come up here to drink and tell stories about how it used to be and forget how it is now.'

I want to laugh at his melodrama, but there's something familiar about one of his ears. It has a notch like a punched train ticket, and I have a vague recollection of seeing it before.

He rises and turns to face me, muscles rippling like cats under a silk bedsheet. He scrapes dirt from beneath his fingernails with a stiletto and kicks a syringe under the sofa while sizing me up.

'Vixen tried to run, boss,' says Mammoth. 'So, I roped her.'

The boss nods and moves closer to inspect me. His eyes wander over my body, taking in my exposed flesh. It's only now I realise I'm covered in more blood than I have ever seen.

'I remember you as a snot-nosed kid,' he says. 'Looks like you lost a fight.'

'You could say that,' I admit, 'but I'm looking forward to the return match.'

He laughs as only a syrinx can, and taking it as a cue to speak, Noomi delights in telling him how she coaxed me single-handed into Mammoth's arms. Ticket-punch isn't impressed and knocks the kid into a corner. Despite her deviousness, she doesn't deserve to be tied up in the darkness that surrounds these people. In better circumstances she'd be selling cookies door-to-door, or learning how to ride a brand-new bike or just passing the summertime on a swing.

'Gianni Serpentine,' says ticket-punch, not offering his hand. 'But you can call me Snake.'

Mammoth unties the heavy rope and I stand completely still. I remember Serpentine now; always on a street corner peddling some drug or other.

'You learn quickly,' says Snake, 'but just so you know, if you unlearn the lesson then I'll get my bolt cutters and remove a fingertip of your choice and a toe of my choice. Understand?'

I nod meekly. I have no intention of testing his patience, but it's the perfect chance to lower my head and check the floor for something I can use as a weapon.

Snake's eyes narrow and, in the relative silence, his breath sounds like gusting wind overlaid with distant screams. Or perhaps it's my imagination. Already the scented air in this poly-wrapped hideaway is playing with my thoughts.

There's a rat walking along a high shelf that supports a row of glass jars, each with a human tongue inside.

I shake my head but the image remains.

'Do you enjoy what you see?' says Snake with a wide grin.

Conflicting emotions fight their way to the surface. My body is a wreck and my heart torn to shreds by what happened to Daniel and the rest of the group. But there's joy too because Mom is back within reach, and Lilith too, who I'd been secretly relieved to be parted from for so long. But what hurts me most right now, apart from my bruised ribs, is being betrayed by a ten-year-old.

I'm torn between remaining silent or dying and trying to take someone with me.

'She came across the chasm,' said Noomi, trying to look small and inoffensive. 'And there was this huge wolf, but I got rid of it. On my own.'

'A half-pint squirt like you fought a wolf?' says Snake.

'It's true,' I say.

Light flares in Noomi's eyes as she holds an expectant hand out to Snake.

'It's like she says,' I offer helpfully. 'Only without the wolf.'

It's repayment time but Noomi doesn't see it. She flies out of her corner, screaming and battering her tiny fists against my chest. I fall away, wincing with the pain of her barrage.

'She's lying, there was a wolf. A big one. And I tricked it. Tell him the truth you festering, shit-ugly, pig-snot, wank-bastard.'

I shake my head and smile sweetly. If she ever gets that new bike I'm going to slash the tyres.

'Take her away,' wheezes Snake. 'And don't waste any of the good stuff on her.'

'But I brought you the girl,' pleads Noomi. 'I need coal. You promised.'

'Then go and scavenge for food like everyone else,' says Snake. 'And maybe we'll do a deal.'

Noomi continues to kick and scream, battering Mammoth's ribcage as he approaches, but she's a moth battling a tank. He grins and turns her upside down, dragging her by one leg out onto the roof. A tiny bit of guilt creeps over me as Noomi gets her comeuppance.

Snake nods approvingly, producing a pipe made from random bits of metal tubing. There's a brilliant red glow as he lights up and, when he finally exhales, a billowing cloud fills the room. He seems so content that, when he finally speaks, I imagine I'll hear the solutions to all the world's problems. I'm hoping one of the answers will explain why Noomi needs coal, but before I can benefit from his wisdom my world turns to a scented blur.

My injuries catch up with me, cloaking my mind in darkness and hurling me at the floor.

Holo-stream Clip
New York, NY – September 23 2083

A surge of emotion floods my senses as I wake. It's not the kid-on-a-mission springing out of bed and yelling 'what shall we do today', but a slow, still-feeling-tired, gradual awareness of the world, like regaining consciousness inside a giant candyfloss machine. Even though I have never tasted the stuff, I can smell the sweet confection in the air, and for a moment it feels like I'm living the dream in Coney Island. Soon though, the smell fades, like the memory of a boardwalk, lost forever from the world.

I'm lying in a cast iron bath filled with hot water and suds, my wound an angry red, but expertly stitched. I can't remember the last time I felt this good. As I stretch back in ecstasy, the old concierge squeezes a sponge over my head, dribbling cool water into the corners of my mouth. It tastes pure, sublime.

The plumbing in this place is pure nineteenth century, but every second I spend here feels like I'm visiting heaven.

I pull myself up and peer through the splintered window frame. There's a view of the FDR[16] and the East River, but where my Mom once bathed in tidal waters there are wispy clouds laid out below us. And below the clouds is a clear view of the scar where a large city once sat. Our passage over Iceland, it seems, is just a distant memory.

'What happened?'

I should be asking a dozen more questions, but this particular one hangs in the air like a wandering meadow. Then I hear a familiar wheeze and slip deeper into the bath.

'Can I assume, then, that I have aroused your curiosity?' says Snake.

He's draped over an old wooden chair in the corner, but as I consider his question he rises and makes his way across the room like a praying mantis. The concierge offers me a brimming tumbler.

'Drink this up, dear,' she smiles. 'It'll clear your head.'

'See that down there?' says Snake. 'That's Murmansk.'

Iceland *then* Murmansk? We travel east to west, so we've done almost a full orbit, which means I've been out for days.

My vision is getting sharper. I stare at the scar where Russia's premier naval city used to be. Around the edges of the crater, certain buildings were left behind, and I can make them out in astonishing detail.

'Remember the slab that crashed into us a while back?' says Snake. 'It was no accident.'

'I nearly died that day,' I say. 'But aside from the mess at Fulton Street it didn't affect us much, did it?'

My ribs hurt when I speak and my fingertips feel odd. I lift them from the bubbles just far enough to check they're all present. In my new found state of bliss, I see a gentler version of Snake.

'You reckon?' he says. 'Did you ever think about that mass of stuff at Pier 86? Huge pieces of that slab, sticking to us like a tick on a dog, dragging us sideways and slowing us down. Just think back a few years and ask how often we fly over Murmansk. Manhattan has been a tundra-wise city ever since Inception.'

'Someone manipulated our course?' I ask. The view from the window is compelling evidence. Snake nods, waiting for his wheezy breathing to settle. Meanwhile, my favourite concierge continues with her exotic soaping.

'We have telescopes on every slab flying past, over or under us,' says Snake, 'especially on the fast-moving ones, or the ones that cut across our path. The data means we can make predictions about orbits and the like. You and me are just the planets and comets and stuff, you dig? We're all sliding around like marbles on a rail.'

'You brought me here to make sense of your data?' I ask.

A memory of Deeby and his unusual logbook entries begins to form. Poor kid.

'Don't flatter yourself,' hisses Snake.

He stares at me in silence and I'm suddenly grateful for the layer of bubbles.

'Get out of there and get dressed,' he says. 'There's something you need to see. Oh, and by the way, sorry about your friends.'

He turns and leaves, but when I try to get up the concierge puts her weight on my shoulder.

'Enjoy the bath for a while longer,' she purrs. 'Finish drinking your water.'

I smile sweetly and slip into the suds, tumbler in hand. I'm intrigued to hear what Snake has to say, but as soon as he's finished I'm going to get out of here, find Mom and punish Chang.

Snake keeps the reason for our little hike close to his chest, but in my mind every corner we turn is a possible clue to Mom's whereabouts so I keep quiet and bide my time. The promise of giving Snake the slip and tracking her down – or eliminating Chang – is a lantern of joy burning in my breast. I'm dressed in a black leather jumpsuit and strong knee length boots we took from a nu-graffiti-covered army store. Mammoth seemed particularly taken with the outfit and, as we head west, I keep catching him looking at me; it's a lust I might be able to use later to my advantage. As we descend a precarious spiral staircase in the basement of the Woolworth building, I begin to get the measure of Snake and how he might have come by his nickname.

'We need to expand, see. Grow or die, and there's no growing to be done south of here, so we need to expand uptown. Problem is the place is owned by some fearsome dudes and we don't got the power to take them down. So, we need help.'

'Yeah,' echoes Mammoth. 'We need help.'

'Sounds dangerous up there,' I say, avoiding the rusting hulks of discarded machines.

'Believe it. There's a shit-high fence across the island at 110th Street, after which it's a crazy show, maybe even cannibals. Nobody knows how much of the island made it into the air and the crews up north aren't going to let us find out. Anyway, not my circus, not my monkeys.'

I have no idea what the expression means, but nod as if I understand. As we descend, walls and floors get dirtier and greasier and I'm grateful for the boots. We pass through an empty basement where a vaulted ceiling drips slimy water from stalactites, then we enter a long, brick tunnel which echoes our footsteps. As Snake raises a cast iron hatchway to reveal subway rails twenty feet below, I'm thinking about what he said. If his territory is bounded by the chasm to the south and he's pinned down by enemies in the north, where will the help come from? We drop with the aid of a knotted rope and walk the tracks south towards the chasm. There's a smell of ancient sewers.

'Did you ever hear of a place called Detroit?' says Snake.

'Great music,' says Mammoth.

It's the first time he's said anything remotely sensible, but I hope it's the last. I want to keep hating all of them so I can exact my revenge with a clear conscience.

Snake lifts an inspection hatch and I peer through. Without warning, the memory of Daniel is in my head, crushing my stomach in a vice and drowning my thoughts in tears. Below us the tracks jut out over the chasm, but there's no sign of his body, just the sound of the wind screaming across girders. In my memory, Daniel is still falling, a grainy film-reel that turns me deathly cold, the flame in my soul quivering. Snake shakes his head, like a teacher who has heard too many questions go unanswered.

'You know when those planes flew into the towers way back?' he says, trying to start a fresh conversation. 'Well, my great-grandmother squared was right there on the street when it happened. You can see her in one of the old flat images, covered from head to toe in dust. And what we got here is similar. You need to bear witness so you can hand down the story. Then you'll appreciate the kind of trouble we're in.'

Snake pauses to acknowledge a motley gathering of 'faces' who appear to be under his control. We stand by and watch as more arrive; smelly children, mumbling crazies and starving adults from different tribes. They look daggers at each other but keep their distance in the spirit of a temporary truce. There's a similar gathering on the other side of the chasm and, for a moment, I imagine seeing Chang.

Snake signals us to move forward to where we can peer over the edge, wind-blown ice shards stinging our flesh. I'm waiting for the clouds to part, anxious for a glimpse of the lands we're passing over, but instead I hear the faint sound of music coming and going on the wind. It's the first real music I've heard since before the chasm formed when me and Mom spent the night in a burned up musical instrument suppliers and we sang as she played guitar.

'That's an old Four Tops tune,' says Snake, sounding for a moment like the person he once might've been.

'This is going to be great,' says a street urchin, jostling for position. 'Do you suss when Clarksville ran into Mont Blanc? Well, this is going to be way better.'

I shake my head in disbelief as I realise he's talking about a slab fall. Me and Lilith once saw a provincial department store crash into the north Atlantic, but until now I'd managed to keep the image from creeping back into my thoughts. It's the fear at the back of everyone's mind, ever since Inception. We're never sure if the day will come when the city tires of flying and simply drops out of the air.

'Hey, look,' yells the urchin. 'I can see something.'

The clouds thin out and we're presented with an aerial view of a city. Behind us a kid with a scarred face is hiring out telescopes. I turn and give him a look that means 'seriously, don't', but then I consider what Snake said. Someone has to bear witness; to keep a record for posterity.

The kid hands me a battered pair of binoculars which bring Detroit rushing up to meet me in a startling closeup. The city is about five hundred feet below us and, with the cloud dissipating, I'm shocked to see how low both cities are flying. My blood turns to ice as I consider how easily Snake's mysterious enemy has manipulated our course, and how simple it would be for them to destroy us.[17]

See how low we made you fly, I imagine them taunting. *And watch what can happen to a city if you don't do as we say.*

The tragic movie of my life reaches a turning point as the accompanying music moves to a dramatic minor key. In every sense this is a requiem for the souls about to be lost. I sob uncontrollably at the thought of all those people and what they must feel as their once magical city sinks towards the freezing ocean.

Explosive charges go off in a crooked line of fire at the prow of the Detroit slab and, when the smoke clears, a small part of the city is completely detached. It loses altitude only to rise again, getting nudged along like a calf being pushed by its mother.

Everything happens in slow motion now. People push cars and trucks over the edge but the city continues to lose height.

'Happy Motown Day,' grins the telescope seller.

The gathering multitude falls silent as the music from Detroit continues. Martha and the Vandellas strike up with 'Dancing in the Streets' as the leading edge of the city folds into the waves. Concrete road slabs fly into the sky like confused snowflakes as screams replace the music and oceanic spray raises a veil over what remains of the proceedings.

I lack the courage to witness anymore and turn away, my hearing strained by the deep bass thump of disintegration.

Immutable Cities 5

PELLARGON – *City of Malevolent Intent*
Squatting at the confluence of three polluted rivers is Pellargon, a desolate mausoleum where obese chimneys retch into an innocent sky and grime-cloaked factories struggle to contain the bestial machinery copulating within. A centre of arts forgotten over gradual centuries, it is said that Pellargon was gnawed apart by giant wasps, its pulp gobbed back out to form a new, alien metropolis. The only safe entrance is across the oil-sheen silk of the harbour, where bright constellated stars hang inverted as a guide to the industrial heart. The miasma of gases and decaying matter is a warning to stay away from the city, said by some to have discovered the secret of manufacturing and transmitting emotion. Successive attempts to sack the metropolis have seen aggressors overwhelmed by waves of reflected grief, their attacks reflected back upon them as an impenetrable barrier of hate. The combined thoughts of innocent children held back this defence for a while, but the city's darkness soon reasserted its iron grip.

QUANG-MEENAK – *The Queen of Resorts*

The primary city of the remedial water province. The population centre is dominated by a massive hotel built in the Ocean Gothic style, popular with tourists who came to see the two main attractions. Just a short walk from the famed hotel there once existed The Noble Zinc, a fabulous restaurant where every menu item was accompanied by a different performance; a short play, a monologue, a violinist, a juggler or even a puppet show. The famed zither master Epic-Nu-Thalam once surprised diners when he played there as a favour to the owner. Squab-Nesh, the noted comedian, also made a brief appearance but went missing in uncertain circumstances after a joke about the food backfired.

The other attraction, now since demolished, was The Bodie Electrum, a kind of prison camp where astral walkers went about their ethereal business safely hemmed in by electric fences. These perambulating souls didn't know they walked since they were merely dreaming, their astral bodies nonetheless visible to those who came to gawp at their nakedness.

Two hundred years passed by, and the grandeur of the resort in general and the hotel in particular faded. Today, those fabulous east-lands carpets are threadbare, the curtains filthy, the mirrors cracked and dark, the silverware dull and the porcelain dinner services pitted and ingrained with dirt. Nevertheless, the aristocracy still insists on staying here, the only address in Quang mentioned in the revered *Cornucopian Almanac of Watering Holes*. The décor may well be shabby, the wildlife in the wainscoting somewhat fearsome and the staff bordering on rebellious, but all of these shortcomings are forgiven for a single redeeming feature.

The world's longest marble bar is stocked with the finest experience enhancing thirst quenchers to be found in the eastern hemisphere. The pinnacle achievement of the resident mixologist – and the headiest of survivable cocktails – is the Holak-mir-Takum, a beverage which is said to erase your life so far and replace it with something much more memorable.

NABANDAR – *City of Harmonious Zither Song*
A closed city populated by erudite souls and musical prodigies.

PENDERENE – *City of Restless Nightingales*
There is but a single size of shoe available in this city, so the majority of the citizenry hobbles about in ill-fitting footwear or goes about their business barefoot. Possession of properly fitting footwear has become a mark of status, so foot surgery is commonplace for those who can afford it. If you intend to enter the city in possession of shoes, it is imperative you obtain a sanction form, properly witnessed by a constabulary Crispin. This documentation must be presented upon exit, along with the footwear it describes, so smugglers be warned! Whilst visiting the city it is essential that you adhere strictly to the laws regarding fragrant shoe-liners, uneven lace lengths and the wearing of mismatched socks. The city fathers employ roving bluecoats who police these and other laws and are empowered to mete out punishment on the spot. At the first hint of this, a small crowd will quickly form, hoping to observe the fitting of the iron clogs which are used to crush the feet of offenders.

STRYFE – *City of Final Breaths*
The art quarter of this city is home to the five seasonal poets. These are laureate posts that last for the lifetime of the holder, each of them linked with one of the seasons: Culmination, Precipitation, Cimmerous, Allegiance and Opposition. The laureates work only in their own season, with the resulting compositions being burned on the last day of the season in a ceremony of renewal. Afterwards there is a celebration of mental cleansing in which each of the works is deliberately forgotten. The punishment for memorising or 'failing to relinquish' a poem is severe.

KARSE-NEV – *Settlement of Cold Untruth*
An ice station closed by the non-proliferation Treaty of Orms-Tahen and reopened after the successful decommissioning of the Pelween Magick Laboratory. Once thought to be beyond the edge of the ancient world, Karse is reached by a convoluted series of airship flights. But traveller beware – the journey to the former thaumaturgical research facility is a ten-day flight in the most inhospitable conditions; crossing barren wilderness and freezing oceans. Also, be prepared for disappointment when you arrive, since the celebrated Raas museum may be closed due to unexpected bear activity. Anticipation trumps gratification though, so every moment of delay is to savour the eventual experience.

The experimental kinetoscope which tells a lie twenty-four times every second is a popular and worthy exhibit, as are the infinite mirror of self and the cabinet containing the disembodied soul of a thief. You should, however, reserve a greater part of your wonder for Morga Krenns, the lightning woman, who's made entirely of electricity. Be careful to time your visit to avoid the monthly respite period, when, to soothe her affliction, the scientists wire Morga in parallel with a network of phase-shifting induction coils.

CHONDU – *Mother of the Filaments*
A nest of energy conducting filaments meets in the nearby mountain range, so Chondu has naturally become the de facto location for the distribution of liquid wonderment. The essence is distilled in the granite lofts of Nela-Firr and makes its way to the city by means of a network of transparent pipes. As twilight falls, the hum of transformers fills the main square and the coil-like devices used to mutate the glowing stream offer their spiked underbellies and inner light to the sky.

OOM-JANN – *The Celestial City of Ink*
The tattooed citizens of Oom-Jann are highly protective of their bodily decoration, believed by outsiders to be the preservation of an ancient heritage. Attempts to uncover the significance of the markings are frequent yet fruitless. One popular hypothesis is that the unique designs represent a folk story which, if the relevant citizens gathered together and stood in a predetermined order, would be revealed in picture form.

BENZIR – *The Adored Place*
A sacred city in the northernmost part of the Shadow Isles, it sits on the banks of a holy river which flows the colour of ginger root. The streets are thick with a musk odour which clings to the air, like a beggar woman grasping a wrist. The time-washed streets ring with the faint

tintinnabulation of mu-metal bells and finger cymbals; unspoken prayers rendered as music.

YAZORDIA – *City of Uncertain Possession*

Many years ago, the underground city of Yazordia was swept by a tunnelling craze when rare minerals were reported found. As the bores went ever deeper in search of dwindling returns, a newer and more frightening madness took hold when a vast warren of ice caves was discovered. This is where the demons were found, apparently abandoned long ago, and entombed in the frozen strata. The decision to leave them frozen in place was unanimous, but in later years, perhaps due to some natural thaw, these same creatures were found in the poorer neighbourhoods, making their living by ridding citizens of unpopular neighbours, scaring wayward children or breaking curses. It soon became known in the upper echelons that shadowy deeds could be performed at a reasonable cost and, in this way, the creatures became useful, gradually insinuating themselves into Yazordian society. Today, as one walks the prosperous boulevards, promenades in fashionable boutiques or frequents popular gambling dens, it is impossible to determine who is a demon and who is not.

NASENHAAR – *City of Improbable Contrast*

A city of exquisite architecture, topped by gleaming silver spires and golden cupolas, which we were diverted from observing by the approach of the annual lottery. Instead of ornate edifices, we instead observed hope, fear, jealousy and sundry other passions elicited by greed. The thronging melee in the main square had a single purpose – to obtain raffle tickets from vendors advertising not wealth for the winner but the promise of a holy pardon from the approaching plague. A visitor seeking science rather than chance may choose instead to venture into the murky streets of the alchemist's quarter where, at great cost, you can obtain a certain and most perfect liquor consisting of sal ammoniac, virgin's urine and a particular sulphur vive.

NORTH OF BARUDH — *Nemo*
There is a certain philosophy which says to name an object is to suppress three fourths of its enjoyment. Three hundred miles north of the Barudhian Wastes is an unnamed city, wherein dwells a people with expressions resembling angry serpents. Their thoughts cannot easily be fathomed by what is seen in their faces, even when presented with a most unusual form of entertainment.

In the living theatre, constructed entirely from bamboo, actors exhibit a seven-year play where thousands of acts run in overlapping cycles, their entire purpose being to describe the history of the city. When not on stage, many of the thespians pay to attend one of the many laboratories dotted about the city where they observe non-actors toiling out their ordinary lives. Critics have pointed out a flaw in the history portrayed here since it does not feature a bamboo theatre showing a seven-year long play.

Katz: Reverse Angle

Ink on Paper
The Movable City of Aeropi::Narjuk
Haksdia 2nd day of Culmination
Passing variously over [Pellargon, Quang-Meenak, Nabandar]
Translations [Penderene]

Troband, emperor amongst men, I prostrate myself in your non-presence. Time for apologies I think, since unfortunate circumstances precluded the timely dispatch of translations. That said, you will be glad to hear I'm still alive; more than can be said for Marisa and Barath. Dina is in a bad way. The poor kid is paralysed and cannot (or will not) speak, so Barando has moved out of the trailer and the boy has taken his bed. Every night, I wake and look across at him, eyelids open, staring at me with that blank gaze. I remember as a child going to a heliographic studio for my portrait to be taken. I knew nothing about the art, but it was clear to me even at that age that the lens was more than polished glass. It was an agent, an actor, a hypocrite in the original sense – the interpreter from beneath. This boy has depths which worry me, not least of which is the tattoo he bears, a raft of esoteric symbols twisting around his leg from bollocks to ankle. Glimpsed, I hasten to add, by pure chance when washing and putting him to bed following the ordeal. Someone has decorated the child for a purpose of which I have no idea, and thus no reason to fear. But fear it I do. That evil shit Parok escaped out of the shop on a rope which somewhat theatrically hauled him up through the ceiling, a direction I seldom consider when indoors. I'm ashamed to admit I suffered no ill effects from the encounter, although if I'd been missing an arm or leg I might have felt more comfortable when Aho Nixx, the Narjuk ringmaster, came visiting. I think now the circuses are combined, he's above Taygorn. The eagle face plastered with Kohl and green eyeliner is an impressive sight in the ring, but close up it's difficult not to turn away in horror. He stole a drag from my pipe then made himself at home on my bed, fixing me with a quizzical stare. I thought he was going to berate me over the deaths. Instead, he calmly explained how eleven cities on the tour had refused to let the circus dock or trade for supplies, even that gentlest of places, the city of [Stryfe], home of the seasonal poets. It's like we're carrying some vile toxin. He also told me about the preparations for taking on urgently needed water from a mountain stream, a challenge that was going to stretch our piloting skills to the limit. I knew both of these things from the usual gossip, but what did surprise me was how he'd kept us all from starving by butchering the animals. He didn't mention what happened in Ocka Julce, I suspect by exercising a great deal of self-control. But he did enquire about the translations (it seems my business is common knowledge) and whether it was true one of them concerned a place called [Karse-Nev]. He was pleased when I confirmed it, then spent the next twenty minutes explaining what might happen to the circus in case of an attack and the retribution and inevitable sorrow which would surely follow. At that point I was glad he left, because I had become quite afraid.

I'll send more. The work is all that keeps me from madness,
Otto Katz

Ink on Paper
The Movable City of Aeropi::Narjuk
Tryndia 13th day of Culmination
Passing over [Chondu]

Now I know it's happening I can hear them. Mournful cries from the abattoir island are clearly audible and sadden me beyond tears. We are slowly consuming ourselves. Today we avoided the City of Thirteen Crimes, better known as [Oom-Jann] on the advice of Madame Sesostris, the tarot card reader. It's a perpetually rainy city, riddled with a maze of canals and aqueducts and fed by waterlogged roofs and generous gutters. Unsurprisingly, it's famed for the manufacture of bamboo umbrellas, the decorations on each of them relating to one of the thirteen crimes. It's also home to Glory Shrike, the crime authoress who wrote *The Spal Zak Affair*, *The Case of the Blockian Crown* and *The Sprechian Murderess*. My favourite of hers though was *Death by Punctuation*, which for me is just an occupational hazard.

Rehearsals continue in Le Grand Chapiteau, even though there's no prospect of a performance. I'm watching

Zarah practice her act as I write this, wondering if we can survive the malaise brought on by the lack of income. I don't know why the various cities rejected us, but they must have sensed or heard something bad and I can't say I'm surprised. We all feel the thunderstorm gathering, all except for Dina, who is still shrouded in a world of his own. I'm unable to shake off the events in Ocka Julce. My nights are troubled by sweats, the filthiest of black dreams and thoughts of being watched, not just by Dina in his frozen dream, but by God. He doesn't usually exist in my personal universe, but his gaze feels real right now. They reckon the visions come if you pray, whether you believe or not. Do you know any good religions? I have time to give it a go, since I remain in the trailer whenever possible, hoping for the Parok incident to blow over. Marisa and Barath's friends are giving me the cold-shoulder treatment and a lot of the other carnies no longer make eye contact. It seems I've finally inherited the bad juju from Dina. Xenobia asked me to destroy the heliograph I'd taken and, when pressed, said she didn't want to be associated with me if the Baem boys discovered my hiding place. I wish Dina had lost the ability to speak before we met because that particular nugget could only have come from him. For the moment at least, I can scarcely bear to be in his presence.

Running on empty.
Otto Katz

P.S. A shortage of tincture has me on the edge of sanity. I dread running out of the stuff. And I know it's wrong to pry, but I've been looking through Dina's sketches. They bear no relation to the city translations, looking more like the covers of the futuristic comics I was forbidden to have as a child.

Ink on Paper
The Movable City of Aeropi::Narjuk
Tryndia 18th day of Culmination
Recently passed over [Benzir]

Dina has begun to talk. In fact, I cannot now stop him from doing so. He speaks night (oh, joy) and day as if possessed, and at such a feverish rate it's impossible to transcribe. The few words reaching my addled brain illuminate a world beyond comprehension where surveillance is total and the only thing that can't be bought is freedom. The boy needs proper medical care, and I don't mean the kind offered by men in white coats. He needs to be understood, not wired up to an electrical generator or pumped full of drugs like an acquaintance of mine once was. My friend didn't deserve the treatment they doled out, but from the doctor's point of view it must be hard not to conclude madness when the patient claims to be from the future. Dina doesn't insist on any such thing, but in my limited opinion he has first-hand knowledge of worlds other than our own. There, I've said it, which probably makes me as mad as him, unless it's all just a misunderstanding.

To cap it all, we're passing over the plains of Ormann which are disputed by three warring city nations. The sight of those so-called civilisations in flames gives me little hope for our future, but provides a perfect map of my mental state.

Sad times.
Otto Katz

Ink on Paper
The Movable City of Aeropi::Narjuk
Faldia 19th day of Culmination
Hovering over [Yazordia]

And so, the misery continues. Janna, the two-headed woman, fell into an argument with herself while we dined on recently deceased animals. I spoke to her a few times prior to this and was pleasantly surprised by her demeanour, so this occurrence is all the more surprising. Her two heads were the best of friends, quite attractive and almost identical in appearance, although the one with the green hair bow has a slightly longer neck and a deeper voice.

When the argument started everyone was shocked, but none as much as me. The disagreement concerned Dina's continuing presence in the circus and how unlucky it was to have someone 'like him' in the entourage. A bit ironic considering the accusation was coming from self-confessed freaks. There were also calls to see our non-existent spear throwing act, but it was the rumour about the kid's tattoos that really lit the fire. They wanted to know what the markings were all about and, when I protested my ignorance, things took a turn for the worse. A bunch of rousties gave me a black eye and two broken ribs, but thankfully the beating paused when Madame Sesostris screamed up her luncheon. Janna had a gun and was pointing it at herself. Or her other self. How do you describe that? I won't even try. I'm a coward and knew the distraction would soon be over, so at the peak of confusion I ran to my trailer and locked the door. This morning I have the muddiest, retchingest, most confused head I ever suffered and will never touch the magickal mood powder again.

I dare not go out.
Otto Katz

P.S. I confess I may have become spellbound by my own spectacle and others aren't impressed with what they see. I was so completely ashamed of not standing up for Dina that I apologised profusely and forgave his little indiscretion with Xenobia. I just hope the word doesn't go any further and Dina understood what I said.

Ink on Paper
The Movable City of Aeropi::Narjuk
Haksdia 37th day of Culmination
Passing over [Nasenhaar], lately [North of Barudh]

We've been cooped in the trailer for days without food or water and Dina is still babbling in tongues which is driving me to distraction. From what little sense I can make, he's dreaming of a ruined city and jabbering about his sister being taken away. For one so young, the poor kid sure does have a lot of baggage. The carnies have a constant presence outside, just waiting for us to emerge. In the meantime, the lesser snake handlers were encouraged by Lady Vyper to set a fire beneath us. Fortunately for us, Aho Nixx came to the rescue and ordered the fire to be put out. I wouldn't say the Narjuk master enjoys having us here, but he doesn't believe the jinx stuff, which is why I opened the door when he knocked. Instead of stepping inside, he ushered a stern-faced woman across the threshold and closed the door. She introduced herself as Morga Krenns and handed me a bloodstained bag of meat.

'This is for you,' she said softly, 'the last of the chimpanzees.'

I don't know if she intended the cruelty, but I vomited on her, which is how we got off on the wrong foot. She doubted me when I said I knew of her, so I rather stupidly mentioned 'the lightning woman' and asked why her name might appear in a thousand-year-old document. Until that moment, I'd doubted it myself, but she reached out and struck me with an electric arc. The flash threw me to the floor with such force I almost lost consciousness, and what little of me was left awake had difficulty processing the experience.

As I recovered my wits, Morga extended her arms to erect a shining nebula lit by a thousand blue fireflies. I tried to get up, but a pulsating electrical pressure held me in place.

'You are a coward,' she said, 'but there is a potential in you to be more. You have a good heart, and you took the boy under your wing.'

'And look how that's working out,' I answered. 'We're not exactly popular round here.'

'Surface impressions,' she said. 'When the time comes, you will find many of them standing by your shoulder.'

'So, you're expecting a fight,' I replied. 'But I don't know who the enemy is and I don't have anything to offer.'

'We are all more than we seem,' she whispered, her voice modulated like a badly tuned radio. Her brilliant gaze trapped me like a fly in honey.

'I'm exactly what I seem,' I said. 'You told me I'm a coward and I'm not arguing.'

'Yet you accepted the mission to care for the boy.'

'How is that a mission? I found him by accident.'

'You translated a document which took you to a particular city, where you happened upon a particular boy. We believe ourselves masters of our own destinies, yet our journeys are marked out through the centuries, like a shining path.'

She released the electrical field and I was able to stand.

'So, we just plod through life, dropping our feet into pre-defined footprints?'

'It's up to you where you place your feet,' she said. 'Fate is not a straight line from one event to the next, but neither is it an infinite sea of choice. Our paths are determined by the actions we take at certain critical points in our lives.'

'Like a tree trunk branching again and again?' I suggested.

'More like a coral or a sponge,' she replied. 'There are many possibilities to divide and recombine. A large but finite number of possibilities.'

She stepped close and cupped my head in her hands, gifting a vision of a battle that felt entirely real with all the pain of the conflict falling not upon the combatants, but on me. My apologies, old boy, but I'm afraid at that moment I lost all self-control and shit myself.

I now know what true pain is, and have no wish to feel it again.

Literally scared shitless and intending
to leave at the first opportunity.
Otto Katz

Diary Fragments 6

Holo-stream Fragment – Para 13.03.47
Brooklyn, NYC – June 3 1968
Bruce Chaka – Photographer

The focus is gritty and the aperture ring requires a stevedore to operate it so I leave it wide open to gobble the remaining light. Raise, frame, focus and release. The reflex mirror bounces and rattles and the shutter's a bit hesitant but experience says the first frame is in the bag. It's an ordinary shot of a bridge and a river and possibly a waste of valuable film, but picture editors like a 'before' and 'after' shot, like we're all psychic. Here's what the sleepy upstate town of Hicksville looked like before the gas main exploded and here it is again when the pall of dust settled. Note the child's stuffed toy placed deliberately in the foreground of the desolation shot. That rabbit is pure Hollywood heartstrings.

I try to ignore the clattering and traffic and yelling behind me, just waiting for what now feels like a half-forgotten dream. The city is getting on with its business as usual and I'm getting stupidly wet. I take shelter under the bridge. There's a guy selling chestnuts like Victorian times, and they smell so good I just have to—

There's a God Almighty crack that sounds like the moon exploding; the bridge pedestal lifts, exposing bricks that haven't seen the light for a hundred years. This time people notice. The chestnut seller screams. Hobos stand and stare as the entire edifice rises for a few seconds then falls again, slowly and with a certain amount of deafening grace.

Panic ignites the air. I run clear of the bridge and get a couple of shots on the hoof, then skid to a halt. When did I reach the point where my eyes would lie to me? Or am I the victim of some elaborate hidden camera show? The entire island of Manhattan is rising, the waters of the East River dripping from its vast underbelly as everything from Battery Park to Washington Heights takes to the air. Instinct makes me frame the shot, but my finger is stilled on the shutter release. Where will this ever appear in print? What will be left when this day is finished? Who will benefit from seeing the image? And there I have my answer. I lower the camera, carefully remove the canister and pull the film out, exposing it to the light of the sun. Some things are just not meant to be seen.

Holo-stream Fragment – Para 12.51.41
Kensington, London – January 30 2021
Countess Valentina di Bruggen-Pomerol – Patron of the Arts

One must always have a helicopter on hand when staying up in London. Not one of those cheap single-engine death traps so popular with the nouveau riche, but a twin-engine jet model certified for crossing urban areas. My pilot is always on hand, so when the unfortunate circumstances made themselves known, I had the concierge arrange for me to board the aircraft in Hyde Park. The park, after all, is there for all to enjoy, is it not?

The dear husband failed to make the flight, of course, no surprise there, but I shan't lose any sleep. Reports from my estate manager confirm all two hundred thousand acres are intact, but I shall ascertain that for myself when we overfly prior to landing. I think it's a big fuss over nothing and will sort itself out in the end, and until it does I intend to stay down in the country. What could be better than larks with friends? I have an idea everything is going to turn out simply wonderfully.

Holo-stream Fragment – Para 03.19.47
Oruro, Bolivia – May 17 1978
Felice De Lorenzi – Primary School Pupil

Sometimes the little island comes closer and sometimes it moves further away, so I have to wait until it gets really close and encourage Tusker to jump. Tusker is my dog, and I pray every day he'll make it back to me. There's no food on the little island. I tried to throw some bread to him last week, but couldn't reach.

Holo-stream Fragment – Para 33.01.23
London, England – September 17 2027
Travis Hausmann – Oenologist and Bibliophile

The tabloids had a field day with the rumours, never tiring of inventing ridiculous puns and playing on words for their three-inch banner headlines. And why would they tire? It's the journalist's perennial obligation to get you to read a story that is not quite as interesting as its headline. Seven dead in local rail tragedy is journo-speak for the much less intriguing *Seven sheep stray onto railway line*. But there is more. I swear on my dear old mother's life I once saw the headline *Chocolate covered kipper factory was a flop* and immediately bought a copy so I could frame the front page and hang it in my study.

I suppose that's the kind of thing that desensitised me to the rumours about the end of days. It seems fortune tellers from all over the world were predicting the same thing; the planet was due to blow up, or some such twaddle, on September the seventeenth. I therefore awoke with great anticipation this morning, wondering if I had time to boil an egg and solve the chess problem in *The Times*.

Holo-stream Fragment – Para 37.22.28
Angel Station, Königsberg – September 12 1919
Terrel Maan – Architect and Psychogeographer

The train is ready to depart and my fellow travellers have a certain look about them. The journey will take us out towards the absolute proof which, to most, looks like the edge of a slab but which others insist is the edge of a flat earth. Some will make the trip in order to confirm what they already know, and some to confirm what they hope is true, a self-doubt which hides nicely behind an unfolded newspaper, although I can still clearly see his reflection in the carriage window. The more massive slabs have survived almost intact, leading to the growth of a movement called Edgeism, whose followers believe the world is still in one piece and, against all logic, remain impervious to the idea of dismantlement. As my own personal pocket of resistance to this stupidest of ideas, I founded an idea to oppose the Edgeists; a utopia created by a myth with no central design. There is no thread to the story, except for what the chosen combination of fragments reveals. The plot is the journey. The stories are the choices. In this place, buildings take form according to what they hear when their own plans were drawn, some assuming the shape of petrified melodies or grand symphonies perhaps, whilst the shape of others is influenced by explosions or marital disagreements or the iron-shod rattle of tramcars.

Holo-stream Fragment – Para 90.03.17
Anne Arbor, Michigan – July 13 1934
Anonymous report recorded from radio

Did you ever stand on a precipice and imagine what it would be like to set yourself free? I read the government advisory book from end to end and not once did it mention seeing a city of eight million inhabitants dropping from a clear blue sky onto the already pulverised ruins of another. Did you know they dumped all the cars over the edge when the gas ran out? All those idiots driving around the city like nothing had happened. What a bunch of jerks. Then there was me, sometime newspaper sub-ed, sometime diner help and failed poet, laying like a nervous crow in an earth-scrape. I watched the passing threat with an intense *blink-blink-blinking*, closing my eyes at the last moment. When I opened them again my ears were ringing from the brutality of the impact and the city was gone; just a curtain of spray washing its hands over the ocean.

Holo-stream Fragment – 04.06.19
San Francisco, California – August 12 1967
Paul Serres – Musician

Monica came round again today. This was both good and very, very bad. At one point during the trip, I saw the ground rise, and it didn't come back down. It's still up there, you know? She showed me the Polaroid too, the one that can't make up its mind what it's a picture of. Man, oh man, this is some seriously good shit.

Holo-stream Fragment – Para 15.85.53
Lundern, Inguland – September 2 1900
Jay Daog Phoenix – Isis Waterman

They say this winter's going to be a right fucker along the lines of '57 and '73. Might even be a frost fair on the river. I don't mind that; I might even go to it myself if I don't freeze my arse off first. What I do mind is when the fucking almighty and all his poxy mates get together and take the bread out of my kids' mouths. Who wants to pay a waterman to take them downriver when they can walk it or skate it? I fucking hate the lot of them.

Holo-stream Fragment – Para 15.56.65
Tuseka, Santeria – December 11 1911
Countess Eliho Troika-Strelitz – Aristocrat

The name of my ancestral mansion is Tuseka, which in the local tongue means a melancholy yearning or deep sadness. The windows are rotted away now, and ever since the forest rose up and the lake disappeared, the walls run with damp or ice, depending on the season. Consequently, I dismantled a decrepit wooden shed and rebuilt it slat by slat in the ballroom where I once danced with a Crown Prince on my twenty-first birthday. The shed is double-lined with mattresses on every surface, inside and out, and can be kept warm by burning a few sticks each day. The splintered wood comes from furniture imported at great expense and smells of polish and subservience.

The weather here is unfriendly, so I seldom venture out unless I need to collect cloudberries or lingonberries or hunt deer, which I do with a bow and slingshot. The rest of the time I amuse myself by inventing stories about each of the rooms. There are a thousand archways, doors and passages and unique combinations of them to take you to each room. One combination will lead me to my secret inner courtyard where many worlds lay hidden. I saw something there once and thought I must be dreaming. The time for exploring those ideas is in the spring though, a joyous event signalled by the cracking of the river ice; a thousand little explosions.

Holo-stream Fragment – Para 22.12.12
Shimla Monorail Route F9, India – March 2 1923
Boradu Quade – Rare Stamp Collector

As I close my eyes and begin to drift, the mental image of my departure point slides into oblivion as details of my destination gather from the wisps of distance. The object of my journey is to lay eyes and, dare I say it, hands, on a twopenny blue 1847 with a unique inverted watermark. The only known example in existence, it was printed from a plate broken immediately afterwards and has languished in the collection of an ignorant provincial brute for thirty odd years. I'm salivating at the prospect, quite literally I find, to the disgust of an attractive woman sitting opposite. This, despite my insisting I have a compartment to myself. I try farting, then tuneless whistling and finally picking my nose, which I urgently need to do anyway, but she remains in place despite having had the opportunity to change compartments at the two previous stops. Undeterred, I decide to engage her in annoying conversation, but to my own great annoyance she responds. Yes, she has indeed heard reports regarding 'new islands of the air' and, no, she doesn't believe in them either, which is a shame. I find myself wishing it were true, since if just a few of those islands were to establish a government and, by logical extension, a postal service, they would obviously need to issue stamps, presenting an enormous opportunity for serious collectors. I put this idea to her and rather than getting out in a huff at the next stop she takes out a pad and begins sketching. After a while she displays her designs for stamps issued by these imaginary new countries. My heart leaps at the sight and, with eyes fixed upon her palpably delicious decolletage, I find myself hoping that romance will blossom during our ascent to the summer capital.

Hannah: Depth of Field

Holo-stream Clip
New York, NY – September 23 2083

The final moments of the city of Detroit have left me numb with despair. I plod along in Snake's footsteps as we follow the subway tracks, alternately wondering if New York will be next and trying to formulate an escape plan. Even if we were above ground though, I'd have no chance of escape. I'm escorted by Mammoth and another low-brow with hams for biceps and a body the size of a fridge. Judging by the way the subway dwellers scatter, he's well-known. We're a clear and present threat and, as such, we're being watched from the many complex angles that underly this part of the city. It's a welcome change from being regarded as a punch-bag, and I might just get to like it.

I've been thinking about what Snake said earlier. Although it's hard to imagine in this subterranean gloom, the midday sun has been lower in the sky recently, which, combined with the entries in Deeby's log book, confirms our orbit has slipped northward. And I just saw the hole previously known as Murmansk.

'Is the change in Manhattan's route worrying you?' I ask eventually.

Snake seems thoughtful, perspiration beading around his eyes. It's getting warm here and there's a smell I can't place. But I don't want to get any closer to its source.

'I showed you that city ploughing in for a reason,' says Snake, his forehead creased like corrugated iron. He seems genuinely concerned.

'The people who killed Detroit have sniffed us out, and they'll kill Manhattan too, just as soon as they figure out a way. That's why I signalled Chang to drive you up here.'

We walk past a decaying body, the gory details thankfully masked by decreasing light levels. But the stink is unholy and matches my growing ire.

The solution to my flashing light mystery is followed by an uncontrollable rage which pauses only to boil in the cauldron of my hatred before spewing out in his general direction. The memory of snuffed lives steams through like a freight train, and absolutely nothing is going to stop it.

'You stinking weasel prick,' I scream, grasping at the first insult I can muster. 'You caused the deaths of all those people just to get me up here?'

'That was just Chang's interpretation,' grins Snake, 'he's unpredictable but efficient. Anyway, I apologised already. You don't get two apologies from the Snake.'

I'm grinding my teeth to stop the words that will anger him and endanger me.

'What could possibly be so important to justify all that?' I yell. 'There's nothing, absolutely fucking nothing that could be so important.'

'You need to have a word with your mother,' says Snake,

all matter-of-fact.

The sheer imbalance of the equation sets me spinning. I can't believe for one second all those lives have a value equivalent to what Snake wants, but the prospect of speaking to Mom after all this time temporarily dials down my rage. I'm still seething though, as I ask him the first of what should be a hundred questions.

'So how did you know I'd survive?' I ask. 'Chang wasn't exactly playing softball.'

'Cassie said you'd make it. So, how about it? Maybe you can have a word with your old lady on our behalf?'

I wonder who Cassie is and how she could know such a thing, but it can wait. I also consider mentioning Deeby too, but it would just complicate matters. I'm not even sure we're on the same side, the way he stood there so calm with Chang.

'So where is she?' I ask, my breathing steadying, 'and why can't you ask her yourself?'

'We already did and she refused. End of.'

'That's all? You didn't argue or try to force her?'

A broad smile cracks his face in two, displaying a gold tooth set with a diamond.

'Did you ever argue with her when you were a kid?'

'All the time,' I say.

'Course. She wouldn't harm her own. No point in spoiling the goods.'

'My mother would never harm anyone.'

'Tell that to Hamilton,' says Snake.

A squeeze on my arm confirms Hamilton is one of my escorts. The fridge.

'He wanted to see her perform,' says Snake. 'So, he made a move on her and she put him down without even blinking. Slammed him against a wall. He was out for hours.'

'It was indigestion,' grunts Hamilton.

'Sounds more likely,' I say. 'I don't know how you found out about her gift, but she would never use it. Ever since we were born she drilled the sense of danger into us.'

'Her so-called secret is common knowledge,' says Snake. 'But maybe you're right. Maybe she just doesn't have it any more and wish casting is dying out like they say. I gotta admit, nobody produces fire from their fingertips these days. And you know the trick where they project their thoughts onto clouds? Well, the last time I saw that was before you were born, missy.[18] All we got now is the remnants of mankind, floating above a plague-ridden planet in virtuous uncertainty. We're sky trash, just waiting to fall, and there's nothing we can do about it. There ain't no saviours anymore. Except maybe for one.'

I scoff unintentionally at his awful prose. He sounds nervous even to me, the thoughts tumbling out of him in a wild panic.

'Manhattan is going down,' he says. 'And your mother is the only one strong enough to stop it.'

I can't help laughing again at the ridiculousness of the situation. I even do a little snort in the middle which makes me sound like a jerk.

'And what makes you think that?' I ask.

'Your friend Pia. You told her your Mom could hold us up and she told us, so in a way it's straight from your mouth. She can do this thing. And she owes us. All of us.'

'So, you help us and we'll help you,' grunts Mammoth, finally finding something of his own to say. All this time his lips have simply echoed Snake's words, like a penitent following the words of a priest.

'You want my Mom to cast a wish strong enough to save an entire city?'

I don't bother denying Pia's lie or wonder how she made contact with Snake. She's dead now, and I won't direct malice against her. But she had a role to play in this and I get the sense that others have their parts too, like we're playing some complicated game and I'm the only one who hasn't read the rules. As I see it at the moment, I end up swinging by my feet in the body room or go along with the Snake and see where it takes me. At least that way I have a chance to find Mom.

'Even if her gift was powerful enough, she wouldn't do it,' I say. 'She swore on all our lives.'

'OK, so what do you think protected you when you were growing up?' says Snake, clearly angered. 'Did you never feel the strength of the wall she built around you? Nobody could ever touch you or your sister. You were those insects with yellow and black warning stripes. Stay clear of me or get poisoned.'

I take a deep breath and consider the evidence that paints Mom in a new light. It's true we were never attacked and, growing up, I always felt safe, even when things happened to people nearby. We felt warmed by a fire and protected from storms, and sure, I guess we always knew what Mom was up to, but I'm not going to give him the satisfaction of confirming his theory.

I'm still thinking about Mom's invisible fence as we emerge from the subway tunnel; the bullies who never approached us a second time; the gang who never approached us at all after finding their leader's disassembled body on our doorstep. I never thought I'd be so relieved to be reminded of these things or so thankful for the protection we took for granted.

As we climb up from track level, the weak lantern light suggests we've reached Fulton Street, but I can't be sure. There's a nu-graffiti covered train standing at the platform, as if the doors are about to close and it's going to move away, a frozen tableau of normality from an unsuspecting past. In a brief moment of confusion, it feels like I've stepped back in time; I've gone back beyond my birth, beyond whatever tore Manhattan out of the ground to a place of innocence and wonder; one that my mother must have been familiar with.

Then I catch sight of the desiccated bodies seated in the subway cars, their gaunt faces animated by our flickering lights. There's a young girl with a dog on her lap who's reaching for a biscuit. A business type with a cell phone to his ear, his other hand searching inside a leather briefcase. A pair of nuns holding hands, as if they had a few seconds notice of their impending fate. A street performer dressed as a circus ringmaster and sprayed from head to toe in faded silver paint. An older woman with plastic bags filled with stuff that only she could have valued. And a young man resting a can on his knee. It's not a soft drink though, but the empty casing of a gas canister which once contained nerve agent. Taking inspiration from the line 'deliver us from evil', a sect named themselves 'Deliverers', their declared mission being to prevent people suffering in a catastrophe they insisted was just about to happen. With Inception lurking a few days in the future though, the city saw them as terrorists and understandably ignored the warning until it was too late.

I reel back in shock at the sight of the bodies. My face and hands are ice cold and I'm having difficulty balancing.

'Have a pull on this,' says Snake. 'You look like you need it.'

As we turn away from the subway car, he hands me a hip flask made of frosted glass. It's engraved with signs of the zodiac, the most beautiful and delicate work of art I have ever seen. My first thought is to question why such a wondrous object should be in the possession of a thug. Shouldn't art belong to the righteous? I'm still trembling as I pull the stopper and take a long sip. It has a warm, pure taste, like tiny prayer bells ringing on my tongue.

'Keep it, as a token of our developing relationship,' says Snake. 'The guy who stole it from MoMA owed me a favour.'

I'm not sure I want a relationship with Snake but say nothing. I like the token, so I stopper the flask and slip it into a pocket before he changes his mind; a tiny fragment of joy in an otherwise bleak landscape.

'This doesn't mean I'll help,' I state plainly. 'In fact, it doesn't even mean I've stopped hating you.'

I turn my back on him, facing the people in the carriage once more and wondering about the lives they led before they were sacrificed. The girl running in the park and playing with her dog every morning before school. The nuns living behind closed doors, venturing out only for confession at Saint Patrick's but buying chewing gum on the way. The bag lady combing the streets by day in search of the ultimate bauble and dossing in a dumpster behind Bloomingdale's at night.

With that thought, I hear familiar footsteps and turn to find my twin sister Lilith standing there, like a distorted vision of myself in a fairground mirror.

I'm transported back to my childhood; sisters running around the neighbourhood like nothing else matters, whispering across the arch at Grand Central, performing on a bare stage at Carnegie Hall and, best of all, searching for the tiny doors that were sprinkled all over the city by an artist, each of which, legend has it, leads to a magical kingdom. But to make things difficult, it's said the doors move wherever they fancy.

Lilith brings all that momentary wonder to a halt with her usual directness.

'We need to have a conversation about Rachel,' she says.

'Is that the best you can do after eleven months apart?' I ask.

I hate it when she uses Mom's given name so I give her the stare we've practised since childhood. As usual, the intimidation kicks in and I fail to meet her gaze. Eventually though, Lilith relents and our eyes make contact. Hers are darker than I remember, as if what she's seen has changed her.

'You're the dirty one,' grins Hamilton. 'But your sister Lilith, she scrubs up nice.'

I bat the creep's hand away and lean back to avoid his stinking breath.

Once again, I'm the dowdy wallflower standing in the corner at Lilith's glittering state banquet. I want to punch his face and keep punching it until he realises my appearance means less to me than what's in my heart and, although I'd never admit as much to her face, that Lilith is far more than a girl who knows a few wish casting tricks.

'Take no notice of him, Hannah,' hisses Snake, 'if brains were dynamite…'

'Yeah, but two wish casters, boss? Three with the mother, huh? Is it enough to stop those guys you told us about?'

Mammoth nods eagerly in agreement and twists my forearms outward to show the stitched and partially healed cuts to Snake.

'Lilith and my Mom have a gift, but I don't,' I say, 'I got the cuts and the other injuries when I crashed head-first into the car park.'

Lilith regards me with suspicion but remains silent.

'Cuts don't necessarily raise the talent,' says Snake, 'emotion will do it too.'[19]

'That's good then,' I say, 'because someone is going to pay for all those lives Chang took, and whether I get to him or not, I'm eventually going to come for you too.'

'You're way out of your depth kid,' says Snake, 'so I'll let that one go, but don't ever threaten me again or something nasty will happen to the kid Chang's holding. Now, why don't you just play nice and go talk to your sister?'

The hired hands release me and I take the lantern offered by Snake, regretting my bravado. The poker hand I've been dealt suddenly feels weaker at his mention of Deeby. Any gamble I undertake now will be undermined by my need to protect the boy.

Snake's idea is reasonable though, if not fanciful, so I'll hear what Lilith has to say. And if I do anything at all, it won't be for him; it'll be for Deeby and Daniel and the others I lost. And to track down my Mom.

Lilith enters the nearest subway carriage and I follow, choosing to settle myself down next to a matronly corpse who's clutching a designer handbag and wearing three diamond rings.

'Nice outfit,' says Lilith, sitting opposite. 'Pity if she gets ploughed into the side of some mountain along with the rest of us.'

She is one callous bitch, but I shouldn't be surprised. Her heart is a blackened cinder swinging inside her ribcage on a length of old rope.

'Just come straight out and tell me what you want,' I spit.

'Rachel did a stupid thing,' says Lilith. 'Snake offered her a way to improve all of our lives and she told him to get lost.'

I let that one slide. I've had a glimpse of what Snake gets up to and I'm not surprised Mom refused.

'He's a good guy, once you get to know him,' says Lilith.

'Why don't you just get to the point?' I ask. 'It wasn't Mom who did something stupid, was it? It was you.'

'OK, so you see right through me,' admits Lilith, 'it's the twin thing, I get it.'

'Jesus, will you just tell me what you did?' I demand.

'Rachel refused to help Snake, even when he offered us real food and warm beds and all the other stuff we went without as kids.'

'Let me guess,' I say. 'You offered to help instead?'

'It was just a few little wishes.'

I feel like an ordinance dump about to explode.

'We've spent our entire lives hiding this shitty curse,' I yell, fuming, 'but you go ahead and perform party tricks anyway because some gangster asks you nicely?'

'It was low level stuff,' says Lilith. 'The kind of thing nobody would ever notice. A gang boss to the north gets unlucky one day. He chokes on a peanut. But he's no loss to humanity.'

'And Mom was good with that?'

'Sure,' she says, playing with her hair.

'Liar! There is no way she would allow it. So where is she, then? What has your friend done with her?'

Lilith is smiling and shaking her head.

'If you've harmed her I'm going to—'

'That's rich,' she spits. 'After what you did on our seventh birthday? You changed the suit of a playing card in full view of the neighbour kids and she took the blame. And I guess you've conveniently forgotten how the parents trussed our Mom up and tortured her?'

There's a rumble at the back of my mind. The blackest

of my dark thoughts are testing the strength of the lock on the casket. When my everyday thoughts of survival surface, I'm trembling and can feel sweat beading on my forehead.

'It was just one wish,' I whisper feebly.

I hear an echo of me chiding Deeby for the very same thing.

'And look where it got us,' says Lilith, triumphantly. 'So, let's not dwell on the past, huh? The bigger picture says wishes were cast and it doesn't matter who did it.'

The script of my life must surely be underlined in red here. It sure as hell does matter who cast the wish. The single action of a careless child leading to so many consequences. It has burned our lives. And my anger and jealously of Lilith lit the match.

'So, what's the problem now?' I ask, eventually regaining composure.

'You remember those low level wishes of mine? Well, it's just possible that Sensitives have picked up on them.'[20]

'Which is exactly why Mom had us laying low all these years,' I say.

Finally, I know I'm right and she's wrong. It doesn't feel like much of a victory.

'If you say so,' admits Lilith. 'Anyhow, Snake reckons some heavy people are on the way, and they aren't bringing us birthday presents.'

I give her the stare again, thinking about all those games of chance falling in her favour or me getting the smallest portion of food or being unable to solve puzzles she took seconds over. It was never good enough for Lilith to succeed; I had to fail.

'Do we know who they are?' I say eventually, tiring of her superior gaze.

'Snake says they're Polar Hegemony.'

'Never heard of them,' I say. 'But in view of what just happened to Detroit, it sounds like I need to speak to Mom.'

'Which is what we've been asking all along,' says Lilith. 'The only thing is, we have no idea where she went.'

With so much information swirling around in my head, I can't think straight, so I just sit and stare at my seatmate's diamond rings and compliment the poor woman on her outfit. This temporary connection to the past somehow makes me feel better, and might even be a comfort to the old lady, wherever it is she went.

I sit quietly and consider my interpretation of Mom's mantra. I always believed it was about hiding our wish casting gifts in order to protect us, but now, after being dragged to a hotel and beaten almost unconscious on the way, I realise we might be hiding a bigger and far more dangerous talent.

Lilith, meanwhile, is in the process of saying something; lying, probably. But as I continue to listen, her speech deepens and gets slower. I watch as her bodily and facial movements slow down and eventually stop, the 'oh' of her mouth neither growing nor shrinking.

Looking around, I can see no movement.

Time, it seems, has come to a halt.

Another strange thing; there's a whiff of damp fur and urine and a *pant-pant-panting* sound. Standing by the carriage doors is a she-wolf, the exact double of the one Noomi killed. The animal is tethered by a braided leash and held by a slightly built girl. She's about my age with long, red hair, brown eyes, and wearing a pale blue summer dress that looks freshly laundered. This detail alone makes her seem like a diminutive magical creature, her presence lifting my spirit by the softest of hooks and the tiniest of invisible ropes. I feel buoyed by her proximity, excited even, and know implicitly that I can place my trust in her.

The girl holds my gaze as the wolf lifts a single massive paw and places it a few inches forward. She's stalking me in slow motion and the girl follows, just as gently.

'Don't move,' she says.

I have no intention of moving.

The silver-grey monster sizes me up, just inches from my face now, jaws opening. I remember the ice-blue stare. Victim, it says. But then I feel the caress of a warm tongue over my mouth and nose and sweeping across my eyes.

The girl holding the leash smiles and I burst into tears. My heart breaks as I consider the bundle of fur Noomi tricked over the edge. Mom always told us wolves were nearby. As children, she said they were our guardians, but even then I never imagined them to be real.[21] They were never like this, with all the breath and the watching and the substance.

'She likes you,' says the girl, stroking the wolf's mane. 'I'm Cassie, and this bundle of fur is Bebe, who was once your sister's protector.'

I glance at Lilith, still frozen in time.

'And the other one?' I ask through sobs. I realise I'm crying for Daniel and the rest of them too.

'Ophelia was your protector,' says Cassie, shaking her head.

I see it all now. Snake, it seems, knows more about me than I know myself. He saw how Mom protected us both as kids and knew exactly how she did it. He may even know about the wolves, which is a good reason to get away from his sphere of influence.

'Snake is a bad man,' says Cassie, as if reading my mind. 'But it's good he brought you here.'

'And why is that?' I ask.

'There's a disaster on the way.'

'Bigger than the one we live in now?' I ask. 'In case you didn't notice, the world has been in trouble for quite a while now.'

Then I see it. The girl is as smart as a whip, but there's an emotional connection somewhere that's broken. I reel my anger back in.

'What's happening with Lilith?' I say, gesturing towards my sister. I have to admit she's even more attractive when frozen mid-sentence.

'Snake asks lots of questions,' says Cassie. 'Hard ones about oppositions and coincidences and parallel courses. And the future. He has a lot of questions about the future, but I don't tell him about anything important. There are bad thoughts buzzing around in his bony head, like flies.'

Feeling a little light headed, I take a final look at my motionless sibling and follow Cassie out of the carriage, walking along the platform to the spiral stairs. I can't imagine what Snake has done to her, but as we pass his time-frozen form she takes out a table fork and jabs it into his shin. Then she places the fork in Hamilton's hand, carefully wrapping his fingers around the weapon. I nod in approval. I believed that helping Snake was the best route to finding my Mom but I have a better ally now, so we need to find a way of ditching the thug and the rest of his crew.

Cassie slips Bebe from her lead and the wolf drops back to walk beside me, her claws *click-clacking* on the hard treads. Following the exit signs, we emerge beneath the old dome of Fulton Street station; a lighthouse in a storm where every single pane of glass survived the collision that created the chasm. It's a message of hope for many.

Just behind the entry barriers there's a memorial wall; a mad mosaic of notes, cards and photographs covering every square inch of its surface. Cassie detaches a piece of lined writing paper and offers it to me. I've been here before and know what the papers represent, so I take hold of the note in a reverent fashion. Many of the dedications mention people who lost their lives in terror attacks before I was born, but thousands more appeared around the time of Inception. Mom said it was people trying to make sense of something impossible to understand, but I never really got that, having seen only the aftermath of Inception and experiencing nothing of the old city.

Now though, I'm beginning to see what she meant, so I take the sheet and read.

Ellie, December 3 2067: The world is in one hell of a mess. Maybe we should gather what remains of the earth's population together in one place and ask the person who broke the planet to put their hand up. Then we can help them to put everything right again.[22]

Cassie stands before a map of the subway tracing a finger along the coloured lines as if she's considering a journey.

'Our island is losing altitude,' she says, as if confirming something she's seen in the map.

'So, we could collide with a mountain range or even a hill?'

Cassie gives a little frown then shakes her head.

'Not on our current course,' she says. 'I'm pretty good at predicting trajectories.'

'You're Snake's secret navigator?'

I'm knocked back by this. If I had to guess at Cassie's abilities, I wouldn't have included anything quite so practical.

'He calls me his ephemeris,' she smiles.

'So, you know the positions of other slabs?'

'Most of them, just from observation and calculation.'

'I get it,' I say. 'Like kids keeping a log, but to the *n*th degree.'

'I'm not telling. Remember?' she reminds me.

'I know what you said about Snake's questions, but you need to trust someone, sweetheart.'

I can see her thinking it through. She's going to refuse, but then she notices Bebe licking my hand.

'The nearest slab is a section of oak forest called Perrin's Ghost,' she says. 'Bearing: two one zero. Range: seventeen miles. Heading away at file miles per hour relative. There are five other slabs within a hundred-mile radius. All tiny compared with Manhattan. The largest is an unnamed patch of Arizonan desert with a functional airstrip. The smallest looks like part of a prison building, from what used to be Albania. There are another eighty-seven slabs within a thousand-mile radius.'

'Impressive,' I say. 'If you didn't just make it all up.'

She shakes her head slowly, disapproving.

'Orbitals are easy,' says Cassie, 'but not every object in the sky moves the way gravity dictates.'

Max F, November 7 2067: So, what do I think holds the city up? Hot air? Who cares? The city flies. So what? It's no more of a miracle than three hundred and fifty tons of tri-deck jet flying halfway around the world. It's just a question of scale. Someone screwed the planet and maybe managed to save themselves in the process, and us poor suckers get to ride around on pieces of broken eggshell.

Cassie takes a measured breath before speaking.

'It's possible when a talented wish caster dies, their wishes can live on.'

She ruffles Bebe's mane. My mind starts to race.

'Are you saying my mother is dead?'

'She is most certainly still alive,' says Cassie. 'But any action we take may change the eventual outcome. Fate is an uncertain mistress.'

I'm not sure what fate has to do with it, but I decide to go along with whatever plan she suggests. She's probably my best hope for locating Mom, and although she hasn't said so specifically, I guess escaping from Snake isn't going to be a problem.

'I need to get some kit together,' I say. 'A backpack, food and water, a rope maybe. And a weapon of some kind. Can you help?'

'Food and water, yes,' says Cassie. 'But weapons are hard to come by.'

'Then I'll make one. Do you know where the nearest Phage market is?'

'People are scared to gather these days,' says Cassie. 'We have anonymous bartering, but you need to earn trust to enter their cliques.'

> *Trent P, December 22 2067: We all saw it in the TV newsreaders' eyes. It was obvious there was something they weren't telling us. But why would they keep it a secret? If I was going to die, and I could stop someone else going the same way, then I'd tell them. They deserved to go to hell. And they did.*

Cassie makes certain she has my full attention before continuing.

'I saw what Snake did to your mother,' she says. 'He put her on the machine, but still she refused to protect herself.'

'She swore she never would,' I say. I deliberately don't

ask about the machine. I don't think I could bear to hear the answer.

'The message she gave me contradicts that idea.'

'She sent a message? Is that what this little diversion is all about?'

Cassie nods.

'Rachel said you shouldn't be afraid to protect yourself and others. And if it means harming your persecutors, then so be it.'

'I don't believe you,' I say. 'Take me to her and let me hear it for myself.'

'That won't be possible,' says Cassie. 'Events will overtake us. But we still have a few moments before we need to return to the now.'

Jenny P, September 1 2067: They say most of the slabs stayed on the latitude where they belonged, nice and tidy like. But Manhattan. Well, that had a mind of its own and ran up north to a freezing backwater where it was cold but safe. I have an idea how it might happen, but it's not a fact yet. I only deal in facts. And dreams.

Whatever Cassie has done to the flow of time, it's costing her a great deal of physical and mental effort. I seem to remember Lilith looking similarly drained when we were kids until Mom put a stop to it. Sweat is beading on Cassie's brow and she seems to have one eye on me and one on a ticking clock.

'In order to cast a wish,' she says, 'the caster must offer something of themselves in return. Do you understand?'

Goosebumps rise at the memory of Mom's arms wrapped in dirty bandages and the zebra line scars visible in between times. This is why I've suppressed any notion of wish casting for so long. It belongs at the back of my mind, along with all those other dark thoughts.

'Harm,' I whisper, thinking of the few circumstances when I saw my Mom use her talent.

'Just so,' smiles Cassie. 'The gift demands blood, or some ill-tempered emotion. It is both fickle and ephemeral. It deserts you when you need it most and will laugh at you and cheat you.'

> *Moby F, October 2 2067: Every day, I think about what I saw. They threw bodies over the side shortly after Manhattan lifted off. And I think some of them were still alive.*

'I knew it when I turned the card,' I admit, suddenly short of breath. 'Lilith was in my face and laughing and jeering and encouraging all those other kids to do the same. How could she do that to her own sister?'

My heart thumps at the memory of what I did next and what it cost my mother.

> *Adam, Alicia, Brent and Tracie, October 7 2067: So, you're standing at the deep end of an empty swimming pool. There's acid flowing towards you, slowly, so you have plenty of time to panic about what's going to happen. Just as the acid reaches you, you jump. The laws of physics are pretty strict about this sort of thing; sooner or later, you're going to have to come back down. But what if you could stay in the air? Problem solved. Only now you belong to the skies. You have become a different creature and exist in a different realm. And the ones who already inhabit that realm do not relish the arrival of newcomers.*

'Afterwards, when I was alone, I cut myself with Mom's

razor,' I confess. 'I wished for something really bad to happen to Lilith, but nothing did. The same happened when I tried to hurt Chang.'

'It wouldn't,' says Cassie, a sympathetic look in her eyes.

'But I once changed a ten of diamonds into a ten of spades and almost destroyed my mother as a result.'

'You were only able to make the change because your sister was present,' says Cassie apologetically. 'I'm sorry Hannah, but you are not, and never will be, a wish caster.'

Immutable Cities 6

TUMNAH NAG – *City of Mysterious Numerics*
A demolished city whose streets are defined by piles of rubble. A mahogany wardrobe stands at the junction of Avenue Eridanus and the Street of Scarabs, a lone reminder of former civilisation. One polished door is locked, the other hangs upon bent brass hinges, the smell of a damp cellar within. Inside, a greening loop of copper wire as may transmit heavy electrical currents is fashioned into a rough hook, and thereby hangs a fine white nightdress and a vial containing a clear, viscous liquid. A note pinned to the door purports to be an investigation into the melodic equations of the heavenly spheres and the numbers governing the universe, of which there are six.

MELAZZAR – *City of Mournful Sensation*
The city is the foremost of the league of poisoned towns, all half-murdered by their own toxic activities. The population is a fraction of its heyday, and those who remain take

extreme precautions to ensure their own safety. The day to day lives of the unfortunate citizens are as toxic as the chemicals they avoid, but there is still one aspect of city life attracting travellers from afar. Each night as dusk falls, an ancient parchment is unrolled to a majestic length, its previous content disappearing as the surface is revealed. Onlookers are soon rewarded though, as ink flows from an unknown source causing profound wisdom to appear upon the freshly erased surface in metaphors of glistening sepia. There is always a rush to copy the emerging tale onto napkins, scrolls and notebooks, or to scratch points on tin foil or slate or anything else capable of taking a mark, but the emerging wisdom is resistant to preservation. Once the ceremony of unrolling is complete, every thought, every mark and every image is erased from the physical and mental worlds, and although the audience is left with a sense of witnessing something profound, it is always accompanied by a deep sense of loss.

MORDEN – *City of Noble Sacrifice*
The citizens of Morden placed themselves in voluntary confinement when a gradual decrease in the birth rate was found to be caused by some unknown pathogen. Supplied with food by a disinfecting conveyor belt for seventy years by the neighbouring city of Nyreum, there are fewer than a hundred living souls remaining in the city. It is possible to send messages, but it is not known how these efforts are received as they choose not to respond. Estimates of population have been established by examining aerial images of the courtyards and a statistical analysis of the movements in windows and mirrors as they reflect the living light. Bodies are thought to be left unburied so as

to avoid possible contamination of the water table. This has been confirmed by long distance heliography, which shows thousands of desiccated mummies, waxwork perfect but lifeless, their cloth-wrapped forms propped up in transit shelters and seldom-used alleyways.

TALIA – *City of Pareidolia*

The citizens of Talia see maps everywhere. Where some observe swirls in stone or stains on damp ceilings, the Talians envisage rolling countryside and unexplored mountain ranges. Where others divine patterns of moss on a barn, the Talians invent vast plains and populate them with cities which grow over restless millennia. Despite their vivid imaginations, the citizens are meek and feeble of countenance and, being reluctant explorers, they frequently draw maps from second-hand knowledge, so, whilst undeniably exotic and beautiful, they are often wildly inaccurate. Entire parties have died trusting these cartographic wonders as exploration tools, and as recently as eight years ago an entire city of the western plain was razed by steam powered machines due to an inaccuracy in nomenclature. The Talians have produced maps of only water. They have produced maps of the clouds on a particular yet unrecorded day. They have drawn charts in immense detail yet with no definable scale. Their particular speciality though is maps which show masses of bizarre detail whilst, nevertheless, omitting important features. Particularly sought by collectors are the migration routes of pink geese and the location of wind chimes ringing in a particular key. Also popular is a summary of fences, sorted by height and material, and a magnificent layout of places where loud or strange noises have been heard. All are exquisitely detailed and embellished with rare inks and powders; even the simplest map-sheet commands ridiculous prices for those customers patient enough to wait. On the fringes of the famed artisans' quarter, the house of Bar-Ellim is both museum and monument to the cartologist and mathematician who discovered the proof of the four-colour theorem. In a room protected by armoured glass, the curious may glimpse early examples of Talian mapwork, chief amongst them being the Reasu-Tosk, an indecipherable mass of plumbing and pipework.

VERNORIL – *Citadel at the Heart of the Sunrise*
The city is home to the Magister Krull, who maintains separate names for his thoughts and his memories, as if they were distinct aspects of his personality. Just a few minutes' walk from his ramshackle mansion is the excellent Kalop-Chan restaurant, where they serve a local variation on the ever-popular crispy Booblenack and the juiciest Frack-Stel in the region. Enjoy!

Katz: Chimera

Ink on Paper
The Movable City of Aeropi::Narjuk
Tryndia 48th day of Culmination
Passing over [Tumnah Nag] en-route to [Melazzar]
Translations [Talia, Vernoril]

A city has agreed to let us give performances over three days in exchange for free access to the freak show for the mayor and his flunkies. I dare not imagine what they have in mind, but the freaks have agreed to the proposal for the common good. Thanks to their benevolence, the place is alive again and I've temporarily escaped the trailer and Dina's screeching mantra-fest, which sounds like a curse in some forgotten language. The place is buzzing with rehearsals in the hope that, if all goes well, we'll resume the normal tour. To celebrate my freedom, I ventured into one of the smaller tents to watch the illusionists at work. They offer a reward to anyone who can expose their methods, but nobody has ever collected. The lovely

Zarah climbed into a painted box which, with a clap from her father, was reduced in size to a cube no larger than a gambling die. He presented me with the object, and with another clap caused the girl to appear in my arms out of thin air. I admit inhaling her perfume and enjoying the touch of her skin just a little too much and was glad Dina wasn't there to see me embarrass myself. I expected the others to applaud, but those present remained silent, regarding the illusionists with a respect that was somehow tinged with sorrow. I then realised they were rehearsing not just for the performance but for something else far more serious. What I had just witnessed was real magick carefully disguised as an elaborate illusion. What could it be that necessitates keeping such abilities under wraps? Moments later, as if in answer to my question, the tent flap blew open and a blast of cold air announced the arrival of the uninvited Lady Vyper, whose gaze seemed a threat in itself. There followed an awkward attempt to restart the rehearsals, but it was clear the desire to do so had been sucked out of them by the snake woman's presence. I have yet to witness Vyper's act, and suspect I might not want to.

Melazzar soon, then freedom.
Otto Katz

P.S. You may receive the final few packages from me at the same time as I plan to dispatch them in a single batch when we get to Melazzar. I hope the city has improved since the manuscripts were written.

P.P.S. I had chance to think over the Zarah thing. The idea of magick concealed as illusion worries me. It feels to me that what we see of these people is the mere tip of the iceberg.

Ink on Paper
The Movable City of Aeropi::Narjuk
Tryndia 48th day of Culmination
Passing over [Morden] en-route to [Melazzar]

We awoke this morning to an uneasy silence. No chatter from the mess tent, no rustle of leaves, nor even the slightest breath of wind. No sound either from the animal enclosures, long since emptied. Even the passage of the islands through the air was worryingly silent, to the point where I felt obliged to hold my breath in order to preserve this great absence of sound. It was obvious to all that something was amiss, yet nothing seemed out of place.

Eventually, a roll call established that five of the clowns were missing, Barando amongst them. A frantic search followed and the fate of the jesters was soon discovered. Five metal spikes were found planted on the ticket booth island, and mounted upon each was a decapitated head in full makeup. Each head was burning fiercely but not yet disintegrated.

Erected alongside this scene from hell, a rudely painted sign: *All epitaphs will burn.*

I have difficulty connecting this horror with anything based in reality. The only way to prevent the annihilation of my soul is to imagine it as a scene from a picture reel. Then I can wait until the end, read the names of the actors and rest happily in the knowledge that they survived in the real world.

I fear for my life. Please send assistance to Melazzar.
Otto Katz

Diary Fragments 7

Holo-stream Fragment – Para 13.39.44
Colón, Panama – May 9 2073
Alyana Olivia Zephyra Briandaso – Socialite

My special pet-name, when translated from the local tongue, means 'dancing between the raindrops', so from that you can maybe guess a lot. I used to be rich. I guess I still am, only in a different way. My apartment is all in one piece, I have a beautiful view over the edge of the slab, and the sun mostly still shines. Today is no exception. Look at me, I've kept my good looks and I'm dressed to the nines; ready to receive my second gentleman caller of the day. Huh? Oh, no honey, don't say it. There are no victims here. It's a good old-fashioned exchange of goods. Barter. We each have what the other wants. If they can climb this far (there are no stairs, so they scale the outside of the building), I know they're physically fit, muscular and most likely virile, which gives me a great deal of pleasure. And if things go wrong? Hey, don't worry Niño. I have a knife and know how to use it. If you doubt it, take a look at those desiccated corpses on my balcony. I sit the naughtiest boys facing the window so I can remonstrate with them by throwing back the drapes. Some of my gentlemen like to keep them open while we perform our bodily dance, and who am I to deprive them of the opportunity to make love with death? And, yes honey, you're right, those naughty boys don't deserve to share my fabulous view.

> Holo-stream Fragment – Para 12.15.12
> Quill Lake, Saskatchewan – August 3 1957
> Junie-Beth Wells – Schoolteacher

With a hundred and sixty miles of road behind us, we stopped to rest at a dimly lit motel diner. We each ordered scrambled eggs and muffins with a side of bacon and hot coffee. When the food came, the girl asked if we'd like to listen to the radio. It was a news bulletin describing cities suddenly floating in the air and terrible destruction the world over. I remembered this situation from before though, when everyone panicked because they thought the radio drama was real. We all laughed and ordered an extra stack of pancakes with unlimited maple syrup, so happy in the moment. We won't get fooled again.

> Holo-stream Fragment – Para 12.16.17
> Tokyo, Japan – February 07 1985
> Jun Murakami – Pachinko Parlour Owner

I had a vision once. It was an old-style pachinko machine in the middle of a barren desert. I wondered in the dream where it had been before and how it came to be there, and who would play this noblest of games in such a strange location. And that's how my obsession with pachinko began. The random fall. The clatter of ball bearings, metal on metal, a thousand balls in every machine and only one of them painted pink. Yes, I know it's not normal. Nobody in their right mind has one of the balls painted pink. But it's my dream.

Holo-stream Fragment – Para 90.03.17
Detroit, Michigan – July 13 1934
Anonymous Report by Radio

I got a long-wave radio signal from Scarborough, England. They traversed the western Kalahari some time ago and are about to cross Namibia's skeleton coast and head out over the Atlantic Ocean. Lucky them. We're losing height rapidly. Ahead of us is the winding red snake of the river Dnieper and the fast-approaching ruins of Smolensk, one of the cities that never made it into the air. It was destroyed several times by Napoleon and Hitler and subsequently rebuilt, and now, like Babe Ruth sliding into third, the city of Detroit is going to finish the job.

Holo-stream Fragment – Para 17.18.62
Dagger Behind Smile Town, Xano-Jung – January 14 2021
Aygul – Factory Menial

It's my own fault, but not the fault of my family. I do not eat pork flesh and have never done so. Not on religious grounds but because I have respect for intelligent animals.

Even so, the state appointed 'auntie' who came to live with us took it as a sign that we were defective people in need of fixing. Maybe it would be alright if it was just the issue of the meat. After all, what kind of government would punish a person for not performing some innocent act? Should I be whipped for not eating carrots, or tortured for not possessing a red bicycle, or executed for not doing a handstand every morning while whistling the national anthem? I don't think so, but I'm not clever enough to understand these things. The clever men are building a road to usher in prosperity, but I heard the cost is very high. I couldn't run a country, but I'm good with tasks requiring dexterity, so I work with my hands. The holy book they object to was given to me by a grateful traveller whose carriage I repaired. It was written in a foreign language so we didn't know the danger it posed to our moral wellbeing (I don't understand what that means, but 'auntie' said moral wellbeing was something we all needed to have). I don't understand how owning a book makes me a defective, but I look forward to discovering the truth when we reach the education camp. Until then 'auntie' insists our souls are dead.

Holo-stream Fragment – Para 33.01.23
London, England – September 17 2027
Travis Hausmann – Oenologist and Bibliophile

As it happened, I had all the time I needed and more besides. Time to catch a train into London Victoria, time to take the underground to Tottenham Court Road and plenty of time to walk the quarter of a mile or so to my favourite bookshop. It's tucked away on Great Russell Street opposite the entrance to the British Museum. I could spend an hour detailing the quaint interior, the irrepressible optimism of the owner when it came to pricing or the faint smell of pipe tobacco, but I do so tire when a story isn't at least concise. I would be remiss though if I did not describe the 'cabinet of wonder' which is Mister Morpurgo's pride and joy. Nestling within are such unique treatises as 'The Theoretical Astrolabe', 'The Powre of Ayngels', 'Opticks', 'Magick without Apparatus' and a singular instance of the 'Letters of Dexter Agorax' concerning his 'Search after Truth'. Also, in pride of place are the 'Wisdom of the Chylde Idiote Ionnas', 'Temporal Artes', 'Ruminations on Magick' and 'The Mirror of Reason'. None of these could I afford. A strictly controlled allowance from my aunt limits the rate of acquisitions, so titles such as 'A Confluence of Vanities', 'Principia Mechanica' and 'On the Flyte of Byrdes' were also out of reach. Today though, employing the magnificent illusion sometimes entitled 'handing over the best part of three thousand pounds', I would become the guardian (books such as these are never owned) of:

> *The Cyclopaedia of Monstres, detailing the privatt interiors and every musculature of the southerne harpy and her fellow fiends. Her vast lungs, the playcement of her numerous air sacs, the magnificent wings with their feather anchors and blood veyns and all ancillary parts of the physique. Complete with Appendices detailing similar treatement of the mighty centaur, the inscrutable dragon and shimmering chimareas, along with mermaids and sirens, minotaurs, hydras and various fearsome sphinxes.*

This magnificent octavo volume comprises the most exquisite hand painted illustrations of beasts and, like its cousin the Voynich Manuscript, is hand written in what appears to be an invented language. I longed to get the precious thing home to study it in detail, so with the sordid detail of payment complete I hurried to the door. It had only moved a few inches, when the handle was wrenched out of my grip and we felt the blast of a tremendous hurricane of wind in the road outside. I watched in horror as the iron railings opposite the shop were torn from the ground and rose up like skeletal wings in front of us. Old man Morpurgo pushed past me (so rude) and ran out into the street where he promptly became a road accident statistic. The poor chap was run over by an ancient petrol driven motor car, which failed to stop and disappeared around the corner into Bury Place. Thanks to my medical training though, I knew exactly what action to take, so I searched the shop for suitable tools and nailed the door securely shut. I must say the sight of the museum's beautiful portico lifting into the sky was quite something, but nothing compares to the view I have before me now. It's a wonderful little mahogany cabinet containing so, so many beautiful books.

Holo-stream Fragment – Para 13.03.47
Brooklyn, NYC – June 3 1968
Bruce Chaka – Photographer

Okay, so I changed my mind once it became obvious what was going on. I revisited the store in the hope of finding any kind of film at all but the place was already looted with no sign of my buddy. New York is going crazy right now, with media crews flocking like locusts in a rush to get something in the can. To me, that spells a lack of foresight because I'm pretty sure the power will be out soon, so no TV, no printing presses, no radio. I heard some of those guys can shout pretty loud though, so good luck with that. And me? Well, I sat watching the East River until I was sure we were completely screwed, then I used up the second roll of film on Manhattan as it finished the process of unplugging itself and gently floated off towards Boston. Then I checked the phone book for nearby studios and set out to find them.

Hannah: Flash Forward

Holo-stream Clip
New York, NY – September 23 2083

I have spent sixteen years of my life hiding a gift I don't even have. Even worse, Lilith has something that I don't. I take a sip from the flask. There's a crackling sensation, as if the sharp taste is making my ears ring. There's a mournful thrumming noise, like a strong wind plucking at steel ropes, and, looking up through the dome, I know we're back in what Cassie referred to as 'the now'.

It's getting hot and there's a potent chemical smell in the air, like some violent elemental reaction. Beyond the glass is a huge yet unrecognisable shape bent into a million fragments by the geometric design of the dome, which appears to be under attack. Pockets of ferocious white heat appear on the outside of the glass, causing it to bubble and melt and drip, forming strange puddles around us.

Hurrying through, we run across the station concourse and into John Street, where I hear the soft pitter-patter of cloth-wrapped bundles falling onto distant roofs or ice-strewn streets. They fizz and spit as the magnesium powder ignites, forming small but brilliant fires across the neighbourhood. Large swathes of the net are aflame and our options for escape are narrowing rapidly.

Snake appears in the street. He's limping heavily and, despite the tough guy image he projects, I can see he's scared. He's staring skyward, open mouthed in wonder.

About three hundred feet above us sits the ominous bulk of an airship, which at first glance resembles a flying insect with dangling legs and veined wings. These remain stationary though since the ship hangs aloft with a combination of combustion engines, electro-jets and rockets. I have never heard or seen anything like it; never imagined that such a magnificent roaring, whining beast could exist in our modern world.[23]

I wonder if Carrie foresaw this, because getting away from Snake is no longer my only concern. I don't know what to make of the airship yet, but if Snake thinks of it as the enemy then maybe it's good for the rest of us. If so, then we have to find a way to contact the crew. Then again, they're flinging magnesium bombs at us, which isn't such a friendly approach.

Snake and his cronies approach and stand alongside us, like we're a team, so I edge away to remind him we're not. Hamilton glances at Bebe who bares her fangs and growls at him. I feel warmer in her presence, even in the reflected heat of the fires.

Above us are the pockmarked doors of a weapons bay and tiny round windows, each one framing the face of a bomb aimer. In the bright scarlet glow of burning architecture, the ship takes on an evil persona, like it's reflecting the fires of hell. As the wind changes, I can hear the twang of catapults delivering dozens of soft, cloth-wrapped bundles.

It seems that we're playing host to visitors. People from another world; a place with the power to drive propellers quickly, to drop bombs, to tear the air apart. To build a ship which steers and carries people. To choose to send weapons instead of hope.

The rain of fire-bombs gradually lessens and eventually stops, coaxing people into the street to douse fires, stamp on smouldering embers, and try to rescue or protect their fragile habitat. Above us, large swathes of the net hangs in ashen tatters, which makes my blood freeze. As I consider who might possess such a machine and why they'd want to attack us, the bomb doors close and the immediate threat dissipates. It seems we've survived whatever warning the captain of the ship intended to issue.

Fewer than ten minutes has passed since we emerged from beneath the dome, but the area surrounding the subway station is devastated.

Further afield, the ropes and bridges remain intact, but escape seems impossible while the airship remains in position. The noise of the engines comes and goes on the wind, but the thing itself is steady, like it's moored to us in some way. Equally worrying are the things we first thought of as legs. These lay mainly across roofs, having dragged themselves there when the airship approached. A few reach the ground though, living tubules that pulse and gyrate, clearly organic; some are transparent, liquid-filled, and resemble the poison-laden underside of a Portuguese man-o-war. Elsewhere, the scaly hull of the beast is pock-marked and battle-scarred, which suggests there is a force somewhere willing to attack the thing. That force is not us though. The sheer mass of the vessel is beyond intimidating. It roots me to the spot. I feel like an insignificant speck in comparison.

'This is a non-orbital object,' says Cassie, tugging at my arm. 'It does not move in accordance with natural forces.'

'You don't say,' I reply. 'I worked that part out myself; absolutely no mathematics required.'

As I speak, the tendrils withdraw into the belly of the ship and the portholes, like vast eyelids readying for sleep, close with a rhythmic whining. Other ports squeal open to reveal new faces at the bomb-aiming windows. I'm too far away to make out their features, but I sense they have an air of quiet confidence that contrasts completely with my own lack of ideas on how to proceed.

I turn to look at Snake and understand why he needed my help. The attack has peeled away the man to reveal a boy underneath, who's quaking with fear. He scans the ship from side to side, but it's impossible to tell where the ends are. Its bulk occupies our entire sky.

'Find your mother and beg her to do something,' he pleads.

I give him a sweet smile and run away with Bebe loping along beside me and Cassie skipping close behind. I'm guessing this isn't the kind of help Snake had in mind, but I don't care. He's shouting after us, but the pleading fades as we head north along debris strewn streets, dodging fires and ignoring shouts from dark alleys. The airship creates a strange twilight, its artificial light beaming through the daylight to create a sky that looks diffused, fragmented.

We travel two blocks and still there's no bow or stern. We pause. The newly opened ports gape, birthing large black canisters that fall silently through the air. I watch as one of them crashes into the street and sprays white sparks a hundred feet into the air. The sparks fall back, deadly flowers of light and, when they reach the ground, people scream and burn and wriggle. Silver fish wrapped in a curtain of flame. They run as though trying to escape themselves, but coils of flame bind them tight, like writhing tendrils of weed. One screaming boy produces a gun and, unable to escape the burning liquid, shoots himself in the head.

Elsewhere, the deadly canisters smash through roofs, igniting buildings from inside and creating a magnificent inner glow that threatens to burst out at any moment. It has a weird kind of beauty, the glow of another more benevolent world that seems out of place amidst the violence. Puddles of molten phosphorus burn in the street and flow into gutters, a river of burning chemistry that threatens to divide and surround us, turning the sidewalk into a sheet of flaming tyranny. I cover my ears to block the screams of those it catches, but there's no way to avoid the smell of singed hair and burning flesh. Bebe raises her head and howls.

The city is on fire and the only way out is to cross a sea of flame and smoke, to fight our way across the hot-stone landscape through indescribable heat. We turn north again, but the heat forces us to take cover in the entrance of a department store. I see a mannequin, her clothes burned off, plastic face melted into a grotesque mask. Her single good arm is bent in an unnatural manner, seemingly pointing inside the shop.

In the circumstances, with every route looking equally threatening, it seems like an idea we can grab, so we push through the heavy revolving door into a dank, dark space. The street behind us is a conflagration fit for the end of days, which terrifies me. This city isn't much, but it's all I have and I want it to survive and, however unlikely it seems, to prosper. And I want to be there to see it. I have no wish to survive for sixteen years, only to be boiled alive in some random attack that makes no sense. I want to understand the world where such things can happen.

The window shatters and the mannequin melts in a wall of flame as the revolving door spits and pops. We duck the hail of flying cinders and fall back inside, distancing ourselves from a heat that threatens to grill us like terrified lobsters.

Cassie moves like she knows where she's going, so I follow, winding my way up a staircase partially blocked by vidscreens, gamercons and commslabs, all still boxed and piled neatly, ready to be sold. Plenty of luxury here, but no electricity to drive it and definitely no food. The way though the toy department is blocked by a wall of shelving, but the route into the restaurant on the fifth floor is clear and will allow us to ascend the levels without climbing up the outside of the building. Cassie skirts respectfully around a couple of bodies and we force our way through a mass of upturned tables and scattered cutlery towards a panoramic window which looks out over the street.

Below us, the p-fires burn the full width of the street, making it impossible to return that way. For those who've made it to higher ground though, the situation is still retrievable. On the roof of the building opposite is an old man, one arm hanging limply by his side. He shakes a fist at the airship with the other. He screams at the crew to come and fight on the ground instead of hiding in the sky like miserable sneaking cowards.

I read his trembling lips with ease as the response arrives.

'What have I done?' he mouths.

The airship fires an immense column of steam, obliterating him from view and, when the vapour clears, nothing but an untidy pile of boiled meat remains.

It's then, in the aftermath of that unnecessary murder, I decide my sixteen years so far won't be a waste. I'm going to survive long enough to get revenge on our attackers.

I wonder if the ship reads minds because the transparent tendrils make their dangling return, a raft of cilia searching the air and sweeping the surface of the city. As they reach the ground, a dark shape appears at the top of each tendril and slides down inside the tube like a weird insect egg. Whatever is happening it seems that science has learned from nature.

'There won't be any more canisters,' says Cassie, frowning in concentration.

She sounds so certain about these things. It's not like she's putting forward a hare-brained idea, more like she has seen some of these events already.

'You'll soon know what the airship crew wants,' says Cassie, apparently reading my thoughts.

Does that mean she knows already? What else does she know?

'I look forward to it,' I say, 'but I'm worried about Bebe. She was here one minute and then…'

'… the wolf is still with you,' smiles Cassie.

'Thank you,' I say, only half convinced.

As Cassie predicted, the airship ceased dropping its deadly black seeds an hour ago but the phosphorous fires continue to burn ferociously. There are dozens of buildings ablaze with no hope of being put out, so the pink light show playing on the belly of the airship is set to continue. It's an entertainment previously beyond my imagination, entrancing me with its dancing flames. I feel guilty watching it, but I continue, well aware that it might be a once in a lifetime experience.

The cilia have delivered their payloads to the sidewalks now – armed troops who stand in position on every street corner.

'We should return to ground level,' says Cassie.

'Safer if we stay here,' I suggest.

'Perhaps,' she replies, 'but our path is not in taking the safe option. I think you know that.'

I'm not sure I do know it, but I owe Cassie a deal of trust so I pull her towards the stairwell and we break into a run. When we get to where the stairs used to be, there's a mass of cindered wood and twisted metal still glowing and creaking from the fiery onslaught. It would crumble if we so much as blew on it.

'Back to the top,' I suggest, wondering if Cassie hasn't already seen this coming.

She nods and we race back up, passing our previous vantage point and continuing out onto the roof. The belly of the airship is so close it seems like we could reach out and touch it, and I have the crazy idea that if we grabbed hold and added our weight then we might bring it down. I'm an ant fighting an elephant, but I don't intend to give up, so I scan for an escape route and spot a makeshift bridge to the adjacent building. Faces watch us from the airship and I wonder if we're important enough to concern them. One particular bomber gives me a stare as if considering an attack, but he eventually turns away. Cassie mounts the crawl boards over to the theatre next door. As I scramble to follow, I take another look at the airship. Rows of bemused faces study our antics like we're the entertainment. They're clapping and howling and laughing at us. There's nothing I'd welcome more than a quick change to the script. If I could have a rocket launcher, even for just a moment, I'd let our audience have it. But there's no *deus ex machina* handing out weapons, so I have to satisfy myself with a single finger.

What's clear to me now is that I'm not, and probably never have been, in charge of what goes on in my life. It's like I'm following a trail of crumbs to a house in the forest, never suspecting who laid it or what awaits me at the end of the journey. I know that all is not as it seems, but until I get a chance to see through the trap, I have no option but to push on and try to stay alive.

A hatch at the end of the little bridge reminds me of the one at our old hideout and I waste valuable time pushing aside my feelings of shame.

We drop into the upper regions of the theatre space. It's a fly gallery way above the stage, where dozens of scenery flats hang in place, waiting for their cue in a long-dead show. Most are wrecked or scavenged but there are still plenty of ropes tied up.

I wonder briefly what happened to the stage hands who last attended them.

'How are you at climbing?' I ask.

There's a thud on the roof and a smell of burning. My impolite gesture has brought a response from the ship's crew.

'Not good,' says Cassie. 'Is this the only way down to the stage?'

I invite her to the edge and show her the possibilities.

'Oh,' she says.

I guess she doesn't know all the answers, and stands awaiting my response.

Cassie looks mystified as I body wrap her in a rope and chuck the rest of it over the gantry. If she foresees what comes next, she hides it well. I push her over the edge and drag-brake the rope, allowing her a gentle descent to stage level.

Before the free end drops beside her, I've clawed my way down a huge red curtain. After the mocking we received from the airship crew, I'm quite proud of the whole roof to stage transfer and sad there's nobody in the auditorium to applaud.

We're walking through the upper lobby before Cassie utters a word.

'Is this how you survived so long?' she asks. 'With circus skills?'

'I know my way around a rope, if that's what you mean.'

There's an Art Deco handrail protecting the fall into the lower lobby. The bands of polished chrome are arranged in groups of three and look as bright now as they would have in the 1920s when the place was most likely built. I'm glancing over the side, thinking of abseiling, but Cassie takes the simple route, descending the broad curve of the main stairway and passing posters from movies made a hundred years before we were born.[24] I watch as she pauses in thought, then selects a door on the right side of the lobby. Inside, there's a sofa, a broken-down view screen and a few feet of film laying on the floor. I'm tempted to hold it up to the light and examine the images; instead I pocket the treasure, a little bit of hope, to be savoured at length if we ever get out of this.

'We should wait here until the fires abate,' says Cassie.

She stares me down, as if any other course of action would be foolish, and I submit to her judgement, flopping into the welcoming arms of the cushions.

'Sleep,' she suggests. 'The fire on the roof is out, so we're safe for the moment.'

We're woken by a commotion outside the theatre and make our way outside, amazed that the rotating doors are unlocked and still work. A couple of roughs push a young woman along the pavement. Each of her bare limbs is wrapped tightly in coils of copper wire, making her look like some kind of modern art exhibit. One of the men is bald and tattooed, the other has long straggly hair and is scarred, a red jagged line crossing his right eye. The woman is about twenty and dressed only in thin underwear. The fires are all but extinguished now and the arctic weather has swept in to replace the flames. The wind is biting. The first man has a rope around the girl's neck. It's clear from the abrasions that he's been yanking it.

'What the hell are you doing?' I yell. 'What gives you the right to treat anyone like that?'

'I know you,' says the long-haired one. 'You're sticking up for this freak just like you stuck up for your mother, and look where that got her.'

I know the voice instantly. He's the one who had his back to me while torturing my mother. If I could, I'd strike him dead where he stands.

I move to attack but I'm halted by an urgent whisper from Cassie.

'That course of action does not end well. You must get revenge some other way.'

'What if I crush his skull with a steel pipe? Would that be allowed?'

With my terrified mother's agonising screams ringing in my ears, I scan my surroundings, desperate to find anything that can be pressed into use as a weapon. I'm closer now than I have ever been to killing someone. It's something I have never even considered, and the idea that I've changed into a potential murderer terrifies me.

Cassie tries to hold me but I break her feeble grip with ease and grab a fragment of sidewalk loosened by the bombing. I charge the long-haired man and am about to cleave his skull when my hand is stayed by a soldier in battle fatigues. He's wearing a helmet and goggles, which lends him a slightly sinister air, but it's the sight of the baton in his hand and the sidearm on his hip that arrests my action.

'Are you attempting to interfere with procedure?' he says.

'What procedure is that?' I spit. 'Mistreating young women in the street? I know we've sunk a long way since Inception, but this is a new low.'

'Keep your nose out,' yells the redneck. 'This girlie's exchangeable for food. First time a wish caster was ever worth anything, I reckon.'

I lunge at the creep again, but the soldier increases his grip and turns me to face a nearby intersection, as if to explain. Set up in the middle of the road and surrounded by whirling snow is a stall like a kids' lemonade stand. Seated behind it is a soldier of higher rank busy processing a well-ordered line of citizens. It's the first time I have ever seen such an orderly queue.

'The Polar Hegemony offers food and medical help,' says the soldier. 'And there's a lottery offering ten lucky citizens a free ride off the island.'[25]

'Is that why you bombed the city?' I ask. 'To offer assistance to the people you just maimed and injured?'

'Deaths were kept to a minimum,' parrots the soldier, 'but collateral damage is inevitable in such a situation.'

'And what situation might that be?'

'They're taking all the wish casters away,' grins the redneck. 'And they'll give food to anyone who helps. A lot of food.'

The captured girl trembles in the severe cold, and it's only then I think to offer her my jacket. In the midst of all this stupidity I'm embarrassed at my own lack of compassion. As she takes it, the soldier grabs my arms and examines my stitched cuts.

'Choose again,' whispers Cassie. 'Your act of kindness changes the flow against us.'

'What you saying there, missy?' yells the redneck. 'You with her?'

'Yes, I am,' scowls Cassie, daring him to escalate the situation.

I wrest the garment back from the girl's grip, which surprises everyone, and Cassie's grim look is replaced by a contented smile, as if a great danger has missed us by inches. I'm about to try and break free from the soldier when we're blasted by the airship's horn. I've heard louder, but only when a billion tons of rock collided with an ocean. This is more threatening though because it's entirely man made. I imagine it's like the foghorn of an old ocean liner.

'Stand by for an announcement,' says the soldier. 'Pay attention to the voice of the electrophone.'

He releases me and snaps to attention. Maybe he's expecting me to do the same, but it's an opportunity I don't intend to miss. Cassie has already seen the chance and runs ahead of me. This is no accident. The girl knew before I did which way I intended to flee.

We cover fewer than twenty yards before there's another blast of sound. Turning towards the source, I'm transfixed by the image of a plague-marked face outlined in a hissing screen of water vapour. The man's lips move in time with the voice that blasts our eardrums and lays waste to the windows in nearby stores.

'I am Morta, captain of the airship Tyche of Gomorrah,' he booms. 'Co-operate with the ground teams and you will be rewarded. Interfere with our search for wish casters and I will destroy this worthless cinder of a city and everybody in it.'

I'm breathless and afraid but grateful to be alive on a day of such astonishments and terrors. Is this what it was like to attend a moving picture show? The image is an appalling mess of random noise and scan lines, but even the poorest quality seems like magic to my unsophisticated eyes. If this is the world of movies, count me in.

Cassie pulls at my sleeve, tearing me from my momentary dream. The soldier has escorted the half-naked girl to the stall where an older woman stands to one side of the ranking officer. She lays her hands on the girl's head and nods. A wicker basket is lowered from the airship and the poor thing is bundled inside. I know it's not a good idea but I need to understand what's going on, so I return to speak to the officer.

'What exactly are you doing here?' I ask him.

He looks me up and down, then scans Cassie in the same manner.

'Do you have a wish caster to offer?' he says.

I shake my head.

'Then stand aside,' he orders.

'But what if I did have a wish caster?' I ask. 'What would happen to them?'

'We'd take them to a place of safety,' says the officer.

'On the ship?' asks Cassie.

There's no answer from the officer, but he hands a food requisition to my Mom's former torturer.

'How much food do you get in exchange for someone's life?'

I'm livid and about to launch myself at the tattooed creep when he takes me by surprise and grabs my arms. I try to resist but he forces me round and shows the cuts to the officer.

'We brought these two as well,' he says, grinning at me. 'The one with the cuts and the one that looks like a fairy.'

'Watch me closely and follow,' whispers Cassie.

She reaches into her sleeve and pulls out a stubby knife which she sticks into the tattooed forearm that's holding me. The torturer yelps and lets me go and, before the officer can react, we're racing away from the stall. Other soldiers see what's happening and flood towards us, but Cassie dodges them with uncanny precision. Our escape plan ticks with the precision of well-oiled clockwork and we soon reach territory that's far more familiar to us than our pursuers.

'Wait,' says Cassie, skittering to a halt in a narrow alley.

'They're not far behind,' I say.

Cassie pulls a heavy steel door open and bundles me inside with a display of strength that surprises me. There's hardly any light but I can make out the looping shape of an old transformer, so it looks like we're in an electricity substation. It's eerily quiet for a moment until we hear running footsteps on the other side of the vented door. They pass without regard to our hiding place.

'Sometimes waiting is the best option,' says Cassie. 'If you're not able to influence an outcome then you should simply pause. The flow of events may change because of someone else's actions, or simply by chance.'

I nod in the shadows as we settle on a couple of wooden crates. I'm beginning to like Cassie a lot and feel comfortable letting my guard down for a moment.

'Things are a bit mad,' I say after a long period of silence.

'But they will settle soon,' whispers Cassie.

I can see through the ventilation grille into the alley. It's snowing heavily now and all I can hear is Cassie's gentle breathing and something I've heard only once before when I was a child. It's the sound of the city creaking and groaning in the air, twisting like an old wooden sailing ship. Usually, when part of a city snaps off it doesn't fall but just peels away, maybe drifting more slowly, or quickening as if repulsed by gravity or some other unlikely emotion. Sometimes it lifts slightly or perhaps drops to a lower orbit. And sometimes, like now, it flexes and bends in flight, announcing to its passengers that significant change is on the way. I have no idea where the mariner's tales of other slabs come from because, to the best of my knowledge, nobody has ever left Manhattan or arrived upon it since Inception.

Until today.

'Do you remember when they shot the birds because they were making the city too heavy?' says Cassie.

I'm grinning in the half-darkness.

'Nobody seemed to remember birds could fly,' I laugh.

I recall old man Katz had a hatred of birds. He always said he couldn't see the point of them and was deliriously happy when most of them were shot. A few days later, the survivors came back and I remember him on the rooftop, screaming at them to stop scraping their poison drenched claws about the place. It was the only time I ever saw the old man lose his temper.

'I think we've all forgotten how to fly,' says Cassie seriously.

She kicks at the floor. It's concrete, but a thick layer of oil has leaked from a circuit breaker and formed a dark carpet of sludge. Her kick exposes a short length of cable which she picks up and wraps around her index finger. It triggers unpleasant thoughts of the young woman we saw being herded through the streets and loaded onto the airship.

'What's the story with the copper wire?' I ask.

Cassie shakes her head, but I sense it's not her final answer, just a notification of delay. She's staring into the middle distance, deep in concentration and I swear I can hear her thinking. I know electrical transformers used to buzz and hum with power but this is more subtle.

'Another twenty seconds and we'll be on our way,' says Cassie.

In the short time since we took refuge in the substation the temperature has dropped another ten degrees and the snow has drifted against the door, hindering our exit. Eventually we manage to heave it out of the way and Cassie steps into the alley. She signals our route and I follow, remaining silent as we crunch our way north through snow-quietened streets. The soft muffle blanket has turned abandoned flyers into anonymous lumps and slows our progress, but the absence of footprints indicates, for the moment, we're safe. Above us, the bulk of the airship still occupies a large part of the sky, but as we move east we begin to see the curve of the hull where the name 'Tyche of Gomorrah' is emblazoned in hundred-foot-high letters. Turning north, we find two fresh sets of footprints. I guess Cassie has been following them at a distance.

'Certain futures have converged,' she says, confirming my theory.

I'm about to ask what she means and who we're tracking when the wind gusts, clawing at the plastic wrapped scaffold behind us. It gives me a jolt, but not as much as the shock I get from Cassie.

'This is the place where those men are keeping your mother,' she says.

Excitement makes my blood fizz, but the feeling is outweighed by the accompanying fear of the unknown. At the same time, I'm wondering how I can release Mom and punish her captors.

Cassie takes her knife and cuts the cords binding the plastic sheets, allowing us to squeeze through. Stepping out of the wind-driven snow, the space within the scaffold provides a welcome respite, but after a few seconds Cassie is directing our course again.

'We waited in the substation so our paths wouldn't cross,' I suggest, as she navigates the maze of scaffold tubes.

Cassie doesn't answer.

The wind blasts the sheeting again as we enter the wrapped building by a side door but, having passed through the doorway, we find ourselves outdoors again. We've emerged on the other side of a wall which forms a part of a much larger shell, the building gutted with the intention of rebuilding its interior, just another one of a million plans that will now never come to fruition.

The massive walls form a box enclosing a central void of rammed earth and an excavated concrete basement which is open to the skies. Fifty yards away there's a collection of site-management and storage huts which look to be in good condition. Judging by the gun muzzles poking from the windows, they are also well defended. The idea we might free Mom without anyone noticing wilts in my breast as we survey our surroundings.

'Come any closer and you're dead,' yells a voice from one of the windows.

'That's good advice,' says Cassie. 'Every possible outcome currently results in your death.'

'Then why have you brought me here?' I ask.

I step back into the shadow of the door frame as Cassie raises her gaze to the belly of the airship. There's an open hatch where a crane is lowering a long steel cable. Suspended from it is a wooden crate, swinging and spinning in the buffeting wind. The crate is caught by a gust and a corner catches the ground, fracturing it and spilling its contents. It's more tinned food than I have ever seen in my life.

'But why are they giving the stuff to...'

'No,' I yell, answering my own question. 'Is this what you wanted me to see? Those creeps getting rewarded for giving up my mother?'

I'm about to ignore Cassie's warning about advancing on the huts when the sound of a winch alerts me to a second cable being lowered. This one is empty though, just a large red hook at its end. The wind buffets the cable mercilessly but eventually it's caught by the pig with the tattoos who emerges from the stronghold. More thugs appear behind him, struggling with a wooden wheel about six feet in diameter. It's clumsily made and looks heavy, but rolls well enough and it's clear they intend to attach it to the cable.

'I'm sorry,' says Cassie, 'but there was no other way.'

I'm trying to work out what she means when the hook is guided down and a loop of rope is attached to the wheel.

'No other way for what?' I ask.

The cable takes up the slack, the wheel turning slowly as it leaves the ground to reveal a woman tethered in a cruel parody of Leonardo's Vitruvian man. Her arms and legs are spread, her hands and ankles bound in coarse twine; weeping red channels cut into her skin. Unlike da Vinci's figure, she hangs inverted, her grim face powdery white and thin with hunger, her mouth a wound whose lips are sewn closed. Her skin is like greaseproof paper touched with fat; it has an eerie translucence and seems only just capable of containing her swollen organs. The woman is bound in copper, her limbs covered in wire that bites deep into flesh. I recognise a distinctive bracelet, but it might have been stolen and worn by someone else.

Please let it be someone else.

The arms are zebra striped with familiar scars, but the effect could easily be faked. And the thin dress the poor woman wears could be looted from any number of stores across town. There is no mistaking her eyes though. Even hanging upside down, I recognise the woman who gave birth to me. The woman who gave me life.

I breathe in, preparing to let out a scream that will put the airship's public address system to shame. And now I'm holding it, a cold tingle playing a haunting tune on my spine. But here comes a familiar vibration, a subtle transformer telling me to hold onto my rage, to contain whatever thoughts of vengeance I have boiling inside my skull. Cassie stands behind me, her hands cupping my cheeks, her mouth close to my right ear. I can feel her breath, but she doesn't speak. Instead, I feel the hum again. A thought comes to me through some medium I don't understand.

'I want you to have something,' says the thought. 'I have had it all my life and done nothing with it.'

'What are you talking about?' I ask out loud.[26]

'Shhh...' whispers the thought.

There's a rush like a hurricane threading its way through shattered skyscrapers. Judging from the heat from Cassie, I expect to feel warmer now, but her gift feels more like a frozen curse; not evil or dangerous but cold and out of reach, like a jar of cookies on a high shelf in a windswept deep-winter barn.

'What was that?' I ask.

'Everything I have to offer,' says the thought. 'Use it well.'

Diary Fragments 8

>Holo-stream Fragment – Para 36.15.28
>Chimbote, Peru – August 17 1993
>Emely Condori – Blackjack Hostess

When I was at university in Lima, I devoured all those stories of dystopian worlds but never believed any of it could actually happen. In the novels, there was always some malevolent ideology at the back of it all, but the situation we're mired in these days just went and happened at random. It might be a strange thing to say, but it would be easier to bear if there were some rhyme or reason to it, some set of ideas we could at least argue against.

    I want to spend time planting crops, but looking after the injured teacher takes up a lot of my time. We have water tanks though, an Indian food store, plenty of shelter and so far we've been safe from predators, so it's not all bad. Some of the cars still work, but since Maria Estavez mangled a stick shift and accidentally backed over the edge we tend to walk everywhere. Some of the families are still in hiding, and there are a couple of hobos who won't leave the old rail yard, so we leave food out for them and get no thanks in reply. We even have electricity, thanks to a small wind turbine and a reservoir in the auto-shop, where we wired hundreds of truck batteries together. On three occasions now we've had slabs rumbling by, broadcasting their stupid pro-independence propaganda, as if it's something to look forward to. Unity, that's what we want. We need independence about as much as we need an extra arsehole.

Holo-stream Fragment – Para 10.10.10
Kaamanen, Finland – January 12 2012
Kati Kankaanpaa – Technologist

I call in most days to see how old man Aaltonen is doing. I think he knows what happened, since he never leaves the shop now. Sophie Laine told me she saw him looking over the edge in the early days, so he must be blocking it out. I wish I could do that. Every day's the same for Aaltonen. After a routine breakfast, he dons the magical garment of his profession; a long brown dust coat with three deadly-sharp pencils in the pocket, all kept in place by a neatly folded handkerchief. Properly attired, he opens the tool shop in the hope someone needs a new micrometer or to get their saw sharpened or wants to replace the seventeen-millimetre socket that's always going missing. (They won't.) But he still finds joy in it; sweeping up, dusting shelves and lining up products. He once told me there's nothing more satisfying than a row of properly aligned screwdrivers, increasing in size from left to right and separated into slot and cross head variants. Before it all happened, I remember coming in to get some nails for my dad, giggling as the old man wrapped them ever so carefully in shiny brown paper and tied them up with string. One day I'll ask him for the same thing and relive a part of my childhood. Sometimes, when he takes a nap in the afternoon I lift the handset on his phone. It's the only one still working. Don't ask me how because all the lines are down, but Aaltonen's is still live. You can dial a number and it'll ring out, but nobody ever answers. I'm soothed by the crackling on the line though, and the fact the bell sounds immeasurably distant. I also like to think that one day, somebody will be there to answer it.

Holo-stream Fragment – Para 44.72.11
Supoi-Na-Pen, Yellow Ocean – February 27 1868
Tran Lee – Fisherman

The fishing has never been good, but we are born where we are and must make do with what we have. Some people do not believe that. They believe they are born where they are, but may take what others have, even if the victim of the robbery lives a thousand Li away. They have claimed the waters we fish and, at every opportunity, they board our boats, making fools of us while they confiscate our catch and cut our nets. Many times, they have rammed our matchwood vessels with their steam powered leviathans. We rescue their drowning seamen and they reward us by building islands and turning them into warships.

Holo-stream Fragment – Para 13.03.47
Brooklyn, NYC – June 6 1968
Bruce Chaka – Photographer

I made a base for myself in a deserted studio on Avenue D which, so far, has survived the looting. I keep a list of everything I use, so if things ever get right side up I can square it with the owner. He'd do the same for me, right? There's plenty of film stock, not my favourite, but good enough, and the darkroom is well equipped with paper and chemicals. Only thing I don't have is power for the enlarger, so I'm shooting in the streets and just processing the negs until I can find a generator. If not, then maybe I'll make contact prints using the sun as a light source. I reckon the story of the city will be told well enough, so I'm making this a record of my personal journey. When it's done I'll squirrel the images away in the hope they reach the future in one piece, each tiny slice of frozen time forming a part of my tombstone.

Holo-stream Fragment – Para 49.19.17
Tshikapa, DRC – July 03 2003
Elim Pranu – Miner

I am the best gem-finder in the mine because I have no legs. No waist either, and only one arm. I start at the chest, which rests on my padded wooden trolley. It has wheels and goes places nobody else can fit.
'Fetch the diamonds boy.'
'Fetch the diamonds boy.'
'Fetch those motherfucking diamonds.'
Boy. That's me. I fetch the motherfucking diamonds.

But nobody knows my secret. At the end of the tunnel called Tumuku-Lah, there's a hole beneath the rails and, in that hole, I see all the lands of the world; different every time. One day I will use the knowledge. Boy knows that Mother Africa flies.

Ink on Paper – Para 11.77.01
Sea Palling, England – September 1 1969
Erica Mae Treacey – Haberdasher and Milliner

Before the thing they said happened DIDN'T ACTUALLY HAPPEN, I was happy to stay in my bedroom all day, listening to the sea and reading my END OF THE WORLD comic or looking at my PICTURE. At mealtimes, they would come and take me to the dining room which, although not as comforting as my own room, was bearable. I didn't mind the other patients as long as they kept to themselves and kept on SHUTTING THE FUCK UP. Once a day, they made us GO OUT INTO THE GARDEN, which I didn't like. In fact, I didn't like it so much they would put the jacket on me. One problem out there was the BOUNDLESS SKY full of FUCKING BIRDS, but the main thing I didn't like about the garden was the HORIZON, where all the TREES LURKED. Between them and me was VOLUMES OF SPACE, which, if you don't know, can fill up with BAD STUFF as quick as a fly can take off; the same stuff that says something BAD IS GOING TO HAPPEN, and when it does there'll be NO ESCAPE. I used to think if I ran fast enough I might get to the place beyond the HORIZON where it joins the lawn, which seems like a good place to be. That was then though, because now it's AFTER the thing that DIDN'T ACTUALLY HAPPEN, so even the place beyond the HORIZON isn't safe. I heard a nurse say it was the end of the world, so I told her it was just a story and not to worry. That was just to make her feel better, but I don't think it helped. In the days BEFORE THE THING THAT DIDN'T ACTUALLY HAPPEN, the place beyond the HORIZON was LUSCIOUS, but maybe only because I never actually saw it. Now though, in the days AFTER THE THING THAT DIDN'T ACTUALLY HAPPEN, I think it doesn't even EXIST. I don't read the comic anymore because the world there GOT DAMAGED. Our world is fine though, because the doors are UNLOCKED, the dining room is REFRESHINGLY QUIET and there's nobody left to make me GO OUT INTO THE GARDEN. Now that things are good, I sit in my bedroom all day, listening to the sea and watching the FIREWORKS that grow inside my PICTURE.

Immutable Cities 7

ZAITEKU D'NI – *The Stillborn Child*
Most if not all cities evolve from small beginnings. Zaiteku D'ni is not such a place. It was conceived as a whole and planned in minute detail by busy commercial minds. A clifftop location was found, where it was thought sickly people would come for the good of their health. Ground was dug. Pipes and wires and troughs were laid and the edges of roads and boulevards and parks were marked out by elaborate stone setts, so a bird of prey might hover there and perceive the grand plan as it came to fruition. But promises were broken, a great war came, workers' lives were sacrificed for some greater good, essential funds were diverted or lost and enthusiasms dwindled. And then time came along and made people forget.

TERENSCHIA – *Home of the Thirteen*
The city where the thirteen books of Thaumaturgy were once kept. It is now destroyed and the whereabouts of its

ruins unknown. The guardianship of the volumes is now entrusted to a cabal of different cities, each tasked with protecting their own book from every possible misfortune. If the cities fail in their bounden duty they can expect a fate similar to Reepah-Teron, a guardian city which was at war with a neighbour. Although they eventually won the conflict, they lost a single battle during which their book was captured. In the years which followed, the city suffered an agonisingly slow fall from grace.

AMARELIA – *The Floating Caravan*
This tiny city consists entirely of a humble caravan slung beneath a voluminous floating gasbag. The gypsy trailer is a strange sight with its curved roof and wooden wheels and shafts to harness some long absent beast of burden. The caravan-city is named for its owner, Amarelia the sky roamer, a messenger from a forgotten age or a meddlesome witch depending on who tells the tale. What is never in question though is her existence. No mere fable this woman, she is sighted often, and once again depending on the teller of the tale, it's a sign of good luck to see the airship and an even greater blessing (or curse) to have its shadow pass over you. Nobody knows when or where she will land or how she manages to stay airborne for so long or how the ship is supplied. There are, however, always those willing to take a guess. She sucks sustenance from the clouds offer some. She's in cahoots with a band of pirates who give her food in exchange for useful intelligence, say others. She is dead and therefore needs no food, except when her ghost must ingest the soul of a child on the eve of the Cimmerous feast. Those fortunate enough to be granted an audience must undergo a ritual purification,

after which they are ushered into her presence with great ceremony. But they must prepare for a shock as they take in the deathly shape of her, a faded corpse reclining in a bamboo cot, her eyes covered with the half-shells of walnuts. It is natural to feel you are in the presence of a dead person until she has examined your mind and deems you worthy of an audience. And then she becomes a presence in the consciousness, a dark octopus whose tentacles encircle the psyche, embracing its deepest secrets. It is hard to prove any of this, since we rely on the word of those who have met her, but all come away with the same lasting impression. The lady Amarelia is a living monument to the 'Domain of the Pentacle', a group of five cities belonging to a civilisation so old their achievements were forgotten before the current occupants of the planet began their evolution.

DIIMENDIA – *The Magpie Pavement*
A city which exists in only two dimensions. To many, the idea is obscene, but a poisonous flower cannot help its nature. The question is, who would visit such a place at the risk of annihilating their third dimension? Although popular with creative suicides, approaching from the side is dangerous, since the city's edges are dimensionless blades of infinite sharpness. Depending on the angle of approach, an oblique path will reveal an anamorphic sliver of the metropolis, its thickness increasing as the angle approaches ninety degrees. At this point, the uncertain city skyline, the massive triumphal arch and its translucent curtain are fully visible and contrast enormously with the reality of our own world. The road to the arch is lined with hovels, chicken houses, rough woollen tents and awnings

of patchwork rags, home to thousands of unfortunates who scrape a living from gullible tourists. Seers and sages are happy to describe what they have never seen in vague terms such as 'I see a chequered pavement', or 'there is a magnificent statue of bronze' or the slightly more creative 'Mine eyes are blinded by the light of a wonderful fountain where falls the rain of a golden fluid'. Despite the presence of stark warning signs, there is always someone prepared to pay the toll which allows them to approach the citadel. Such pilgrims are watched with great interest as they approach the veil, pass through the arch and disappear, never to return. Some have held the curtain aside by prior arrangement, but anyone hoping to peer through the gap invariably has the eyes burned from their skull by the powerful telescope which is available for rental at reasonable rates.

Katz: Gate Check

Ink on Paper
The Poisoned City of Melazzar
Faldia 49th day of Culmination
Translations [Zaiteku D'ni]

Our arrival in Melazzar came unexpectedly early, so we were already docked when I left the trailer in search of breakfast. I expected the smell of coffee and bacon on reaching the kitchen tent, but instead found a dithering of hungry souls toying with their eating utensils. The servery boy said supplies were late because the landing bridge wasn't yet in place. His announcement was met with a round of questions, groans, sighs and complaints that were still in full flow when the public address system crackled into life. This startled everyone because it was rusted and battered and considered to have expired. The message it conveyed was unequivocal. Return to your trailers, tents, beds in trees, quilts under wagons, rags inside packing cases and all the other hiding places in which you rest your head. Lock yourselves in and under no circumstances come out until you're told.

If the idea was to prevent a panic, it didn't work, because the entire circus entourage (including myself and a silent and rather sombre Dina), headed to the ticket booth island as if by prior arrangement. All wore a resolute expression, some clearly scared while others appeared to be bristling for a fight with an as yet unknown foe.

The bridgehead was obscured by a curtain of noxious fumes, like the entrance to some spectacular show which stilled the advancing crowd. Nobody, it seemed, would be crossing the bridge today. A murmur went up as people enquired what was going on and the answer was swift in arriving. Snake heads emerged through the curtain, sniffing the air with forked tongues, estimating the strength of the opposition. The crowd fell back as each reptile emerged spitting fire, steam, air, stones and venom. As the tenth and last of the heads broke through, the driving power behind them emerged. Clothed only below the waist, all eyes were fixed upon Lady Vyper's defiant pose and the fumes trailing behind her as she appeared from the poisonous nebula. Her emergence felt like a declaration of a war between worlds, or the inevitable continuation of hostilities between warring families. The air fizzed and crackled as she approached Morga Krenns, standing proud at the head of our contingent. For a moment, it seemed that Vyper's ambitions were doomed to fail, with her standing on one side and everyone else on the other. Then the balance shifted as those faithful to the snake woman emerged from the gaseous curtain.

I have no words to describe the phenomena that appeared thereafter. The result of a technology I don't understand, perhaps, or the purest magick. The opposing sides called down abusive powers from the sky, filling the air with tragic screams and the smell of burning flesh. I saw just a few of them fall, but when the smoke of battle cleared I was surrounded by thirty or more crumpled and lifeless forms, Aho Nixx, Morga Krenns and Lady Vyper amongst them. Other than that, I cannot bear to offend mankind with an exact choreography of the deaths. The methods and means of extinction should not be made a spectacle, especially since I now believe the entire purpose of the battle was to protect myself and Dina and allow us to reach the safety of the city. I feel deep shame at that. Is it something about the boy, or do the tales of those ancient cities mean something more than the sum of their ashes? It feels like we have won an important battle, but only just begun the process of war between good and evil. If you know anything at all I implore you to explain the significance of these events. Take care old friend. This poor coward must bid the survivors farewell and determine what the city of Melazzar holds in store.

Ink on Paper
The Poisoned City of Melazzar
Faldia 49th day of Culmination

We entered the city as dusk approached, grateful for the clothing and masks gifted by the people of the Aeropi::Narjuk, whom I fear we may never see again. Our dress was Arabian in style, the masks more suited to the noxious atmosphere of a chemical plant or foundry, which I confess the city resembles. The central part of the metropolis though, known as the atrium, is fume free and resides beneath an enormous glass dome protected by airlocks. I'd like to say we were welcomed, but the citizens of Melazzar are as poisonous as their own suburbs and, after a humiliating personal search, we were refused admission. Eventually we enlisted the help of a travelling puppeteer who spotted the golem amulet I rescued from Prem's mutilated body. It hadn't helped the clown, but I was grateful for its assistance and muttered a little prayer of thanks as we climbed inside the travelling show's capacious wagon where we changed into suitable costumes. We waited until the guards changed shifts and were admitted to the dome, adjacent the area where the nightly ceremony took place. I tried to reward our puppet friend with what money we had left but he took the amulet instead and went to set up his show. We watched for a while as the trailer expanded this way and that with doors opening, panels extending and flaps sliding so the stage eventually occupied almost three times the volume of the original vehicle. This in itself was well worth watching. Children gathered rapidly, eager to get the front seats; a sight which brought a tear to my eye. I hadn't witnessed such unbridled happiness in years. It was the anticipation of an entertainment so wonderful it would remove them from the reality of their existence, if only for a while. I swear I saw Dina smile as the little play unfolded and the puppet characters paraded up and down in their private world, unaware of events beyond the confines of their stage. We watched the thing from end to end before applauding enthusiastically and turning to the main event of the evening.

As dusk fell, the crowd rearranged itself on either side of a central causeway marked out by vitreous cobblestones. Everyone, it seemed, knew the part they were to play, including the many tourists who had probably never witnessed the nightly unrolling. Dina grew excited as the trunk containing the scroll was opened, but I think I was even more enthralled than him. I was about to witness an event that had taken place for thousands of years, the description of which I had only recently translated. In some bizarre and completely self-centred way, I felt my revelations had created the fabulous ritual from nothing. A 'creatio ex nihilo', with myself playing the part of the Angel, who, according to Madame Sesostris, created the universe. I was wrenched back to reality by a resonant gong whose sound was left to decay away to nothing, signalling the start of the ceremony. A pair of heavily muscled men approached the trunk and took hold of the free end of the scroll, preparing to draw the vellum out along the length of the cobbled channel. The crowd fell silent as the operatives began their walk, a quiet *click, click, click* marking the unwinding of the drum and the emergence of the scroll. I hadn't expected to smell anything, but the vellum had garnered a distinct aroma over thousands of years and I wasn't sure what to make of it. Is this what the others are experiencing or does everyone get something different from the ceremony?

With the first few body-lengths of scroll now visible, the previous day's symbology rolled into view, provoking a scurry amongst the crowd as they tried to write down or draw what they saw in the hope of retaining at least a fragment of meaning. No sooner had they emerged, however, than the markings on the scroll disappeared and, as the vellum continued to be drawn out, the air filled with the frustrated sighs of citizens and tourists alike. And so came the end of the beginning.

The opening of the slit in the air caused a mass intake of breath. I imagined even those familiar with the ceremony couldn't help feeling awe at the unmistakable 'otherwhere' emerging from the reverse side of the phenomenon. Onlookers gasped as the ink began to flow. I'd expected to see a single column of fluid, unable to imagine how it could arrange itself on the surface of the vellum. Instead, we witnessed the delicate pouring of thousands of streams, each distinct in colour and thickness, clearly anticipating where and what was to appear once the inking was done. The inks didn't colour the scroll as I'd expected but disappeared beneath its impassive surface, hiding in wait for the time of revelation. It was frustrating in a way, since I'd hoped to see the writings and illustrations appear as if performed by a hand, for no other reason than my hope that such a spectacle was controlled by man. Because if not, then by whom? Wonder returned in an instant though as the surface of the vellum took the appearance of a number of gentle streams, gradually gaining energy until they were the surface of an angry ocean, roiling and boiling in a spasm of creation.

Dina tugged enthusiastically at my sleeve as unfamiliar language and esoteric symbols emerged from the waves, gradually gaining form as the waters settled, first to a ruffled surface, then a mirrored lake, and finally flattening into the ordinary vellum we saw emerging from the trunk. The crowd fell silent for a moment, as if forgetting their purpose, then the scratch of pens and pencils and the skitter of charcoals began in earnest. The attempt to capture this evening's mysterious insight had begun. I stood in awe, wondering if Dina saw the same thing I did laid out on the glowing vellum.

The brilliant symbols, the flickering letters and glyphs represented no single intent I could divine; instead, they were a taunt, a warning, an invitation to participate, and I found myself staring in awe at their infinite landscape. It was like their linkages, discontinuities, correspondences and glowing junctions contained every bit of intelligence in the universe, if we were only prepared to look long enough. I tilted my head back and across the slippery undertow of time breathed the subtle fragrance of a distant and wildly unfamiliar city; a citadel dominated by the presence of monstrous insectile airships; a place where we might find answers to mysteries, but which was bristling with uncompromising foes and unfamiliar dangers.

I recognised the sensation at once from Dina's sketchbook; no longer a series of anonymous charcoal smudges, but a living, pulsating place, its magnetic attraction pulling us like a soft iron bar in an electrified coil. A glance at Dina confirmed the nature of the choice facing us; it was not as simple as good versus evil, because none of us is that virtuous. If the power behind recent horrific events was not evil though, then I dare not imagine what true evil must be like. What chance is there for the souls who remain behind when such dark malevolence is on the loose? Who will stand for them, if not us? Do we settle for freedom and answers or engage our loyalty and continue to ask questions? Dina's smile contained his own answer and mine too. The tantalising glimpse of his sketchbook world was pleading for our presence, but the siren-song of Aeropi::Narjuk and her denizens was unimaginably stronger. The voice of the circus was calling to us in time of need; an ineluctable force beckoning us back to the fabulous Theatre of Dreams.

Diary Fragments 9

Holo-stream Fragment – Para 01.34.29
Tarrasch, Dark Joy Plateau – March 23 2022
Mariam Glonti – Border Guard

The guardians from the other side come out at night and move the rearmost roll of barbed wire so it sits at the front. Every night they do this, stealing our country, inch by inch, and by that same stealth enlarging the size of their own. One day we will rise up and take back what is ours.

Holo-stream Fragment – Para 36.15.28
Chimbote, Peru – August 17 1993
Emely Condori – Blackjack Hostess

We try to keep lights covered so we don't advertise what we have, but it didn't stop a passing slab from trying to snare us with a steel hawser and hook. They scoured a channel down the main street before gaining purchase on a steel lattice that was once part of a railway bridge. Luckily, the cable wasn't strong enough and it flailed back at the pirates. Another set of attackers rained molten metal down on us, which I never understood. Why waste their resources to do that? I wrote that one in red ink, in case it might explain something later. Every ship has a log book, so I'm guessing an airship that used to be part of the earth's crust is no different. All we need to do now is find some way of steering properly, something that's currently done in a half-assed way by one of the hobos who has mental problems. To be fair, his idea of using the advertising hoardings as ailerons is brilliant, but he has a habit of slow-steering us into trouble, so we need to dispose of him in a kindly way. He showed an interest in the telescope I removed from the casino, so maybe we can make him the lookout instead of the steersman. The view through that scope is hypnotic. There are great swathes of land left behind on the surface and nine tenths of them are covered by what looks like forest. It's difficult to tell with the wispy cloud cover laying between us. Over the 'sea' though it's a different matter, where the ruins of ships of all ages dot the dried-up ocean bed and newly exposed mountain ranges bathe in long awaited sunlight. Above us there's nothing but cloud and the occasional glimpse of silver fish that might just be optical illusions, shining with the kind of blinding light that bounces off chrome bumpers and sears your eyeballs.

Holo-stream Fragment – Para 13.03.47
Brooklyn, NYC – June 17 1968
Bruce Chaka – Photographer

I eventually found a generator so I'm busy making prints now, making damn sure I get rid of all the developer and fixer by washing them three times longer than usual. I used to work in a newspaper darkroom with a guy who didn't bother to wash the prints at all. They were trashed the next day with chemical staining but as long as they made it into that night's edition he didn't care. What matters to me now is to make these prints last. That, I guess, and not getting blood all over them from the shotgun wound I picked up. Pity about that. Looks like they really will be my tombstone, so I better find them a really good hiding place.

Hannah: Crane Shot

Holo-stream Clip
New York, NY – September 25 2083

I'm surrounded by a thousand or so people who have gathered to watch proceedings outside the old NYPD building, where the soldiers have set up more wish caster stalls. I have never seen so many people gathered in one place or smelt so much concentrated body odour, but it suits my purpose, just so long as I can keep to the middle of the melee and out of sight of my pursuers.

The rednecks who gave up my mother turned on me as soon as she was on board the airship, no doubt hoping for another food bounty. I didn't want to leave Cassie but something told me they wouldn't – or couldn't – harm her, and that's exactly how it played out.

Since they knew the neighbourhood and I didn't, my only defence was speed, which worked up to a point. I managed to keep ahead of them for four or five blocks and eventually found somewhere to hide, hoping that might be the end of it.

Now it's only a matter of time before the crowd parts and I have nowhere to hide. I have no plan, no guide and, with Deeby and Cassie out of the picture, I have no responsibility for anyone but myself. I feel like I'm in freefall.

If I could follow Mom aboard the airship I'd do it in a heartbeat but, as Cassie kindly pointed out, I am not and never will be a wish caster. I'm beginning to wonder if I'm ever going to be any use to anyone.

'You here for the lottery?' says a boy.

I turn, expecting to see someone I know, but it's just a hopeful stranger, a couple of years younger than me. He's sweeping the falling snow out of a thick mane of dark hair.

'You really believe that?' I ask.

'Nine people went up already.'

'So where do we get a ticket?'

'No tickets,' he replies. 'They drop a red ball out of the ship. You catch it, that's it.'

As unlikely as this sounds, I believe him. He has the sort of face that can't lie. I wish I'd met him in different circumstances; we might even have become friends.

'Good luck,' he chimes.

Near the recruiting stall, an officer stands on top of a wrecked bus, obliged to shout above the gathering wind and the racket of the airship engines.

'The final ball will be dropped soon,' he yells. 'In the meantime, we will continue to process wish casters.'

I glance at the line near the stall. There's a woman at the front of the queue who's attempting to prove she's a wish caster with an old-fashioned magic trick.

'Why do you want to get on board?' I say to the boy.

'I could ask you the same question,' he replies.

'They took my mother,' I snap. 'No, actually they didn't take her; some set of shit-arse bastards gave her up. There's a difference.'

'Tough deal,' he sighs, 'but it can't be any worse on the ship than it is here, can it?'

I glance around our battered city. It could be patched up, but I see his point.

'No use looking at the line,' he says. 'I've been here a while and they aren't impressed by much. They only took one guy in the last hour or so and nothing before. A few hopefuls turned up with their friends or family all roped up but they know straight away if you've got what they're looking for.'

'Which is what exactly?'

'Dunno,' he admits with a toothy grin.

The line moves up. It's the turn of a woman who thinks her words get truer the louder she shouts. She has a girl on the end of a rope who refuses to look the officer in the eye.

'This one killed a man with a single glance,' she yells. 'A rampant, witch-hag like that must be worth something. Some bread maybe? A little chocolate?'

'Look at me,' demands the officer.

The accused girl maintains her floorward gaze.

'Next,' he says, dismissing them both.

'Her mother had wicked thoughts when she was in the womb,' screams the woman.

A pair of soldiers step forward to drag her away.

'Burning fire guided us here,' she yells, struggling to get free.

I spot an unwelcome face in the crowd. The tattooed pig has seen me. I duck low and crawl on hands and knees in a forest of legs, hoping to emerge somewhere he doesn't expect. Instead, I get rolled on my back in a frenzy of jostling as a deafening fanfare announces the release of the ball. Through a gap in the bodies above me

I see it float towards the crowd, bucking and swaying in the wind. It disappears as people around me gather closer to follow the trajectory. They're yelling and screaming so loud the noise drowns out the sound of the airship's engines, but they fall silent again as the ball approaches. There's confusion above me as desperate hands stretch out towards the prize. I briefly catch sight of it again as it hits grasping fingers and bounces out of sight.

At floor level, all I can see is a shifting forest of legs, but having seen the ball drop into the crowd I have an intuition where it will end up. I can't explain my next actions logically, but it seems that Cassie's gift is guiding my clumsy hands, and eventually, grazed by concrete and trampled by feet, they close around the pliant surface of the ball. I'm unable to stand, but for the moment I don't care because, laying here beneath this smelly pile of humanity, I know I have what it takes to board the ship.

The crowd is confused by the absence of a catcher and, when they finally part, I'm laying out in the open where tattoo can see me. The nameless boy runs to my aid as tattoo approaches and, as I'm getting to my feet, he stands between me and my foe. There's a short delay while tattoo sizes up his opponent and then he strikes, confident that he has the upper hand. The boy is dazed and drops to one knee, shaking his head. It's then I slip the ball in his pocket and take a step backwards. I hold my hands out, signalling submission as I call to the officer who's overseeing the stall.

'This man wants to hurt me,' I yell. 'I'm a wish caster and I'm trying to give myself up.'

The crowd parts, allowing two soldiers to march over and take hold of me. Tattoo slinks away with a look that says we have unfinished business.

'And that boy there?' I yell. 'He has the lottery ball.'

The kid manages a few words as he's dragged away to his fate.

'Thanks,' he says, 'maybe we'll meet on the ship.'

'Be careful what you wish for,' I reply.

The irony is not lost on the officer who's standing before me.

'We've seen eight wish casters from the entire city,' he says. 'All of them were brought to us against their will and mostly at the wrong end of a tether. What makes you so different you'd give yourself up voluntarily?'

'You have my mother,' I state plainly. No point in trying to intimidate a man who has a weapon levelled at my chest.

'Ah,' he smiles. 'A family reunion. How touching.'

Tattoo appears in my line of sight again, some way behind the officer. He stares for a moment, drawing a hand across his throat in a slashing motion. Then he uses some pretty crude sign language to indicate what he will do to me first. I really hope I made the right decision giving the ball away because the rest of the rednecks have shown up, waiting for me to get thrown out of the line and back into the crowd.

I turn my hands, palms up, and display the scars on my forearms, but the officer isn't impressed.

'Those are irrelevant,' he smiles. 'We only care what the device tells us.'

I hadn't noticed it until now, but there's a flat silver rectangle on the table between us. It looks like an old-school tablet, but there's no screen, just an outline of a hand where I expect to lay mine any second now. I reach out, but the officer slaps my hand away.

'You want to be electrocuted?' he says.

I'm stunned into silence as I consider why he might lie.

'You have electricity?'

'Place your left hand on the device,' he says.

If he's trying to make me anxious, he's succeeded. I no longer know which is the bigger threat, the soldier with his half-suggested electro-death or tattoo with his sexual assault and explicit slow-bleed. I've heard an electric shock can burn a person for minutes before death finally grants them release, but I choose to place my hand on the pad anyway. Better reduced to charcoal than submit to the apes who defiled my mother.

I place my hand on the pad, feeling a slight tingle as my skin makes contact with the cool metal surface.

'Keep it there,' says the officer.

I hold his gaze as the tingle increases. A wisp of steam puffs out from the pad as small points of illumination appear at each of my fingertips. I've never seen artificially generated light before today, so I guess I should be excited by the array of dancing colours. I fear what the lights say about me though, and I'm afraid of what will happen if I'm rejected.

'Absorption and Glimpse,' says the soldier, as the lights announce their verdict. 'Take her.'

The engines strain and the airship gains altitude before we're fully winched in, so the wider impact of the p-fires becomes clear. Historic architecture is burned and smoking all the way down to the Battery and up as far as Central Park and, contrary to what Snake believes, there's nothing beyond the fence at 110th Street except a dense mass of jungle. The trees form a close packed canopy that reaches all the way to the Hudson, where thousands of twisted vines hang over the waterless edge like a poorly maintained haircut.

Directly below us, the crowd near the NYPD building has swelled so much it looks like the entire population of Manhattan has gathered. They are angry, screaming abuse and waving fists as we leave, suddenly aware that the opportunity to leave the city has passed. I really wish I could help, but a single plastic ball was my limit and I'm not even sure I did the boy a favour. For all I know, we're heading for execution.

We continue our winch journey, the soldier assigned to me staring at the copper coils which now encircle my limbs. I only got a brief look at his highly athletic frame when I first laid eyes on him, but what really marks him out is the tribal marks that cover his head and neck.

'You were chasing those children across the net ways,' I say, challenging.

'Guilty as charged,' he admits. 'It's my job.'

'Killing children?'

'Don't believe everything you see,' he says. 'Wish casters are masters of deception.'

'So, the boy didn't die?'

'That's a lot of binding,' he says, ignoring the accusation.

Outside our wicker basket, Manhattan swings like a drunkard's dream as our ascent continues.

'Why is it so tight?' I ask. 'And what's the point? Wouldn't rope be simpler?'

'If you don't know why you're wearing the coil,' he says, 'then I don't understand why they think you need so much containment.'

I wonder what he means. Maybe the rednecks wrapped my mother to suppress her power. And if the soldiers believe I'm a wish caster, then perhaps they're doing the same thing. I rummage in my thoughts, desperate to find the gift Cassie thought she had given me and what the officer thought he saw in the lights.

There's nothing, but I do recall some of my Mom's science lessons.

'The wire wrapping thing,' I say. 'Is it supposed to be a Faraday cage?'

'I can't believe you have to ask,' he grins. 'What kind of desolate backwater have you been living in?'

'Hey, this is a great city,' I snap.

It's the only home I've ever known and I feel obliged to defend it, even if I'm starting to think he might be right. My entire view of the world has been turned upside down and I'm no longer sure what I know. I'm pretty certain the coils are designed to suppress unusual talents though; like wish casting maybe. That would explain a lot.

'Maybe it was great once, but now it's a pariah,' he says. 'Why else do you think you had no contact with other slabs?'

'I didn't know such a thing was possible,' I say.

'But you know how a Faraday cage works?'[27]

'My mother taught me. We're not savages.'

'You could have fooled me. Most other slabs we've chased stuck to the civilised latitudes. They didn't go slumming about in the arctic.'

'I'm not certain we had any choice,' I reply.

Maybe Snake had a point. If these invaders have made contact with or maybe even conquered other slabs then Manhattan is just a small piece of a much larger puzzle. I wonder how he'll deal with the situation now that Mom and, hopefully, Cassie are no longer under his control. Then I wonder if my Mom ever was under his control. I doubt even Lilith would allow her to be treated so cruelly, so it must have happened after Mom refused to help and struck out on her own. It all depends on the timing. My thoughts turn to my guard and the gold oak leaf adorning his lapel.

'That insignia you're wearing,' I say. 'What rank are you?'
'You'll be debriefed once you get aboard.'
'But you're part of the ship's crew?'

He nods and a fraction of a second later I see a little facial tic.

He knows I have something on him.

'You were chasing those children before the airship arrived,' I say, 'and wearing ordinary clothes, just like us poor desolate backwater people, which means you were already in the city on some kind of undercover operation.'

'You'll be debriefed once we're on board. And then it will all make sense.'

As the basket nears the hull of the airship, I feel a vague vibrating sensation which grows as we're hauled through freight doors and into a transitioning area.

The ship is alive with the hum I first heard when I was with Cassie. Here though, it's not a single note but a harmony of fifty or so tones, each signalling the presence of a chorister so clearly it's like they're standing in front of me.

But almost as soon as the joy begins it ends again when I'm grabbed from behind and a bag is pulled over my head.

I'm pulled off balance and fall onto one knee. I feel a ribbed wooden floor with my hand but, when I'm helped up and propelled along by a hand at my back, my footsteps echo off a much harder surface. There's a vague smell of ozone filtering through the bag and some distant voices too, but whoever leads me remains silent. Judging by the breathing pattern, it's not the man who escorted me aboard. Even with the bag in place, my senses feel more alive than they have ever been, as if my mind is waking up.

The engines are muted now, as we move deeper into the ship's belly.

'I believe this place will suit our purposes,' says my guide eventually.

It's a woman. She places her hands on my shoulders and orders me to walk backwards, all the while steering me like we're aiming for somewhere specific.

As I step backwards, a cold shiver guts me like a fish. I haven't the slightest clue what I'm doing here. I followed my mother blindly, which seemed like the only way to help. Now that I'm captive and blindfold it feels like volunteering might not have been the smartest move.

'Sit,' says my female guide.

I feel for a seat with the backs of my legs and settle down carefully. I remove the hood without being invited and am immediately reminded of how much I don't know about this brave new world of airships and bombs and people from other slabs.

The copper lined room is a perfect sphere. It's about sixty feet in diameter, with an iron mesh floor dividing the upper half, where I'm sitting, from the lower half, which is perforated by regularly spaced windows giving a panoramic view of the city sprawling below us. The effect is unsettling. It's like having a dream about flying in an old leather armchair.

Standing in front of me is a matronly figure in a grey military uniform and wearing fish-eye glasses. The kind of person who might work in a pawnshop, delighting in locking other people's dreams behind bars.

'You were thinking about how it all stays up,' she says, sitting down opposite me.

Her chair has the look of Mr Katz's, which is comforting, but the fact that this woman just read my thoughts feels like a personal violation. I feel dirty; infected by her unwelcome and intimate probing.

'Aren't you worried I might attack you?' I ask.

'Is that something you're likely to do?'

'You just bombed my home,' I say. 'People were killed. I saw them die.'

'Of course,' she says. 'It's not possible to fight a war without incurring casualties. In the days before Inception, I believe they called it collateral damage.'

'That doesn't make it right,' I say.

'There are no rights in a war,' says pawn-shop, 'only wrongs. Please feel free to remove the copper bindings if you wish. This room provides ample protection.'

'I don't understand,' I say, not attempting to remove the coils. 'I thought they were to protect you and your crew.'

'Protection from you?' she says, clearly amused.

An explosion in the city below diverts her gaze towards the panorama. The skeleton of a building burned out before the airship arrived looks like it might topple at any minute. The possibility doesn't seem to interest my interrogator.

'You must have many questions,' she says.

She's right. There are dozens. But the one I ask first isn't the most important.

'How is it possible you have electricity onboard this ship?'

'Because we wish it,' she says. 'And so will you.'

I really want to know if she's using a play on words to tease me, but before I can ask another question, a pair of blinding lights trails across the sky below us. A fraction of a second later there are two loud thumps, so close together as to almost sound like a single explosion. I feel the airship rock like a dinghy in a maelstrom, but my host doesn't seem bothered.

'What the hell was that?' I yell.

My interrogator is puzzled for a moment and, glancing down at the city, her look turns quickly to one of abject terror.

'I think I understand,' she says quietly. 'Look again.'

The sky below us is clear except for a few wisps of vapour separating us from a view of the city's grid. On the roof of a nondescript building, overlapping doughnuts of smoke expand, giving birth to a pair of fireflies which, in turn, form bright rings of fire. Even at this distance, the missiles seem to be tearing the air apart.

'Those were installed to protect the city against terrorists,' I say. 'I never expected they'd still work.'

I feel a strange calm as the points of fire rise towards us on columns of black smoke. It's like I know they cannot harm me. My interrogator has no such confidence though and rises from her seat. She's about to make a run for the door when an ear-splitting *ba-dumph* announces the impact of the missiles and the deck shakes below us. With years of experience balancing on nets and ropes, I think nothing of it and remain standing, but my host loses her footing and hits her head, firstly on a railing and then on the metal floor. Her rich ruby blood navigates the angles of the mesh, pooling on the underside of the grid before falling in great dark splashes. Judging by the severity of the wound, she'll bleed out before I can bring help. Before I have to decide her fate though she twitches and lays still. I check for a pulse but there's nothing. It's time to find Mom.

I'm heading for the exit when I realise exactly what just happened. I saw the missiles pass below us and felt them strike the ship about ten seconds before the events actually took place.

And it's then, as further explosions rock the ship and the floor lurches even more violently, that I manage a little laugh. Cassie's ability to see the future has shown up just in time for it to die again, right along with its unremarkable new owner.

For the briefest of moments, it seems like I'm nowhere. Before the missiles hit, I thought they'd be no more annoying than a bee sting to a ship this size but, as the bulk of the vessel turns in the air like a falling elephant, I sense we've reached a turning point.

Where I am now is a time between times, as if the universe is trying to decide between differing fates, choosing to split along a line of probability or buck the trend and maintain a steady course. Do we kill hundreds in the ship and many more in the streets below or do we take an alternative path, leading perhaps to an even more dangerous conclusion?

I don't know how fate works, but I'm all for taking my chances. Airships don't hit the ground at hundreds of miles an hour from this height. If they don't catch fire (and we haven't) they deflate slowly, falling to earth like leaves in slow motion. And if there's stuff to absorb their velocity on the way down, all the better. Except, no, that can't be right. Ten seconds ago, the idea of metal beams flexing and bending in a graceful manner was not a concept I'd ever even considered, yet suddenly I'm willing to bet my life on a favourable outcome. Not that I have a choice. It's going to happen regardless of tensile stresses and structural deformations, so let's deal with what we have.

The best place to be is the upper surface of the airship's dirigible envelope, since we're sinking on the level and, by the time the impact reaches that far, most of the collision speed will have been wiped off by the deformation of the lower layers. But panic has crept up on me and now it's whispering. I wish it would shut the hell up and let me focus on my premature death, but I find myself listening. It's Cassie talking, but in my voice, and to be honest I'm not keen on what she has to say. 'You want me to relax?' No, scratch that, I'm talking to myself. I'm telling myself to relax.

A metallic tearing sound signals our initial impact and I drag myself towards a gash in the envelope and peer out. We're sliding and screeching down the side of a tall building and the deck is tilting. My new knowledge tells me this is nowhere near as survivable, but then we snag a cable and our descent first slows and then stops. There's a groaning, creaking sound, suggesting we'll be on our way again soon, but for now we're swaying ever so slowly about a hundred feet above Madison Avenue.

She's here again. Cassie, telling me to relax. No, it's me telling me to relax, telling me to exercise the possible futures.[28] My conscious self doesn't know exactly what this means, but there must be some part of me that does, so I try to block out the screaming of the crew and the groaning and creaking of the ship and concentrate on nothing.

I need to see a future of my own choosing. When I saw the missiles launch, I was seeing events that hadn't yet happened and ten seconds later they did. What if I direct my mind to simply imagine my own actions and see where that particular future leads? And what if I don't just do that once but twice? I could see two possible futures and, depending on which one of them is best, take the action that led me to the preferred future.

It sounds crazy but I know now it's what Cassie meant. And if I don't stop at two possibilities, but imagine myself in ten different scenarios, I'll end up with ten different outcomes and ten actions that will lead me there.

I pause and then mentally jump through the gash in the hull. Two seconds later, on impact with the street, my leg snaps but there's no pain, only disgust at the sharpened bone sticking out through the flesh. Then I feel the pain. It wants to shatter me into a thousand fragments and stamp on what remains. I'm alive but haemorrhaging blood.

A femoral artery, a period of silent fading, then silence.

I decide to imagine another action, see another outcome.

I'm back on board the airship, my leg intact, so I stay put this time. The creaking intensifies and something snaps. We've resumed our fall. My stomach turns as we descend and when we hit the ground at a moderate speed it seems for a moment I'm safe. Apart from the twisted metal stanchion piercing my abdomen.

Not going to work. Try another action.

We're falling again, so this time I move towards the dorsal surface. On the way, the air turns fiery-orange and I'm screaming as flesh drips from me and the world turns black.

Try again.

This time I'm clanking along metallic corridors that simply won't stay level. Ahead of me there's the fizz of burning phosphor so I change course and traverse a gallery overlooking a cargo hold. And there, still strapped to the wheel of torture but head upwards now, is a cruel caricature of the mother I once knew.

Her face is a tragedy of pale translucent skin and a mouth that, although no longer sewn up, fails to curve into a smile at the sight of me. The copper wire wrapping her limbs is greened with corrosion and, where it bites into her flesh, there are tiny fizzing points of energy, bluish discharges that describe her resistance and her captivity in a single cruel glow.

I clatter down the stairs three at a time and hack at the ropes holding Mom in place, but then step back to consider what I'm doing. The future I'm seeing now shows the storage hold as a burning cauldron of hot gas following an explosion, and there's nothing I can do to stop it. Being able to glimpse the future, it seems, isn't quite the same as being able to change it, and the look in my Mom's eyes tells me that she already knows that.

I try to create a calm space around me in order to stop time like Cassie did, but that particular gift refuses to surface and I end up cursing the poor girl for gifting me a supernatural doodad and leaving me without a user manual. But that's me all over I guess, ungrateful and uncaring. Putting those around me in danger to serve my own needs and getting them killed in the process. I really don't deserve to survive this.

Mom is shaking her head slowly.

'I tried so hard to find you,' I say softly.

'I know you did, I know,' she croaks. Her lips are cracked and scabbed.

'And we don't have much time, I've seen what…'

'Don't fret, Hanny, it'll soon be over.'

I'm crying now, unable to bear what they have done to her.

'I'm scared, Mom. I don't know what to do. And the thing that happens next? The thing that takes you away for ever? It's getting so close.'

'Shush,' she says. 'Just hold my hand for a moment.'

I take hold of my mother; I bathe in her warmth.

'Could you wish for Manhattan to stay in the air?'

She smiles, and I can see it hurts to do so.

'I could try,' she says, 'but that's not the way the city dies.'

'Then how does it?'

'I want you to enjoy your life, Hanny. So, stop asking questions and let me ask one of my own.'

I nod and smile.

'What would make you the happiest girl ever?' she asks.

Every night before falling asleep and every morning when I wake, the same thoughts batter me with their accusations. How could I be so selfish, to attract attention to myself by performing that vain little trick? And not even by my own talent, but one I stole from my sister. How could I lay my mother open to such punishment?

'I want to say sorry, Mom. I was selfish and stupid. And you were the one who suffered.'

'I know, Hanny,' she says. 'But you were forgiven that very same day and every day since. You just didn't believe it.'

'But Mom, what they did—'

'It was horrible, I know, but you don't deserve to suffer for the rest of your life. So, listen to me. I forgive you, Hanny. And I love you. Take it now, and never forget me.'

I caress her zebra-stripe scars and gently remove the bracelet, placing it on my own wrist.

Choking back the tears, I tell her I love her too, knowing that I'm pushing my escape window to the absolute limit.

My mother smiles and closes her eyes, managing a look of repose even in distress and, unable to bear it any longer, I turn and run, the catwalk ringing out as I sprint towards the bridge. On the way, I hear a thunderous explosion and feel a punch of pressure at my back. I know at that exact moment my mother has died.

Immutable Cities 8

XHIVA – *The Shy Citadel*
On the first full moon of Inundation, take a quantity of parrafinous spirit and fill a crystal bowl until a meniscus forms in the vessel. From a tiny pipette, gently float enough oil of vulcanite to form a lens the width of a pea. By the light of the glorious moon, examine the lenticular area closely with a magnifying apparatus and observe the tiny city of Xhiva. Be swift in your observations, for the vulcanite will soon burn away and render the city invisible once more. Until then, wonder at the magnificent towers and spires of this 'somewhere' place as you trace rays of light which, whilst they describe the city most adequately, will never fully reveal its true nature.

PARRANOXIA – *The Travelling Demon Show*
Some profess that dream states may be stored in the cathedral of the mind. One such is BadLadd-Querril, described by his dearest and closest friend as a threepenny

mummer impersonating an elderly badger. There is no record of a description attributed by his enemies, but there must certainly be many, which is a good reason to keep the show in constant motion. The city of Parranoxia is a painted waggon drawn by a pair of down at the fetlocks animals which are nonetheless treated well by their owner. Not so the miniature citizens of that same municipality, who are imprisoned in an enormous book-press between performances. They are never fed or provided with water and have no social interaction save for their time on stage when they recount tales of long-ago in the form of well-rehearsed plays. Audience members fall into two camps. Those who take delight in the acting skills and differentness of this mesmerising demon show and those who ignore the spectacle, objecting to the mistreatment of the tiny actors and demanding their immediate release. Sadly, for creatures who wear angelic sigils as tattoos, there is no law to ensure the well-being of those conceived by the folding of pages torn from a magickal grimoire.

BHEEBEE – *The Lightning Rod*
The explorer Tamas Ranok claimed to have spent a month here as a guest of the monarch, while an aviator known only as Parookey described his flight over the city as the most significant event of his life. Others have claimed knowledge of the rites, the traditions, the cuisine, the religions and even the styles of wallpaper to be found in this mythical city, while one trader cites the place as his main source of mechanisms and devices devoted to the pursuit of pleasure. A museum in Brona Xeak displays a range of artifacts supposedly manufactured here, but they are without provenance. A child's spinning top, an altimeter

of novel design, a set of cutlery with nine-pronged forks fashioned from an unidentified alloy, a tiny pair of ballet shoes, a crystal cabinet filled with curious stones, a solid heliograph of a bizarre circus scene and many more. But none of these artifacts is accompanied by evidence of their fantastic origin. Ranok was discredited when the time supposedly spent drinking with the King of Bheebee was found to overlap with his stay in a sanatorium, and Parookey has failed spectacularly to produce the stereoscopic plates which he claimed to have exposed. The appetite for stories is insatiable though, and the loss of these two favourites simply led to even more fabulous inventions. Balazs Quoon took an expedition to the region and observed a city packed with towering glass structures, claiming he was prevented from approaching the golden gates of the metropolis by a river in flood. Later the same year, Oriel Panna witnessed far more modest spires glinting in the sunrise when he saw an onion-domed temple of Proxis attempting to rise from the ground. It was held back by thousands of citizens, each pulling on a tether. Neither of these or any of the other tales have attracted support, but there is one recurring story thread which describes an iron tower known as the 'Getter'. With the aid of a sharpened finial, this monstrous construction pulls blue-plasma lightning from the sky. It is surrounded by the charcoaled remains of a forest and a carpet of eager green shoots.

TORBEN-BRAX – *The Beautiful Dreaming*
A floating city kept aloft by art.

Diary Fragments 10

Holo-stream Fragment – Para 15.85.53
Lundern, Inguland – November 5 1900
Jay Daog Phoenix – Isis Waterman

Fucking, fucking fuckers. Fuck the fucking lot of them. I had to pull the boat out of the water at Wapping to stop the river ice crushing it, and now I'm having to pay a mate to store it in his yard. No, on second thoughts, he's not really a mate, otherwise the fucker wouldn't be charging me two bob a week. Still, it's an ill wind. I got a few little jobs with a real mate, absolute diamond geezer, no questions asked and run like fuck if you spot a peeler. Not strictly legal. Totally fucking bent if I'm being honest. Anyway, we're all well fed now and there's a few shillings left over to bring the dustbin lids to the frost fair. The river froze above the bridge a few weeks ago on account of the slow-moving water behind the arches. It seized up on the seaward side a few days later, and looks like staying that way for the rest of the year. Fucking weather deities, sitting around in the sky all day excavating their fucking noses and pulling daffodil bulbs out of their spotty fucking arses. They can all fuck the fuck off and take their fucking wintry weather with them. Just fucking saying, right? Now, where was I? Oh yeah, like I say, I wasn't bothered about the fair; all those tricksters and pickpockets and snake-oil salesmen, oh yeah, and actors, especially the fucking actors with their fucking clever little plays. And those pissing twats with their souvenir engraved spoons. Who gives a fuck about all that? Turns out it's my nippers, that's who. They wanted to be at the frost fair when the Imperial Flagship arrived and I confess I fancied a look myself. You know what? I am so fucking glad we came. What a fucking monster that thing is, like a fucking great insect just hanging in mid-air without a thank you or a by your fucking leave. I pity the foreigners who get on the wrong end of that fucker. The little 'un pissed himself when he laid eyes on those tendrils, and the eldest shat his britches when they blasted that fucking great horn. And when the captain appeared on that fuck-off sized kinetic painting? I had to work like a fucking navvy to keep my sweaty arse cheeks squeezed shut. Talk about sixpence and half-a-crown.

Holo-stream Fragment – Para 00.03.88
Hopi Sovereign Nation – April 2 1961
Ankti Chaka – Educator, Mother and Shaman

Our traditions are an echo of age-old wisdom, of which our memory is incomplete. We are nonetheless taught to understand the mechanisms of the planets, the means by which stars affect the climate and crops and the importance of the open door by which we converse with the Creator. In the tongue of our fathers, there is no tense. The past, the present and the future? They are all one. Our sovereign nation has lifted, is lifting and will lift.

Hannah: Lap Dissolve

Holo-stream Clip
New York, NY – September 25 2083

Up ahead of me there are snatches and squeals of radio traffic, a sound I have only ever had described, like voices emanating from a new world. The bridge crew are surprised to see me, but equally busy trying to stay alive, so when I dive into the captain's seat he simply shrugs his shoulders, as if to say 'enjoy your final few seconds'. I realise it's not him I'm interested in though, but his female second officer. There's a look in her eye that reminds me of Mom, and I know straight away that she has a variation of my mother's talent; ironic, given the airship's mission is to sweep up wish casters. I also know that whatever action I take, her future ends in a few seconds, so I cross the bridge and demand her side arm. Having decided we're all about to die, she hands me the weapon without question, willing to clutch at any straw. I'm just following my intuition at this point, so there's no guarantee it'll work, but I shoot her in the stomach, hoping to severely injure but not kill.[29] The look she gives me in that moment is pure terror. I've seen it only once before when I stabbed Lilith in the arm with a pencil and used her talent to change the suit of a card. Now, having inflicted infinitely more pain on my subject, I'm hoping to borrow whatever talent she possesses to change my run of luck.

We have seconds to live. The Tyche is in free-fall and I expect to see my life flash before my eyes; just like a movie, they promised. With the exception of galloping horses, I've never seen a real movie until today, but if it's like falling through a holograph album with an infinite number of pages then yes, this is most certainly it. The movie of my life or, more likely, my death, as shown by the broken down and out-of-focus projector of my childhood.

Mom forgave me, so it's about time I forgave myself.

Holo-stream Clip
New York, NY – September 25 2083

I make my wish.

I recall a feeling of deep regret the time I stole the talent from Lilith, but the gut-wrenching emotion I feel now hollows out my being and freezes what remains of the cadaver. I know instinctively that no time is passing while I consider what I'm doing. Either that, or time is running at the normal rate and it's taking me zero time to think. Whichever it is, nothing is happening. I expected the situation to resolve immediately in my favour, but there's no sign of change in the woman whose blood is spilling out between clutched fingers. If anything, she looks sorry for me, as if I ought to know what to do at this critical moment. I try the futures again, but those silken ribbons of time I've recently learned to follow lead only to darkness. I can't see what happens in those shadowy dead-ends, but I think Katz might have called them the endings of the soul during one of his scarier tales. All I know is I don't want to go there.

Thinking of Katz reminds me of the golem. As a child, we were having tea with the old man in his shop and I swear the little clay figure moved of its own volition. Katz insisted it did no such thing, but I reminded him how a figure could be brought to life by writing a Hebrew inscription on its forehead and he admitted it might be possible. 'You need the letters for certain,' he'd said, 'but you must also make the universe listen to what you want.'

I knew he was hinting, but I didn't want to say it sounded a lot like wish casting, so I edged around the subject. He knew what I meant though, and told me I could call it whatever I liked, but to remember that nothing in the world ever happens without desire. It's a lesson that has waited years to bubble to the surface, but now it's here I know how to complete my wish. My imminent death gives a sharp edge to the wish, to the need, to the desire, and it's that edge that punctures the mental aura surrounding the officer. Suddenly, she's relieved that her own death will mean something and she visibly relaxes, eager to loan what I need. But she still sags when I borrow her talent, channelling it into my soul like a golden stream of energy. She smiles through the pain as we complete our pact and, when it's done, she untwines her fingers and brings her bloodied hands up in prayer, thumbs touched to her lips in thanks. And in that moment I see her mind; she's thinking of some other place where the earth is an undisrupted whole.

Only then does the girl known as Hannah Keter die on Madison Avenue.

Milford Junction
Milford, Kent – 16 December 1944

The afterlife is absolutely nothing like I expected. I'm in a high-ceilinged but dingy room, a refreshment salon with a service counter, numerous wooden tables and chairs all heated by a cast-iron stove. The light outside is failing, and there are blackout blinds on the windows, so the interior is illuminated by opal lampshades in the shape of flower petals. Beneath their dim gaze, patrons sit drinking tea, reading newspapers, chatting and, in some cases, gossiping, while a couple in the corner engage in furtive conversation. An imperious woman, her hair piled high, surveys the scene from behind unpolished tea urns. She breaks her conversation with a ticket inspector and carries on polishing a glass as she turns and examines me from top to bottom.

'Are you one of those modern dancers from the palais my love?'

That wasn't what I expected, but in this place nothing is rational, as I will soon discover.

'Why would you think that?' I ask.

'I couldn't help but notice your clothes, very chic, and you're so thin,' she clucks to the ticket inspector. 'We've seen it all, haven't we Mr Godby? We get all sorts coming through here. Now, what can I get you?'

The transition from what I was to whatever I am now has dulled my senses, but there's a glorious aroma of fruit and spices, amplified a thousand-fold as Mr Godby lifts the glass dome from a cake stand.

'I reckon a Bath bun,' he says, 'judging from the way she's eying up these little beauties. And a piping hot cup of tea to wash it down.'

'Yes,' I say, somewhat stunned, 'how much will…'

'All taken care of, duck,' smiles the manageress.

I finish the bun before I reach my table, which attracts some amused looks. I don't mind because it's the first proper food I've had for years. And the first time in my life I have ever been in a situation you could describe as remotely normal. As I sit down and look around, I get the feeling it's impolite to stare, so I concentrate on stirring my tea without chinking the spoon against the cup. I fail though, probably due to the same nervous impulses that are driving my limbs crazy. There's a rise in the level of conversation as if I've committed a mortal sin with the teaspoon. I glance at the old-fashioned wall clock, alerted by the sound of the minute hand clicking over to twenty before six. Presently, the air fills with a thunderous sound, a rumbling steam-powered presence accompanied by the shrillest of whistles and a *clat-clatter-clat-clattering* of steel as a passenger express thunders through the station. It's just the way Mom described it in one of the many stories she told us as kids, a thought that, now I appear to be experiencing it for real, sends a shiver of winter cold through me.

I leave my tea to cool and wander out onto the cold platform. Dusk is approaching rapidly, so passengers waiting for the next train stand beneath benevolent lamps, reading their newspapers and chatting, or guarding their suitcases and staring into the middle distance. When an express hurtles through in the opposite direction, the light from the coach windows illuminates the waiting passengers with a flicker-flick-flick like frames in a black and white movie. I watch them closely as the train flashes through, taking in their appearance like the moment is significant and I need to remember every little scrap of it. The red tail light of the express disappears beyond the signal gantry and I make my way to a somewhat musty and dimly lit ticket office. Wooden benches line three walls and centred in the fourth is an arched window set above a metal ticket tray. The window blind is pulled down, so I sit and wait, despite the lack of heating. The painted brick walls display large, colourful posters inviting the traveller to visit exotic but unfamiliar destinations like Blackpool, Whitby and Saltburn-by-the-Sea. The one that attracts my attention most is an impressive illustration of Battersea Power Station, a squat leviathan of a building with a pair of white chimneys that threaten the sky like massive guns. I have no idea why I favour it, but it seems to me that a decision is required. As soon as the thought enters my head the blind rolls up and the ticket seller's face appears. It's moon shaped with pebble spectacles and is red-blotched from the heat of the coal fire roaring in the room behind.

'Where to, Miss?'

'Um, Battersea Power Station?'

'You fond of architecture then?' He smiles and passes me a rectangle of cardboard. 'Or do you just like breathing in coal dust?'

'I like the look of the building,' I reply. 'It seems exciting.'

'Platform one in ten minutes,' he grins, 'change at Manchester London Road. Gets you into London St. Pancras at a quarter to midnight.'

Hannah: Wrap

>Heading 082, approaching Corque,
>Republic of the Air – 4 November 1900

I force myself to ignore the icy reptile clawing its way down my spine and take a moment to gather my wits and take in my surroundings. I joined the train as planned, sharing the third-class compartment with a nanny and her schoolboy charge. Neither spoke, beyond the initial polite greetings, but it was clear from their body language that I didn't fit into whatever world they inhabited. I'd like to say that I spent the journey getting to know them better as we passed through town after town, all the while gathering knowledge of this strange new country, but I'm afraid the exertions of the past few days caught up with me and I fell asleep. I'll never know if they were real or if they objected to my snoring because I never saw them again, and neither did I see my destination. Instead, I regain consciousness on the bridge of an airship similar to the one that crashed over New York. The landscape lurking outside is swathed in darkness with the odd pinprick of light, the whole vision swaying slightly as the gondola swings in the prevailing wind. I'm flanked by officers in black uniforms piped with deep blue and gold, functional and plain with the minimum of rank badges or medals. This is a fighting ship and, judging by her air of authority, the woman on my left is the ranking officer; the man on my right most likely her second in command. Which just leaves me, stuck in the middle, ten-times drunk and stunned by bizarre circumstance. I have no idea what's happening here, except for the conviction that I'm no longer in Kansas. I do, however, have a growing sense of who I am and how I feel. I'm here under sufferance, not as part of the crew but not to be ignored either; a civilian standing amongst the military, a voice respected by many, but not all. Even in this new place, I am something 'other'.

I was Hannah in New York and, apart from my plunging death onto Madison Avenue, I was moderately content with that life, as much as one can be when starving. Now I'm Hannah in Lundern too, and whilst definitely not starving, my life is neither simple nor safe. Somehow, on the bridge of this ship, we're both Hannah; a confection of minds in a single body, our aspirations and dreams intact; our … oh shit, no, not now. Please. A tsunami of vomit is boiling in my stomach, preparing to gush into my mouth and out onto the deck; an unwelcome splatter of stinking mess that will do absolutely nothing for my social standing.

'If you'll excuse me,' I say.

Take time to breathe, breathe, and breathe.

'I have matters to attend to. You will alert me on final approach.'

'As you wish, Lady,' replies the commanding officer, obedient but without humility.

I make a show of leaving the bridge with a swagger and dragging of silks, then, safely out of view, I stagger to my day cabin and fall into the tiny rosewood bunk, hands covering eyes that refuse to focus, feet elevated to get some blood into my brain. It's a mistake. I vomit.

I decide to try water, resulting only in more vomit; hands trembling, vision fuzzy, balance uncertain. I turn onto one side as a choir of purest soprano notes rises in my head.

Was it too much to ask that this might disappear with whatever change has just come over me?

I am an addict, but regardless of the knowledge, I remove the ornate flask and take a small sip, closely followed by a couple of large slugs. Despite the immense feeling of well-being flooding my senses, I'm ashamed of this weakness that now inhabits me.[30] Wherever I go from now on, it seems the abyss will be waiting to swallow me. And as the maelstrom in my head settles into patterns of more reasonable thought, I curse Snake and his damnable coal. Calm, calm, calm. And rest...

> Heading 005, approaching River Isis Marker,
> Inguland – 5 November 1900

With my mind fairly clear, given the circumstances, I rise and peek through the porthole where the seasonal pre-dawn stars are just setting. My soiled robes have been replaced by a stealthy aide, so I dress in replacement silks and head towards the bridge, where a full complement of officers have assembled to observe our approach. On the other side of the armoured glass, the drumming of our engines accompanies a gentle but freezing dawn. Two hundred feet below us, and three miles dead ahead, the ice-locked river Isis is a frosted serpent, winding through crystal glades on its way to the city of Lundern. Having hit our navigational marker, we turn west again, slowing our progress to match our speed with the city slab that's now approaching us from behind.

With the new course laid, we make our way aft to the secondary bridge where the captain instructs the flag officer to fly a message in the traditional manner.

*Imperial Flagship John Dee
requesting permission to dock.*

For a while, the pennants look marvellous in the golden sunlight, but after a few moments the rising sun is swallowed by dark clouds and our vision of the approaching city is cast into deep shadow. Just visible, nonetheless, and almost directly below us, is the frost fair; an entire temporary town built on river ice and wearing a crown of brilliant fireworks. The folk gathered there are waving arms, flags, firebrands and anything else that might signal their joy. Oh, to be in Inguland, now that winter's there. A few moments further into our descent, Lundern's only bridge emerges from the gloom, the manifold stone arches topped by snow dusted houses, shops, chapels and halls along the greater part of its length. And then, like the disappearing fair, it's gone again, slipped along behind us like an imaginary winter palace.

As we begin our descent into docklands there's a *click-click-clicking* of claws on the metal decking and Bebe comes to my side, muzzling her damp nose into my hand. Seventy-five feet now and approaching river level. The Kingdom-Brunel cradle surrounds us, its gigantic ribs reaching for the sky like the upturned skeleton of the last leviathan.

Fifty feet, twenty-five, ten, five and ... contact.

Engines dying and clamps engaging, we've made it home and, from our commanding position in the dock, able to take in the finest view in Lundern. Flying off our starboard side and tethered by immense forged chains is a recently captured slab. It's a city of towers and tall buildings, concrete canyons and lights, broken bridges and net-scapes that once called itself New Amsterdam.

Appendix A.
Notes

1. Original document held by the Hagstrom-Xi-Hawking Institute. Handwritten by the blessed Hannah Keter (HK), cursive script, black ink on heavy art paper. Such materials were scarce, circa 2080. Date may be inaccurate due to water damage on the script and the fact that the blessed HK had limited access to accurate timekeeping or calendars. Subsequent dates are reliable, having been obtained from holo-stream time stamps. This item is currently on loan to the World Cultural Exposition.
2. Despite significant effort, none of the blessed HK's juvenilia has so far been recovered. Holo-stream coverage of the years prior to puberty is limited to just six examples. Access to sensitive material is limited to senior fellows.
3. Two similar pages were recovered in the dig of 5981, the only known fragments of Deeby's (DB) logs. The child has never been properly identified.
4. Typhus was the main factor in the reduction of the

population. The New Jersey mega strip was in financial difficulties and closed eighteen months before Inception. It's likely one or more of the five controlling families contributed to its collapse, but documentary proof is sketchy and of doubtful provenance.

5. Geographical analysis of the holo-stream data suggests the blessed HK was over Alaska at the time, which calls into question the accuracy and thus historical reliability of some of the available log entries. These would naturally resynchronise when the 'slab' overflew easily identifiable regions and then gradually drift into inaccuracy again as the flight path took in areas of blank self-sameness.

6. This fragment was never found, but the institute's collection contains thousands of such diaries, some of which may have been gathered by the blessed HK herself.

7. The fear of individuals wielding 'uncanny power' features in every historical age, as does the persecution of the unfortunate practitioners. Whether the object of fear is described as 'magick' or 'wish casting' or simply 'unfamiliar science', the fear persists today, as does the sanction, the first primitive impulse being to destroy what is not understood. The seminal paper on this subject is *Prospero's Magic Abjured*, Roentgen, Carew, Karsh et al. EIT 5828

8. See *Gangs of the New York Slabs* – Trowbridge, Zain, McQueen. 5243.107

9. The topology of New York has been recreated many times using available data, but the best reference is probably the one which instructs the reader on how to investigate it for themselves. See *Remapping the Eternal City* – Yeats, Waite, Crowley. 5315.223

10. Historians are divided on this point. Is it a sign of prescience in the blessed HK? Is the blessed HK offering up a conscious message to the future?
11. The first mention of Judaic symbolism. There are no holo-stream records of the period that the blessed HK alludes to in this section.
12. Rabbi Katz was a Judaic scholar of parallel 00.11.82. His better known Doppel in parallel 00.07.29 was the translator of *The Immutable Cities* from the original manuscripts, now lost. Katz' covering letters are held by the institute, part of collection 2F. The translated text of *The Immutable Cities* forms part of the catechism of the Holy Edifice. All Glory to the Cities of Old.
13. The Holaroid image is part of collection 1A and holds fragments of the blessed HK's DNA. Each year a lottery selects three citizens who are permitted to examine the exhibit in a location of their choice. Currently on loan to the World Cultural Exposition.
14. Many theories exist as to the significance of various numerical observations made by the blessed HK directly or indirectly. The main theory suggests links with Hebrew numerology or 'Gematria', a complex discipline in its own right. There is currently no proof of any causal link, but the idea remains a popular one.
15. Once again, it seems that the blessed HK offers herself to the future.
16. Franklin Delano Roosevelt East River Drive – roadway along the eastern side of Manhattan Island.
17. Competition between co-orbital slabs was fierce in the early days as their inhabitants chased dwindling resources. Cooperation would not begin until early 2124.

18. Apocryphal.
19. The traditional enactment of magick has a cost, whether physical or emotional. A physical simile is the conversion of matter to energy. Energy is created at the cost of matter. See *The Scientifick Mechanicks of Magick*, EIT, Ponder, Webb, Krige, Werner, Dirac, for one of the better introductory texts and follow up with any of the papers and publications in the bibliography. *Applied Magick*, EIT, Galton, Rae, Strindberg, is probably the best of these. NOTE: all publications on this subject are subject to special license. If in doubt, consult your tutor as the punishments are severe.
20. Those who are able to detect magick when deployed, but are unable to practice the art themselves.
21. Wish creatures are magickal projections of the host's psyche in physical form.
22. One hundred and seventy-seven similar 'messages of hope' are held in Vault 2C.
23. Many of the larger slabs retained the means of industrial production, including the creation of hydrogen. Consequently, they were able to build airships which they used to threaten and prosecute war. In most parallels, the largest of these was the 'Tyche of Gomorrah' mentioned here, although in some existences the ship bears different names.
24. The blessed HK exhibits a fascination with the ancient movie genre which recurs throughout her fragmented story.
25. Although the stated aim was to round up 'wish casters', it's possible there was another motive for the raid. The over-heavy initial bombing suggests the Polar Hegemony were also attempting to destroy

something or someone. Historians have no supporting evidence for either argument.
26. This is the first recorded instance of ability transference.
27. The Faraday cage was a clumsy and sometimes ineffective method of magickal containment. Superseded in 2123 by the neurological clamp, originally designed as a suppression mechanism for sapient constructs.
28. The process of using the 'glimpse' talent to examine multiple futures by mentally enacting them and examining their outcomes to determine the most favourable result. Effectiveness dwindles as the period observed (and thus the potential number of probable future paths) increases.
29. Magickal ability is enhanced by physical or emotional pain. In this case, the blessed HK enhances the officer's ability and 'borrows' it using her 'absorption' talent.
30. The effect of 'coal', an addictive substance distilled from contaminated rainwater.

Appendix B.
Reading List

Soma Bed Mk 7 User Manual
Serpentine Corp. 2589.100

Early Magick Practitioners
Tromso, van Diemen, Black, duPre. 3107.187

The Immutable Cities – An Historical Treatment
EIT. Jasper, Joshua. 2565.001

Primitive Ideas on Quantum Branching
EIT. Trood, Argand, Keller. 2707.312

Many Worlds Mechanics
EIT. Stryke-Paulsen, Evarg. 5561.003

Frame Analysis
Erving Goffman. 1974

Magick Under Control – Suppression of the Final Taboo
Quirke, Mbele. 5225.301

Travelling Circuses of the 1930s
Carter, Gold. 1941

Excavating New York – a Psychohistorical Perspective
Morgan, Flitch, Cooper. 5982.119

Modern Lexicon of Parallels
Barras, Quaid, Ferraro. 5982.110

Perception of Reality: Whiffling through the Tulgey Wood
Loew, Flack. 4071.203

Manhattan Slab Power Struggles
Tora, Lackey. 2273.111

Media Steganography – Hidden Messages in Plain Sight
Maya, Tuckey, Slinn. 5151.113

*Determining the Broad Future – Mass Observation
    as an Economic Tool*
Harlano. 5777.126

How Parallel is Parallel?
Magellan, Joosten. OIT 5423.113

Early 20th Century Circus – The Art of Spectacle
Beamish, Stout, Brandon et al. 4122.153

Understanding Media: The Extensions of Man
McLuhan. 1964

The Orb: Transluminance
EIT. Secker, Davos, Chiang, 4472.221

The Blessed Hannah Keter – A Life
Abiyah, Sawgrass. 5151.013

Yankee Cultural Idioms in the 26th Century
Parooni, Lessing, Stevens et al. 5789.101

Social Interaction and Religious Mores in c26 Euramerica
Virag, Spetz, Logan. 5812.323

Commercial Synaesthesia – Cultural Blindness Versus Profit
Perez. 5822.107

Mechanical Thought Transference
UIT. Van Flett, Trace, Eden. 2592.077

The Emergence of the Second Sino-Russian Alliance
SAA. Xi M, Xi H, Brenner. 2400.217

Animating AI. The History of the Body Electric
UIT. Torvald, Shark and Richie. 2606.115

Social Control and the Five Families of Commerce in c26
Broadback and Prior. 3122.107

*The Dancing Albino Leopard Who Smokes Cigars
    and Speaks Fluent Polari*
Jensen, Klammer, Thorisdottir. 5166.287

The Human Cost of Interactive Entertainment
Branagh, Crick, Lawrie. 4501.113

About the Author

Mark Lamb is a documentary photographer who spent his formative years in 1960s New Zealand, going barefoot until the age of twelve. When not being schooled by rugby-playing nuns he loved to create fantasy games which were played out with friends in the 'bush' surrounding his childhood home. After a spell in the Royal Air Force he spent time as the Sultan of Oman's bodyguard and subsequently founded a successful scientific software company. These days he can usually be found exploring the urban landscape where he enjoys meeting and photographing people who have interesting stories to tell.